THE DANCES THEY DO

Also by Harry Elliot:

COURT CARD, REVERSED

DIVORCE, DUKAKIS STYLE

4-16-00
Dear Norman —
I've got a feeling,
my friend

THE DANCES
THEY DO

It's now or never!

BY

HARRY ELLIOT

love —
Al

PLYMOUTH ROCK PUBLISHING
P.O. Box 1298
Plymouth, Massachusetts 02362

Copyright © 1999 by Harry Elliot
ISBN 1-890791-95-4
Library of Congress Card Catalog Number: 99-085806

Printed in the United States of America

THE DANCES THEY DO is a work of fiction derived entirely from the imagination of the author. No names, characters, or incidents are real, and any resemblance to actual persons living or dead, or events, or venues, is purely coincidental. Moreover, nothing in these pages should be interpreted as legal advice.

Jacket and book design, typography and electronic pagination by
Arrow Graphics, Inc. Watertown, Massachusetts.
Fred Astaire photo courtesy of Photofest, used with permission.
Harry Elliot photo © 1999 by Morton Bardfield, used with permission.

FIRST EDITION
Published by
Plymouth Rock Publishing
Plymouth, Massachusetts

ACKNOWLEDGMENTS

To Claire and Morty Bardfield for their encouragement and support during my difficult times. To Dorothy Jane Seymour Mills, author of "The Sceptre," for taking time from her own works in progress to help me with mine. To Norman Thomas DiGiovanni, a family friend, for his insights into the world of publishing and for his reassurance that I may someday find myself in that world. To Nancy and George Mumford for their loyalty over the years. To my daughter Liz, the light of my life, my pride and joy, for her love and devotion. To my granddaughters, Elaine and Alexis Mumford, for their hugs and kisses. And, finally, as ever, to my lawyer and friend, Jordan Ring, for his unstinting efforts on my behalf.

DEDICATION

To Claire Bardfield:

You warm us with your smile,
and uplift us with your spirit.
        You keep the flame.
You remind us about love every time we forget,
        and we are always forgetting.
You are the presence that holds us all together.
We travel around you in wobbly circles.
                You are the sun.

Your reassuring smile, your British accent,
you are the unseen force that holds us all together.
        Our gravity.
You keep our feet on the ground.
You hold the oceans in your hands,
        the tides.
You are the moon.

August, 1999
Harry Elliot

Chapter I

Emergency phone calls for students, coming as often as not in the middle of the night, were directed first to Nils Gulbrandsen, president and chancellor of Sylvanius College, a small liberal arts college nestled in the Berkshire Hills of western Massachusetts. Not to the dean of men, or women. Not to the small college's interdenominational chaplain. No, Gulbrandsen would have it no other way. To him, Sylvanius was a family, and a crisis to anyone within its walls was his personal crisis as well.

"We can't locate him," Paula, the student switchboard operator, told Gulbrandsen when he arrived. She was an older part-time student with a number of jobs on and off campus to help pay her tuition. "The proctor in his dorm thinks he might be at the Orleana."

"Can you call him there?" asked Gulbrandsen. It was a snowy Sunday afternoon, one-thirty, and he had rushed over to the administration building in wrinkled corduroy trousers, a faded flannel shirt, and an olive-green Army surplus field jacket.

Paula smiled. She knew the Orleana well, having bartended there on weekend nights since she had turned twenty-one, the legal drinking age in Massachusetts. She also knew that the student Gulbrandsen was seeking, Denton Ricker, was underage, and that his I.D. was one of the readily-available counterfeits used by students with ties to certain disreputable off-campus circles—in his case, the motorcycle crowd. But Ricker was older and bigger than most of his classmates; he did not appear out of place on his stool at the far end of the bar, and so with a nod from the owner, Paula refilled his glass with draft beer and listened to his attempts to impress her with stories about growing up on what he referred to as a "quasi-aristocratic" horse farm. Lucky I'm on the switchboard today, she thought, glancing over at the pacing Gulbrandsen, if Ricker was at the Orleana, whoever was on duty would tell her so and put her call through to him.

"He learned about the death of his parents yesterday," Paula told the beleaguered college president, after her short conversation with Ricker. "He's leaving school this afternoon, but he says he'd like to speak to you before he goes. He'll let you buy him a beer, he says. 'One for the road.'"

"Are you in trouble," the bartender asked, taking the phone from Ricker and putting it back in its place beside the cash register.

"Nah," replied the young man. Except for ordering his beer, he had spoken to no one in the near-empty bar.

"Well, for what it's worth, we like you here," continued the bartender, their weekend man, a young man who, it was said, had married an older woman with a number of children from previous marriages. "We'd hate to see you in trouble with the school. Speaking for Paula and everybody here at the Orleana, we'd hate to see you kicked out."

Acknowledging the man's words with a nod, Ricker went back to his beer. He saw himself at a turning point in his life. He saw himself at that moment, in that bar, in that college town, as someone singled out from his fellow classmates for a purpose. He imagined an invisible spotlight shining down on him from above. The thought comforted him. He needed comfort. Except for his elderly aunt, he was now all alone in the world.

Denton Ricker viewed academia as alien territory, even from the start. At his family's horse farm he was comfortable both with the horses and the genteel ladies who came to ride them, but he was a poor competitor himself. The same lack of discipline that disqualified him in the dressage ring proved to be his downfall in college as well. The confinement of dorms and the deadlines for term papers and exams proved too much for young Ricker. As the first semester wore on, he spent more and more time off-campus. He felt much more at ease with townies than with his classmates, whom he considered pretentious and full of themselves. Of the townies, he preferred the motorcycle crowd to the benign group in front of Friendly's Ice Cream. Leather best expressed his rough, unshaven persona, he thought. Leather and insignia patches.

Soon he had his own Harley as well as a small, intricate tattoo just below his left collarbone. It was a bird in flight, a stormy raptor as seen from above, gliding—wings outstretched, each minute feather drawn with fine-line detail. A banner held in its beak was inscribed with a motto. It read, "Ride the Wind."

Hardly had Ricker shed the scab that forms from tattoo needles when he received word of the death of his parents. The call from his Aunt Grace came a day before the distraught woman was put through to Gulbrandsen. Ricker's parents' truck and horse trailer had skidded on some back road in Vermont. The truck hit an icy stretch, jackknifed, broke loose from the trailer, and fell 450 feet into a half-frozen river.

That night, Ricker had a dream: He was in his father's place behind the wheel on a mountain road high above the clouds when a majestic bird called his name. Entranced, he followed it into the abyss where, gasping for breath, he tumbled endlessly in free fall. "Ride the wind," it cried out to him. It spoke in the voice of a woman.

The next day Ricker awoke prepared to put his academic life behind him forever. For a final time, to leave Sylvanius College and his unadorned dorm room, a room so austere a monk might have occupied it. He intended to slip away unmissed and un-missing, telling no one, taking nothing. After all, was there anything he had any use for? Surveying his monastery-like room from his bed, he saw little of himself in his surroundings. Papers? Books? Alas, there wasn't even a poster on the wall to make his living space his own. Not even a framed photograph of a loved one to rescue from the hands of indifferent strangers, to save from consignment to the trash heap.

Prepared to leave with nothing but the clothes on his back, he dressed slowly, carefully, giving thought to what he chose to wear. Foremost was his prized possession, a western-style denim shirt—worn out, faded to the perfect degree of softness. It was like an old friend. The girls always had their eye on that shirt. On chilly mornings in their rooms or apartments it would be the first thing they'd reach for before getting out of bed. When they made his coffee and scrambled eggs they'd be wearing nothing . . . except for that shirt. Days later, putting it on, he'd think he detected their perfume on it.

Patchouli. Sandalwood.

So this was college, he mused, pulling on his well-worn cowboy boots—his motorcycle boots. Was it totally lost on me? Or did it have some message, some hidden meaning that I'll realize later?—that I'm too stupid to appreciate now? He decided to prolong his departure as much as possible. Revel in his misery. Let the pain of it wash over him. His parents: dead. His days as a student: over forever. Like an itinerant knight or heroic cowboy he saw himself saddling up and riding off into the sunset.

He planned to spend his last few hours getting in touch with his emotions. Total immersion, he decided. A drink or two might help. The Orleana might be the perfect place for his personal *Commencement* to commence.

Or so he thought after his first few sips of beer.

Then the phone call. Gulbrandsen was on his way.

Besides his duties as president and chancellor of Sylvanius College, Gulbrandsen took it upon himself to teach one course. A single course to incoming freshmen. "Introduction to Western Literature," he called it. It began with the Sophocles tragedy, *Oedipus the King*, and, more often than not, at semester's end had not progressed much beyond discussions and term papers surrounding that same piece of literature. Loosely surrounding it, for the most part, with his incoming students' papers on the subject or related subjects serving to define themselves to him— a definition that often followed them throughout their years at Sylvanius.

"Who am I?" asked Oedipus. If his students advanced to the point of asking themselves that question, thought Gulbrandsen, he'd be given a window into their minds. More so. He'd have a window into their very souls.

For Ricker, Gulbrandsen's one-hour course was the high point of his week. One hour of intellectual fireworks. For Ricker, it meant a week not wasted.

Chapter 2

Ricker's ancestral family, the Dowlings, had been in America for generations, but their numbers never seemed to increase; their family tree remained long and thin and deeply rooted in the servant class, until, in the early nineteenth century, the family was overwhelmed with a bequest in the will of one of their employers: three hundred acres of forest north of Boston in what was known in those days as the Essex Townships. This gift came as a surprise to everyone, especially potential beneficiaries of lineage, who challenged it in court; but, in hushed tones, behind closed doors, certain facts emerged, and the case was silently dropped. No messy scandal, no lingering grudges—the best deal, actually—and the Dowling family took it.

In the years that followed, the inheritance dwindled. Lots were sold off or traded to pay for one emergency after another, even to finance an occasional commercial venture or two. But that was before the time of Ricker's great-grandfather, Hosea Dowling, and before the 1902 influenza epidemic, which reduced the already-small family to near-extinction. Dowling, a blacksmith by trade, was into his forties and unmarried when the epidemic struck. As sole family survivor he took possession of his inheritance—and a wife, in quick succession—but alas, the newlyweds found that of the original property, only twenty-five acres remained.

Fortunately, the best twenty-five. The crown jewels. The highest ground. Ponds, potable streams, and, above it all, a breathtaking view that could reach to New Hampshire. A glimpse of the White Mountains. This property, he optimistically asserted, taking title, would be the sacred birthright of future generations of Dowlings, preserved with restrictive covenants written into the deeds making the mortgaging, transfer, or sale of this land difficult, perhaps impossible to accomplish.

Dowling, his wife, and, in the years that followed, their young son, Joshua, lived in quarters between stables and foundry. The youngster was a gift from heaven; to carry on the Dowling name; to insure the family's survival. Precocious, helpful, he lent a hand at an early age. A blessing for his overworked dad—while it lasted—before school beckoned, and long before the opportunity in Sudbury: his apprenticeship with a farrier who specialized in treating, and sometimes curing, lameness in horses.

In the early days of the twentieth century, with veterinary medicine in its infancy in this country, farmers had little choice in the treatment of animals with orthopedic problems. Calling in a veterinarian was a luxury few could afford. They would either devise home remedies, ask a neighbor's help, or, most usually, seek the advice of their farrier during regular horseshoeing visits.

When Joshua returned from Sudbury, a young man eager to put his newly-acquired techniques into practice, he was well-received; indeed, soon found himself successful beyond his dreams. With time he built a house larger than his needs, on a hill to provide a view of his rugged land. Where others saw rocky woods, he visualized white fences, grassy meadows, and grazing horses.

Joshua Dowling's reputation grew as a man who could save horses for whom all hope had been abandoned. Many measures were available to him short of shooting the animal; some simply required a change of routine or diet, but most involved corrective shoeing. (No shoes at all for six months, or, at the other extreme: high wedges, pads, heel-plates, even shoes put on backward when a low toe was called for.) Risky, empirical remedies were not a timid man's game; self-assurance was a must, and no small measure of salesmanship. "Try it for a while," he'd say. "God blesses those who do not destroy their animals too quickly. Have patience."

They did. Eventually, the legend of Dowling's accomplishments spread beyond the North Shore, in part because of the itinerant nature of his work; but at auctions, horse shows, state fairs, or wherever farmers' paths might cross, one subject was sure to come up: the man who was no ordinary horse shoer.

Dowling's services did not come cheap. Prestige led to wealth in a spiral that elevated the young man out of the journeyman class into something resembling professionalism. Indeed, he could have married well but chose to marry for love. A poor girl. Like himself, without family.

Of his two daughters, Grace and Millicent, it was the elder, Grace, who helped him in his work. She tried to please him, to do chores as well as any son he might have had. The baby, Millie, was spared responsibilities in the busy household and allowed to pursue an education with college in mind.

Things went along predictably for Millie until, at the age of nineteen, she accompanied a few of her friends to the 1948 Olympics trials. Later, she learned that she had qualified for the United States Equestrian Team and was invited to compete that summer in London.

Meanwhile, reeling from the war and bitter memories of the 1936 Games, the members of the Olympics Board of Governors were determined not to make the same mistakes that hurt them so badly in Berlin twelve years earlier. They would try to subdue nationalistic zeal in a competition that was almost, by definition, patriotically motivated.

At least in the equestrian events they had their answer: Conrad Ricker was their unanimous choice to run the show. "Cap," as he was known to all, had competed in the 1936 Berlin Games for his native Germany and had witnessed the ill-fated "three-day event" first-hand. He had ridden the impossibly difficult cross-country course that caused the death of three horses and where only twenty-seven riders out of the fifty entered managed to finish. He assured the Board of Governors that under his aegis, history would not be repeated.

Cap's political credentials also proved exemplary, his only ties to religion or politics having been occasional appearances at Quaker meetings in college. Denied Conscientious Objector status under Hitler, he set his sights on the Olympics—qualified, competed, then defected to England in the aftermath, amid the chaos of departing teams, mingling with British athletes, their horses, trainers, handlers, and staff.

He spent the war years in the English countryside, ostensibly with horses but occasionally meeting with mysterious strangers. They'd appear in shabby Bentleys up from London, have their little chats, then return the same day.

Tall, dignified, with a pleasant demeanor, Cap enjoyed a remarkable degree of acceptance in his new country, even during the War, even with his foreign accent. But why not eliminate that handicap entirely, he thought? He took courses in English, engaged tutors, and even performed in Shakespearean plays before local audiences. Eventually, his efforts were rewarded. Not only did he remove all traces of his native tongue from his speech, he accomplished what was of paramount importance to the British in assessing one's station in society: his newly acquired diction was unmistakably that of the "upper classes."

Then, after the War, he was again called upon to serve his newly-adopted country, this time with the 1948 Summer Olympics.

Things were going well, the Games were progressing without

a hitch, when, on a Sunday, he received a phone call from a constabulary near Walsingham Downs, an exclusive hunt club preserve outside London.

"Sergeant Portersfield reporting, Sir."

"Go ahead," said Cap.

"We have a young lady here," said Portersfield. "She's apparently with one of your foreign teams. American, I should say. Violated all sorts of ordinances, you know. Has the authorities all in a dither. Could you send someone down to fetch her?

"Have them bring one of those horse lorries, if they could."

It was, of course, Millie Dowling, eliminated in the early rounds of competition but unable to resist riding the immaculately groomed bridle paths that weave their way through the parks and gardens of London. She was 3,000 miles from home, on her own horse, the weather was perfect, the countryside gorgeous—so what's to stop her? Without a helmet and in jeans and a tee shirt, she rode wherever she pleased, disregarding signposts and ornamental barriers, and heedless of local ordinances and restrictions. They're to separate the *classes*, she thought; silly, and certainly not applicable to me.

"You trespassed into a restricted hunt club reservation. A private game reserve," said Cap, who, feeling responsible for the young American, had come for her himself.

Among the smallest athletes in size (Millie carried the flag in the opening ceremonies, a mascot-like honor), she was nevertheless a team leader, respected for her tireless competitive spirit, even in defeat. "Hotheaded, outspoken," some said, but in matters of principle, she insisted on her rights. Gazing up at Cap in silence, she tried to abandon her usual good-natured smile for an apologetic expression, a prayerful look—as best she could—one of contrition.

"The Queen, or somebody from the Royal Family, was due to come riding through the very path they found you on," added Cap. "You could have caused an *incident*."

"I'm sorry," she responded, staring up, hopefully. "Thanks for coming down and rescuing me. I don't know what I would have done. They seemed so upset. I must have ruined your Sunday."

"Not at all," said Cap, the hint of a smile emerging at the corners of his thin lips. "I wish all my other problems were as easily resolved."

"Is it resolved, then? Am I free to go?" she asked, beaming.

"Except for one small thing, you're as free as a bird," he replied, taking an engraved silver case from the breast pocket of his regimental blazer. Opening it, he removed a calling-card which he handed to Millie. "I'd like you to be my guest at a reception tonight. A gala, rather exclusive get-together, but informal nonetheless. The Lady whose flowerbeds you trampled getting here should be in attendance. I'm sure she'd welcome an apology from such a charming young lady as yourself . . . most graciously."

Could it be, thought Millie looking at the card, the most important man I've ever met is attracted to me, an uncouth American still in her teens?

Her question would soon be answered, when, for the second time in as many Olympics, Cap Ricker packed up his belongings and departed for a new country along with its homeward bound national team. This time his destination was America, in the company of the young woman he intended to marry.

The newlyweds settled in quickly on Dowling's land, and the Old Man couldn't have been more pleased to have them. His wish to see white fences crisscrossing his green pastures became a reality. Stables were built, and a carriage house for overnight guests. Soon sheds to house tractors and other labor-saving farm equipment went up. A riding academy was emerging, with facilities for boarding and training the horses of the wealthy North Shore smart set.

Success came quickly to the young couple. Overwhelming success. Owners leaving their animals in the expert care of the Rickers during their long travels abroad would find, upon their return, that those particular horses outperformed all others, would not be stale from disuse but would be well-schooled and ready for competition. Cap had turned their pets into serious athletes.

At social gatherings, no conversations were as compelling as those concerning the minutiae of one's horses. Indeed, among the elite, the horsey set, the remains of the American aristocracy, and those with vast amounts of "new" money who aspired to it, things equestrian provided a common ground, a universal language. The Rickers spoke that language fluently.

Dowling lived to see his family leave generations of servitude behind them forever. It happened on his watch, and, to a great extent, by his efforts. His father would have been pleased. The land was intact—even improved upon—and their family assets were on the rise.

Millie and Cap had one child, a son, Denton, whose upbringing was entrusted, for the most part, to his Aunt Grace. She had been caring for her remaining parent, her ailing dad, but when he died her attention shifted entirely to her nephew. "Grace, you've sacrificed everything for us," Millie often told her. "Your own life, a career, marriage. We could never manage without you. You keep our family together."

And so, with Grace tending to household affairs, the Rickers, free to pursue their goal, ultimately managed to attain it: national recognition for their competitions. Winning a "Blue" at *Rickers'* was becoming a coveted achievement for riders throughout the country. The future was looking bright for the family and its heir apparent. It wasn't until later, after the young man had reluctantly given in to his father's wishes and was attending college, that the family's fortunes began their decline.

Chapter 3

Gulbrandsen was no stranger to the Orleana, a nonde-script roadhouse too seedy for faculty wives but where bikers were not entirely comfortable either. Its clientele consisted of the over-forty locals, the Merle Haggard-Johnny Cash-Willie Nelson crowd. Gulbrandsen was reputed to have held a literary *round table* there when he first came to Sylvanius College, back when the Orleana served food and overflowed with students. The story was passed down from one class to another, often with embellishments; indeed, the pass-ing-down process itself achieved the status of student rite, not to be abandoned and forgotten: the legend of Gulbrandsen's *Orleana Round Table.*

It was said that in his early years he'd invite the most scandalous of the faculty and/or their spouses to join in his free-wheeling brand of intellectual elitism. But there were consequences: A trip from an open air seminar on a hot spring afternoon to a mental institution and eventual suicide for one young female instructor. Expatriation for others, some never to return. There would be a price to pay for freedom—political, artistic, and, above all, sexual. Unwanted pregnancies. Divorce for all who had been married at the time. . . . But some good came of those heady years. For some, the creative spirit was born, later to manifest itself in literature, the theater, art. For others, those with intellectual freedom bred into their bone, Sylvanius was simply a stop along the way.

Gulbrandsen spoke little of those years, especially to students, who interpreted his reticence as proof of his suffering in the aftermath of some romantic tragedy. He did not disabuse them of their fantasy. Fact. Fiction. He saw little distinction when it came to human emotions. When it came to love.

Patchouli. Sandalwood.

He noticed Ricker at the bar and headed in that direction.

Gulbrandsen walked with the slightly stooped-over gait characteristic of tall thin men. He had brown Jesus-length hair, steel-rimmed glasses, and, on that Sunday afternoon, he wore the same corduroy trousers, faded plaid flannel shirt, and olive-drab field jacket he had hurriedly put on after taking the call from Ricker's Aunt Grace. His hair was uncombed, and his reddish-blondish-greyish beard was scraggly, unkempt. "I'm sorry to hear about your parents," he said, approaching Ricker. "I spoke with your aunt earlier. Let's go to a booth in back where we can talk."

"I'm out of here," said Ricker, taking his motorcycle gloves in one hand and his half-empty beer glass in the other. He was dressed in bikers' black, a Harley double-wing emblem across the back of his leather jacket, a Brando cap. "I'd just like a word with you before I go, though. It shouldn't take long. My tuition's paid up for the whole year, but I'd say I got a year's worth of college in my one semester, if you could just clear up a few nagging questions for me."

As the young man spoke, Gulbrandsen, heading toward the back of the dimly-lit room, gestured to the bartender for two glasses of draft beer to be sent to their table. "Don't expect too much from me, Denton," he warned, finding a booth and easing himself down on one of the benches. "I'm only human, but I'll try to help."

"I don't want to blame others for my failures here," said Ricker, making his side of the booth his own, "but I got the feeling that I was at war with my teachers. They seemed to be acting in concert against me. Were they? Am I imagining it? Or did they all get together and discuss me before they decided to give me *incompletes*, or flunk me outright?"

The bartender arrived with two overflowing glasses of draft beer. With a fixed gaze at Gulbrandsen, Ricker, sitting sideways in the booth with his back up against the wall, waited for an answer. Sure, I've got a chip on my shoulder, he thought—why not? I'm an orphan. I'm entitled.

Gulbrandsen took off his delicate glasses. Holding them between two fingers, he slowly wiped his eyes with the back of his wrist—wiped his *weary* eyes, he thought, as he squinted at the young man staring at him from across the table. "We touched base," he confided, deciding that candor, uncomfortable as it might be, would be the best approach. "We discussed you only to make sure that our particular course wasn't a fluke. To convince ourselves you really *weren't* doing anything for any of us here. But no, Denton, there was no conspiracy against you. The faculty didn't gang up on you, if that's what you think. Some of us even liked you and hoped you could make it."

"Were you one of those?" asked Ricker, his eyes narrowing.

"Not especially," responded Gulbrandsen between sips of beer. "I thought you were a pain in the ass. No. I take that back. I see a lot of myself in you, Denton. You're a rebel, a lot like I was at your age, but braver, more willing to take risks. Anyway, I enjoyed having you in my class. Quite a bit, in fact. I'll miss you."

Ricker remained silent.

"Unlike many of your classmates, Denton," added Gulbrandsen, "—and I think this is important—you can look me straight in the eye. I have honors students who drift through their classes like leaves in the wind. They do their homework, which is more than I can say for you, but they can't make any more eye contact with me than someone who stole my wallet."

"What do you think will become of me?" asked the young man.

Gulbrandsen put down his glass. How many times had he been asked that same question over the years?—each student expecting his or her own special, well-phrased answer. And he wouldn't disappoint them. He'd give them the best he had to offer. Not platitudes or academic bullshit, either. He extend to each of his students as much respect as he would to colleagues, parents . . . dignitaries. He saw his words on a par with, or better than, anything their own fathers could provide. Or their family doctors. Or their priests.

"'What will become of me?'—Oedipus asked the Oracle that very question and was told he would murder his father and marry his mother, a most unwelcome prophecy to say the least.

"I'm no oracle, Denton," he added, "but I'd say oracles are to be avoided. They'll fuck with your mind if you let them. They're trouble." Gulbrandsen lapsed into silence. He went back to his beer.

"So?"

Gulbrandsen seemed to shrug. Ricker couldn't be sure. The only other customers, two bearded men in canvas coveralls, finished their drinks and left. Silence.

Gulbrandsen, as well, emptied his glass. "Let me tell you about a skit I heard recently on the Garrison Keillor Show. Have you ever heard of him?"

"Is he the *Lake Wobegon* fellow?" ventured Ricker.

Gulbrandsen nodded. "Well, there's a character on that radio program, a 'talking chicken,' who doesn't actually *talk* as such, but responds in a sort of clucking-speaking combination, a marvel accomplished by Keillor's sound-effects man, Tom Keith. In difficult situations and often against overwhelming odds, the 'chicken' acts with bravery and with an indomitable spirit. . . ."

As Gulbrandsen continued his discourse on "the chicken," Ricker thought: What's happening to me? I'm stuck here, on the last day of my academic life, listening to the president of my college go on and on about a talking chicken. A talking chicken!

"... I listen to the show every week with one purpose," continued Gulbrandsen: "To find out what that chicken is going to say to me. To me personally! To learn what that brave little bird will say or do that will help me cope with my problems, or improve me as a person. [Were there tears starting?] To gain some special wisdom from that chicken that Fate or God intends for me to hear.

"Now, Denton," added Gulbrandsen, pulling an oversized, red print bandanna from the pocket of his field jacket and loudly blowing his nose into it, "while we're on the subject of 'talking birds,' what about yours? Tell me about your tattoo. Your ally . . . your totem for life."

Chapter 4

Cantrice was no stranger to Rick's stables when she learned that he was back from college. As a youngster she had taken riding lessons from his parents, entered junior events at local shows under their aegis. Later, after it became apparent that she had neither the aptitude nor the desire for competition, she was allowed to stay on as a casual rider, to continue boarding her horse there; after all, she enjoyed so many aspects of the sport: the quaint rituals, the etiquette of horsemanship, the powerful beast surging between her legs.

Now she hung around for different reasons, some unclear even to her. She occupied her time mucking out stalls, toting wheelbarrows, sweeping up. Grooming, watering, and feeding the horses. Turning them out. Bringing them in. Ever present, she became privy to the inner workings of the stable, knew some of the problems facing the young owner, and even had a hand in solving a few. In Rick's absence, she'd answer strangers' questions—answer them with confidence, with authority. Her pronouncements would be allowed to stand; the changes she made would be there the next day, the next week.

Cantrice had the tall, severe beauty often found in French

models: black, shiny hair in a "Dutch" clip, small turned-up nose, pointy breasts that knew no bra. She had a self-assured manner that inspired confidence—in her ability, that is, not in her principles. She had few friends.

At the stable, she didn't crowd Rick. (At home it was Rick; never Denton, never Ricker.) Cantrice knew how to keep her distance, not violate his space. She knew it instinctively. She didn't follow him up to the house, and she paid her boarding fees as before—before she put in so much unpaid labor, for one thing—before she learned he didn't need the money, for another.

Indeed, the insurance claim from his parents' accident had been settled. Rick and his aunt Grace shared equally in the proceeds from a $750,000 policy. He was a rich young man, a most eligible bachelor, and it seemed only Cantrice knew about it.

It wasn't long before Rick began to look forward to her appearances. It pleased him when he looked out of his bedroom window and saw her small red sports car parked down beside the barn. And when he was pleased, she knew, and when she knew, she spoke freely:

"Where do you go on your motorcycle? Do you have a girl? Does she ride with you? hold on to you tightly?"

Rick was taken off guard by these questions, personal questions asked during chores—inappropriate, but somehow exciting. "Once in a while," he said, turning his attention to her. Cantrice had been working hard, perspiring through her tee shirt—her breasts, barely a cleavage; her nipples prominent, erect, holding his gaze.

"Does she wear leather?" Cantrice persisted. "Tease you with a crop?" She took one of the riding crops from a hook on the wall behind her and touched Rick lightly below the ear with it.

Rick indeed enjoyed the bikers' brand of sex: the groups, the chains, the acting-out of fantasies. But he kept that life, that part of his personality, separate from the stable—from his work, from home.

Cantrice continued her probing: "What are they like, these motorcycle girls?"

Rick allowed himself a boyish smile, then shrugged. "Like everyone else," he lied, adding, "only they smell worse."

"Where do they smell worse?" she quickly responded. "Where it gets wet when you kiss them?" She took the Coke she was drinking and poured it between her thighs, staining her tight-fitting jodhpurs. "Mine's sweeter, do you want to taste for yourself?"

The surprise of her act startled him. And then moving toward her, bending, kissing—it all seemed awkward, off balance, somehow inappropriate. She sensed his discomfort. "I'm a virgin," she whispered heavily into his ear. (It was part of a new game, now. She would make up the rules as she went along.)

"I'm not ready. Not yet," she continued, her hand moving slowly. "But I just want to see you. I want to see that white stuff come out of you. What does it taste like, Rick? Let me taste it."

He watched her sticky jodhpurs climb the ladder into the hayloft, followed after them, and when they were around her ankles he was ready. From then on it was simply a matter of their blood chemicals doing the talking, guiding the primordial ritual from which few escape—smiles quickly fading, unstoppable urgency taking over—and then, later, smiles again, wider than ever.

Sex in the barn was just fine for Cantrice—for the first time, that is. Next time—and there is *always* a next time—it would have to be more comfortable.

Where? When? It is all the two can think about. A motel? Her place? His house? Ah, the carriage house.

After a week or two of daily interludes they find themselves at the next plateau: overnights. Weekends first, but then, eventually, every night. Friends are curious, but Cantrice begs off. Secrets, *intrigue*.

They announce that they're "living together." Then comes the question: "Why not make it legal?"

"I'll make all the arrangements," she says. "Poor boy, you have no parents to fuss over you. I'll take care of everything."

Chapter 5

Rick's Aunt Grace found life increasingly stressful, living in the big house with Cantrice, and so she moved herself and her few personal belongings into the carriage house next door. I should have done this sooner, she thought. Two women in one kitchen. Impossible.

She had never learned to drive. Never felt the need. But after her sister died and her only other living relative, her nephew, was sent to jail, she found she had needs she never dreamed existed. At least her transportation problem could be easily solved:

Otis Graveline, who owned and operated one of the two local taxicabs, had been driving in town since the end of the Second World War. He had known Grace since their days in a one-room schoolhouse, and later, off and on over the years, he worked for her dad. He welcomed any opportunity to catch a glimpse of her back then—now, well, his feelings still remained pretty much the same.

Grace, a wisp of a lady, attracted people to her with her forthright, genteel charm. She always dressed carefully—took pride in her grooming, her appearance. Growing up, she had been naive, trusting of others, and earnest. Now, in her waning years, only her earnest, serious approach to life remained.

Otis's "Veterans Cab" pulled up regularly, twice a week, to take Grace shopping or on any other errand she might require. He seemed to have worked out some mysterious, embarrassingly small flat rates and threw in, as well, such complimentary services as lugging bundles and doing odd jobs around her tiny carriage house. He accepted payment—usually involving change, often pennies, but declined tips. Their relationship would be all business, he insisted, in spite of his warm feelings toward her—out of respect for her station, out of devotion, out of emotions unfathomable to him.

It was Otis who drove Grace to court to visit Rick during his first few weeks in custody. Although she didn't understand the proceedings, she knew her nephew was in trouble, and his lawyers seemed to be unwilling or unable to help him, and the trouble he was in—somehow, divorce-related—seemed to be getting worse every day, and the worse it got the angrier he'd get, and the angrier he'd get the worse his chances became for putting his problems behind him.

That she understood.

But she didn't understand the proceedings. And she didn't understand what led up to the proceedings. Basically, she didn't understand how they could have plucked her nephew out of his house, the Dowling house, without anybody able to stop them. Night after sleepless night, as weeks turned into months, she'd lie in bed pondering the question, turning it over in her mind, trying to make some sense of it. Perhaps Rick could provide answers for her. She'd visit him and see. Now that his trial was over. Now that he was no longer in court. Now that he was in jail.

She decided to bring a bundle of his clothes along with her to the visit, something decent for him to wear in the event his case was appealed. She envisioned it going to a higher court: *Superior Court* or *Supreme Judicial Court* or, best of all, *The United States*

Supreme Court. Courts with understanding far greater than that of the lower courts that had punished him so unfairly.

The bundle consisted of one suit—his best—and ties, dress shirts, cufflinks, and expensive shoes. The banker's-blue, three piece suit, she packed folded between sheets of tissue paper; the shirts, plastic-wrapped in laundry boxes; the cufflinks, in a velvet snap-top case; and the shoes, which she had painstakingly shined, in flannel sleeves. Her reasoning: if you dressed like a gentleman, you would stand a better chance of being treated like one. You would be less likely to be dismissed as riffraff. A well-dressed Rick would be perceived as a credible witness, acquit himself with dignity, and earn the respect of the high courts he'd appear before. With that expectation in mind, she wrapped the package in the same yellow-with-age paper in which her sister's wedding dress had been wrapped, and tied it with a delicate grosgrain ribbon she found among Millie's other possessions in a hope chest in the attic.

A shuttlebus from the parking lot dropped Grace off at the main building of the Merrimac County House of Correction. Once inside, she learned from a guard behind the counter, that to be granted a visitor's pass she needed a valid driver's license or suitable picture I.D. She had neither. The guard summoned a lieutenant from an upper floor of the building, using a hand-held transmitting radio, one of the walkie-talkies that took the place of guns as symbols of authority within the prison. The senior officer seemed to resent the inconvenience over such a trifle; nevertheless, he waived the regulations and issued her a pass. She had no such luck with her nephew's clothes.

Prison regulations prohibited visitors from leaving articles of clothing for inmates except by following a special procedure: Garments deemed appropriate for court appearances and outside A.A. meetings could be left with the Property Clerk during working hours a few days prior to the visit. (No Sundays, no evenings, no holidays; no obscene tee shirts, no leather jackets.) If approval were granted, the articles would then be tagged, bagged, and put into an assigned cubbyhole in the property room for the inmate's use.

In theory.

In practice, any clothing was fair game to be used by anybody, inmate or guard. Articles lost or stolen . . . well . . . Could you describe them? they might ask, if they chose to respond at all.

The guard behind the counter stubbornly refused the old lady's pleas. Could she prevail on the lieutenant again? Impossible. She gave up and placed her package with the guard—by then, losing patience with her—for safekeeping. She had wasted half of a one-hour visit and had no intention of wasting more time bringing the clothing back on the shuttlebus to Otis in the parking lot.

The visitors' room, more than twenty-five feet wide by sixty feet long, throbbed like an overcrowded, overheated beehive of noisy, intense humanity. Stepping inside was like entering somebody else's party—their chaos, their madness—a party in full swing, going strong.

Four double rows of folding chairs formed narrow aisles that ran the length of the room. The rows of chairs faced each other: one for the inmate, one for the visitor. The rule against contact between them was not strictly enforced. They invariably exchanged kisses or handshakes at the beginning and end of each visit.

Grace spotted her nephew waving to her from halfway down one of the center aisles. She made her way hesitantly. "Excuse me," she repeated, interrupting each conversation as she slowly approached. "Excuse me . . . excuse me."

Here in this teeming room few white faces could be seen. The darker skin colors, like shades of coffee, ranged from black to milky tan. And what language did they speak? Grace thought it might be Spanish, but much of it, spoken, to be sure, by white men, was lost on her. The variations of the word *fuck* did not register in her brain. All races used the word in every sentence, sometimes two or three times. They would even insert it into multi-syllable words such as *Mass-a-fuckin-chusetts*. Was this caterwaul an expression of pain, wondered Grace? Or, like the cacophony of atonal music, was it upsetting only if you paid attention, only if you made the effort to listen?

For almost everyone, the room provided excitement, noted Ricker, as he watched his aunt's slow progress down the narrow aisle. Visitors and inmates alike seemed to have difficulty restraining their exuberance under the watchful eyes of the guards, who were stationed at twenty-foot intervals around the room. Small children too squirmy to be held for long ran amuck around the chairs. Why was everyone in such good spirits? he wondered, so euphoric? Was life in an American jail so superior to what passed for freedom wherever else they came from, that these inmates could celebrate so? Was the food so much better, the beds so much softer, cleaner, and drier, and the TV so much more entertaining? And these were the wages of sin, he mused. The price of crime. The consequences of getting caught. And this was punishment?

As Grace drew nearer, Ricker noticed how his aunt had changed; aged, since the last time he had seen her. Her white hair had grown thinner; she appeared to be more frail, more ethereal than ever. She looked confused, disoriented, her hands trembling slightly, her head, her whole body, unsteady.

Observing his elderly aunt in this setting, Ricker was struck with a new emotion, one unfamiliar to him: shame. Ashamed of himself and all those around him. I should never have allowed her to come, he thought, envisioning her ordeal: negotiating this monstrous gauntlet, passing so close to these coarse people, edging between their sordid conversations—their talk about friends and relatives arrested for this or that, and now in some jail or other, or perhaps even in some part of this jail! Their street gossip blending with their prison news, all flowing together into some homogenous babble from which it would be impossible to tell where the street left off and jail began.

Every visiting period would always unfold in the same way: the din would grow louder and louder, reaching a crescendo as the hour neared its end. Then a buzzer would sound, and the visitors would file out at one end of the room, turning in their passes, while the inmates would congregate at the other end, to be taken in groups of two or three into another room to be strip-searched before being allowed to return to their tiers.

Finally, Grace reached her nephew and sat opposite him, all smiles and eager to please. What could she do to help him gain his freedom? she asked. The question seemed familiar to her. Had she asked it before? In court? On the phone? Was she repeating herself?

"We've tried everything," he answered, forcing a smile. "I thought I had the best lawyers. The biggest divorce firm in Boston. You spent your life's savings on me. Your retirement money went to my lawyers." There was nothing further she could do, he told her, touching her arm (a guard, frowning, approached . . . hesitated, then backed away slowly, his narrowed eyes lingering). She should put her mind at ease, carry on her own life as best she could, not worry about him.

She fought back tears. The tears of frustration, of disappointment—ultimately, the tears of loss (once they started there would be no stopping them). She'd have to change the subject quickly, she thought, or the torrent would begin. But no new subject came to mind. Her difficulties with Cantrice? What could she tell her nephew of her life at home or ask him of his in jail that either would enjoy hearing? And so their visit was marked by what wasn't said, by their silences—ideas considered and rejected out of kindness, their words edited in their minds to nothingness.

They found safe ground, finally, talking about the early days. Anecdotes from his childhood. Ah, for those happy times, she thought, how did they slip away from us so completely? The toddler, who, when his mother was absent, came to her for comforting, for love, and later sought her out even with his mother close at hand. And the intervening years—they held such promise. The hopes, the lofty expectations.

And then the death of his parents, his return from college,

and his wedding—not the glittering social occasion that she expected and he deserved. The bride's family made no effort to conform to the social protocols of its class. Their cheap reception had been attended by noisy, drunken people whom she did not know. And afterward, her own position weakened more with each day of the couple's six-year marriage—more habits conceded, more values abandoned.

A cloud had descended on her once-happy home. Rick, often moody, depressed, unable to cope, would ride off on his motorcycle with friends, sometimes for days. And later, with the arrival of Cantrice's mother—the silly woman constantly underfoot, taking sides shamelessly against her son-in-law and his aunt . . . well, Grace soon found herself little more than a shadow in a stranger's house.

And then, worst of all, the nightmare of losing Rick. With him in jail, what was to become of her? He was not only incapable of protecting her, she thought, now he couldn't even protect *himself*. She was certain that hidden forces were at work planning their destruction. Not Fate or bad luck, but actual people hatching malevolent plots. Lawyers, taking aim. Firing legal bullets.

Halfway home, she remembered the package of clothing. Alas, she had no intention of returning to the prison for it—her nephew's clothes, the clothes of a gentleman.

Just as well, because no sooner had visiting hours ended than someone claimed the package. The guard with whom Grace had left it slipped it into his locker and later took it home with him at the end of his shift. (His wife, pleased with the windfall, hung the items carefully in the back of her husband's closet. You could never tell, she thought, when he'd get in trouble and need them for a court appearance of his own.)

During the ride home, and for weeks to come, the visit kept haunting Grace: *How can he protect me, when he can't even protect himself?* How did this come about? To ruin our family so quickly? To wipe us out so totally?

The old woman had always believed that if bad things were

deliberately visited upon good people, some mechanism would be triggered to remedy the injustice; that in America, weak, gentle people like the Dowlings would somehow be protected from the strong and powerful seeking to harm them. Furthermore, she had always expected the courts to defend her and her family, not willingly join in their destruction. Now, with the realization that society's promise to her had been broken, that the social contract upon which she relied was an illusion, she could only ask herself: why?

The old woman imagined a balance sheet upon which her family's fortunes were written. In her mind, she saw a record of their tranquil years, albeit those of servitude, vs. the ambition, opportunism, and social pretense that had come to characterize them lately. On one side of the ledger she saw words like duty, selflessness, charity . . . on the other, the more recent side, she saw vanity and greed.

In the days and weeks following her visit to Rick in jail, Grace became increasingly isolated in her tiny carriage house, no longer attempting to dress or shop or touch the world outside her door. She no longer attempted to enter the house she grew up in, her house, the house that Cantrice and her mother now seemed to regard as their own.

Concerned when the old woman showed none of her usual signs of activity, Cantrice checked the carriage house, and, discovering that Grace had taken to her bed, called in their town's Visiting Nurse. An examination revealed a severe case of osteoarthritis, a diagnosis later confirmed by Cantrice's personal physician, who prescribed pain-killers and suggested bed rest as the best interim remedy; but when the condition further deteriorated, he insisted that Cantrice move her mother-in-law to the local hospital, where he and his staff could keep a closer eye on her.

Later, as Grace improved, transfer from the hospital to a nursing home impended—without Cantrice's consulting her, without her approval. Later still, the question of money came up, and it, as well, was expeditiously resolved:

Lawyers were called in and the old woman's assets, the insurance money and entitlements from the family estate, were litigated in her absence. Cantrice Davis was appointed Grace Dowling's legal guardian. Arrangements were made between the bank and the nursing home. In a subdued, oak-paneled, inner chamber of the Merrimac County Courthouse, men in three-piece suits cut through protective covenants like a hot knife through butter. Nothing extraordinary. Their *ex parte* requests were approved and implemented without debate.

Finally, briefcases in hand, the same lawyers left the courtroom. They left with a special satisfaction known only to their profession: they had accomplished legally what members of a less civilized society would have fought for with fists, or swords, or guns. And they did so amicably, without ever having to raise their voices. And at no time did perspiration ever appear on their brows.

And, moreover, their clients, in appreciation for what they had accomplished, were willing to pay them handsomely for their efforts, even going so far as to pick up the tab for the leisurely lunch that followed the proceedings, and then—incredible as it sounds—even to compensate them for the time they spent eating it!

Grace shared her last thoughts with no one: American courts had, uninvited, stepped into her life. Lawyers, judges, and later police and prisons stepped into her life. It seemed like only yesterday her nephew was a baby in her arms; now he wore a blue scrub uniform that smelled of bleach and sneakers that reeked of disinfectant. And who was wearing his true clothing? she wondered. Who deserved to wear it? A gentleman's clothing.

Later, at the end, the quiet epiphany: the old woman looking at the intravenous solution dripping into her body, realizing the futility of her plight, giving in to the hopelessness of it.

Ricker, as well, suffered in the aftermath of his aunt's visit. He fell into a depression as he saw his prospects vanishing—five years without anybody on the outside to persevere on his behalf—or, failing that, without anybody to serve simply as an ally, a street address, a yellow ribbon, a light in the window.

But depression rarely lasts in prison. Routine lumbers on—unstoppable—dragging everything and everyone along with it. A mysterious, organic, institutional flow soon overwhelms all personal affairs, forces all outside problems further and further into the background—and the *real world?*—well, with each passing day the real world becomes less important, less relevant, less *real.*

Ricker was not informed of his aunt's hospitalization. He learned of her death months later, and then only indirectly. As his money was nearing depletion, his interests were being served less and less. Finally, his lawyers, to their great relief, were allowed to withdraw from his case, and he was assigned court-appointed public counsel.

Chapter 6

Lying on his bunk with his hands behind his head on the pillow, Ricker watched the new man put away his things. From a plastic bag, issued downstairs, came all you'd need in small, medium, or large. The new man was an old man by prison standards—fifty, maybe sixty—with a dazed look that Ricker had seen on many men locked up for the first time. Ricker enjoyed watching these new arrivals. Their worst nightmare was about to come true, and he had a front row seat for the event.

Ricker kept his eye on the newcomer as the cell's steel door rolled closed and slammed. Did the old man's shoulders droop slightly at the sound? Was the color draining from his face? Did he feel faint when he sat down on his bare mattress?—or, was he trembling out of fear? Ready to sob? About to break down and cry for his mommy, his teddy bear, his psychiatrist . . . his lawyer?"

"What are you in for?" Ricker asked, rising slowly from his bunk.

The new arrival, sitting on his discolored mattress, looked up, startled. The big man standing before him reminded him of someone. Who? Elvis? Brando, as a young biker? Soldiers he had encountered in his Army days? "Umm . . . a divorce," he replied. "*Contempt of court* from a divorce." His words sounded apologetic as he spoke them, as if *armed robbery* or *assault with a deadly weapon* or even *murder one* would have given him greater status in his cellmate's eyes. He stood up to shake hands. "Ben Larkin's the name."

"Ricker," said Ricker, and he went back to his bunk.

"What do you do on the outside?" Larkin asked him.

Ricker looked over and smiled. In all of his four years in prison, no one had ever asked him that question. This old man was the first to ask him what he did on the outside. "I own a horse farm," he replied. "I board horses for rich people. I give riding lessons.

"I mean I *hire* instructors to give lessons," Ricker went on to explain. "I've had champions come out of my place. My stable competes at the highest levels. . . ." He got up and began to pace the small cell.

"Did I say I *own* a horse farm?" he repeated angrily, stopping in front of Larkin and staring into the old man's eyes. "I mean I *owned* one. My ex-wife grabbed it on me. Boom!—just like that—one day I turned around and I was in jail and the bastards had my place." Just then he began retching. He rushed over to the metal toilet in one corner of the cell, knelt, and, with his arms spanning the toilet bowl, attempted to vomit. He produced nothing, though. He stayed in that position for five, maybe ten minutes, then got up and went back to his bunk.

Later, Larkin noticed traces of blood inside the dry toilet bowl. He flushed it clean with a stream of urine.

Chapter 7

Cantrice made herself a cup of coffee in the mini-kitchen tucked in the back of the law offices of Stanton & Shaw. Davis, Stanton & Shaw when she was a little girl. Before the death of her father, a man she couldn't conjure—try as she might—in spite of the many black and white photographs she'd unearth every so often from her mother's mélange of treasures and junk. Fortunately, Archibald Shaw was there for the confused ten-year-old. He and her mother served jointly as her legal guardians.

With time she took comfort in the fantasy that, all along, Archy might have been her real father. Why not? Didn't she see looks and body language between him and her mother, or recall *almost* embraces broken off when she came into the room? But how can I get at the truth, she thought? They guard it so jealously. Mitzi Davis, too selfish to make the sacrifice, too selfish to give to her daughter the secret that might open the door to more secrets and the difficulties they'd surely spawn. And Archy, a fussy man (meticulously dressed, even at odd hours at home), always evasive, a master at anticipating problems. (His words coming back at him some day.)

No, thought Cantrice, the truth is a card they'll never play. An adult card held close to the vest. Part of what adults do, she concluded: holding cards, dealing, bluffing, walking away from the table when it suits them.

"Would you like a cup?" she asked, entering Shaw's office and choosing a comfortable chair near his desk. How many times had she approached him over the years across that very desk? Marched right in with a Shirley Temple smile. (All heads turn. Stenographers put down their pencils.) Interrupting what? Adversarial stand-offs? Intimidating depositions? Bankruptcies? Foreclosures? Who knows? Who cares? *Darlings* do that. It's expected of them.

"No thanks, Honey," he said. "You know, I don't see enough of you lately. You're getting to look more like your mother every day. There are some great genes for beauty in your family, it's a shame you don't have any kids to pass them on to."

What about me looks like my mother? wondered Cantrice, whose beauty was that of a model: tall, severe, angular—big eyes, near-anorexic body—while Mitzi Davis, her mom, had always been soft and cuddly.

"Your Rick episode might have been a disaster," continued Shaw, "but there's no reason you can't get out now, meet some men of your own class, and start a family of your own."

The young woman managed an agreeable smile. "Strange you should say that, Archy. I'm here because of Rick. He's due to be released soon."

"How soon, Honey?"

"Less than a year. Who knows? Any time now, maybe."

"Hmm," mused Shaw, up from his desk and pacing. He had developed the habit because it put his clients on the defensive— gave him a slight advantage over those seated. Now he did it automatically. "Are you afraid because of his outburst in court?"

Cantrice, once settled, remained seated during her sessions with Shaw. Her only activity, aside from occasional gesturing with her hands, was crossing and recrossing her legs, which she did often, especially when annoyed. "Of course I am, Archy," she responded with exasperation. "Who wouldn't be? He threatened my life, remember? Vowing to feed my body parts to my cat isn't something I'm likely to forget, is it? The man's a lunatic, and I'm petrified. That's why I'm here. I want you to take steps to protect me. I'm not prepared to have him come at me. Not now, not yet."

"But Cantrice," argued Shaw, "you can't take a little tantrum in court all that seriously. When he's done his time he'll come out meek as a lamb. Sure, men like Rick threaten at first, but five years is a very long time in the can. They cool down. They forget. They only want to get out and get on with their lives."

"That's just it, Archy," asserted Cantrice, turning in her seat and fixing a hard stare at him, "five years *is* a long time to brood over what he thinks is an injustice done to him. He'll want revenge. I know Rick better than you do. Do you know what he once said to me? It was during one of our weekly fights—daily fights, toward the end. It showed me how paranoid he really is:

"I was simply questioning him as to why he didn't include me, his wife, on any of the deeds to his real estate, and he said I'll never break the *Dowling Covenants*. As if I even knew what the *Dowling Covenants* were. And coming from Rick, a biker, not some country squire.

"The scary part was that he could change personalities so easily then—and what about now? Who knows what he's like now? I'm sure it'll be no gentleman who will walk out of that jail!"

Shaw had noticed a scuff on one of his shoes. He inspected it with a frown, a gesture that annoyed Cantrice. She continued, petulantly: "What life does he have to get on with, anyway? We took all his property, don't forget. Thanks to you, it's ours now. And the court gave us his bank accounts, his parents' insurance. Even his aunt's money is gone. The nursing home took care of that. No, Archy, I want you to keep him in. I'll never have a moment's peace with him on the street. You *can* keep him in, can't you?"

"I'll tell you what I'll do," said Shaw, seated again, jotting on a yellow legal pad. "I've known the warden up there since his law . . . um, enforcement days. I'll call him and have him check on Rick. He'll find out if that ex-husband of yours has been making any threatening remarks to anybody. We'll learn if he's bragging about any plots for revenge. They'll interview a cellmate or two. They know how to get information."

"I'm not happy with that, Archy," said Cantrice. "I can't imagine what you'll learn that will put my mind at ease."

Chapter 8

"D o you believe in God?" Ricker asked Larkin a week after the old man's arrival in prison.

Larkin, into a hunger strike and suffering, did not object to Ricker's attention. Any diversion, he thought, lying on his bunk in the foetal position, his head gripped with the worst migraine headache of his life, his whole body aching with flu-like symptoms.

"God?" He looked up, smiling. "God?"

Ricker was pleased to see the old man smile, although he thought he had asked a serious question. Smiling is rare in prison. Humor rarer still. Among inmates—psychopaths, angry men with hair triggers, human time bombs ready to explode— laughing at the wrong time or mocking the wrong man could lead to violence. As a result, most jailhouse inhabitants, guards included, opt for long faces.

Preferring Larkin's smile to the old man's former pained expression, Ricker continued: "Do you pray. Do you ask God for anything? Do you pray to get out?"

"No. I don't pray to get out," Larkin replied, in little more than a whisper. "God or Fate has put me here for a reason, and I don't want to second-guess what it might be, or question it, or interfere with it."

"Then you believe in God," asserted Ricker.

"I don't believe in *religion*, if that's what you mean," explained Larkin. "But I do believe in *something*. Something has shaped my life, and I trust it. It's helped me out. I listen to it. It sends me signals all the time, and I listen to them. They reassure me that my destiny will turn out all right."

"Jail?" noted Ricker. "Is jail a signal?"

"Could be," replied the old man, running a hand through his thinning hair. "I could be sent on a mission. Maybe not so much for myself, but maybe as part of somebody else's destiny turning out all right. Yours, for instance." He looked at Ricker, who had pulled up an overturned wastebasket and was sitting on it facing him.

"Mine?"

"From what you've told me, Ricker, you obviously come from a good family. Your people go way back. My guess is that you may even have aristocratic blood in your veins from your mother's side of your family, and maybe from the German side as well. You might be destined for better things in this world, and my being sent here might be part of some grand design to head you in that direction."

"You mean God ruined your life to save mine?"

Once again Larkin smiled. "You had a visitor yesterday?"

"An old girlfriend."

"Something to go back to when you get out?"

"I'm never going to get out, Larkin. That I'm sure of. People who have power over me wanted my possessions . . . and they got them. Now they want me in, permanently . . . and they're going to get that, too."

Chapter 9

STENOGRAPHER:

Do you swear that the testimony you are about to give will be the truth, the whole truth, and nothing but the truth, so help you, God?

CANTRICE DAVIS:

I do.

BRIAN HURLEY:

For the record, my name is Brian Hurley. I've been appointed by the court to represent the defendant, Denton Ricker. If there are no stipulations or objections, Mr. Shaw, I'll begin questioning your client.

B.H.:   Could you state your name?

C.D.:   Cantrice Davis.

B.H.:   Are you married to the defendant?

C.D.:   No.

B.H.:   Are you divorced?

C.D.:   Yes.

B.H.:   When did you obtain your divorce?

C.D.:   After Rick was in jail a few months, maybe a year.

B.H.:   What were the grounds for your divorce?

C.D.:   *Adultery.*

B.H.:   I'm surprised to hear you say that, Miss Davis. One would think with your husband's sentence . . . mmm. Why weren't the grounds *"Cruel and abusive treatment?"*

ARCHIBALD SHAW:

You may answer.

C.D.:   I think we had better evidence with *adultery.*

B.H.:   What was the nature of this *better evidence?*

C.D.:   We had videotapes. Photographs. Private detective affidavits.

B.H.:   Who was the third party? Or parties?

C.D.:   My friend Eve.

B.H.:   We'll get back to her later, but first I have a few more questions about your ex-husband. How long were you married?

C.D.:   Six years.

B.H.:   Were you happily married?

C.D.:   No.

B.H.:   Why not?

C.D.:   Rick was abusive, violent, and—of course—unfaithful.

B.H.:   Did he ever strike you?

C.D.:   Yes. He threw a beer bottle at me. It shattered in my sink. Shards of glass flew everywhere. I was petrified.

B.H.:   Please continue.

C.D.:   I could go on for hours. There was the Christmas tree incident. He threw a pair of pruning shears at me.

B.H.:   Yes. Please continue.

C.D.:   He was putting up the tree. I told him he was shaping it unevenly. He became furious. Threw the shears at me. Missed me by inches.

B.H.:   Did you report those assaults to the police?

C.D.:   Of course.

B.H.:   And that wasn't why you divorced him?

C.D.:   I didn't *say* that.

B.H.:   What *did* you say?

C.D.:   I said, "Those weren't the *grounds* for my divorce."

B.H.: Do you have any children?

C.D.: No.

B.H.: Could you explain why not?

C.D.: Rick didn't want to bring kids into this world against their will. "Kicking and screaming" is what he said, honest. He said it a lot, too.

B.H.: Did you use birth control? If so, what kind?

C.D.: Condoms. At first. It didn't make any difference. I think Rick was sterile, impotent.

B.H.: Do you *happen to know* the difference?

C.D.: Of course I do.

B.H.: Was he ever tested for sterility?

C.D.: No. But his family had a history of marriages without kids, or no marriages at all: bachelors, old maids. Whereas my family was normal. My mother was the youngest of six brothers and sisters.

B.H.: What about impotence?

C.D.: The last couple of years we had little sexual contact. None, actually.

B.H.: Did you work during your marriage?

C.D.: No. Rick wouldn't let me.

B.H.: What kind of work would you do if he'd let you?

C.D.: I was trained as a paralegal in college. Um, junior college. My dad was a lawyer. I had connections. I could have been a legal secretary. A highly paid one, at that.

B.H.: What made you think your ex-husband wouldn't let you follow the career of your choice?

C.D.: He said he didn't trust me around lawyers. No. Erase that. I mean he said he didn't trust them around me. Sorry.

B.H.: What did you do to pass the time?

C.D.: Nothing much. Went shopping with my mother.

B.H.: Were you close to your mother?

C.D.: Yes. She lived with me. She moved in a few years before my divorce. I wanted her around in case Rick became violent.

B.H.: Now let's return to Evangel Wells.

STENOGRAPHER:

Is that first name two words? Hyphenated? Could I get a spelling on that?

C.D.: E-V-E A-N-G-E-L W-E-L-Z. Two words in that first name, no hyphen.

B.H.: Could you tell us who she is?

C.D.: My best friend. We were at Pemiquabbin Community College together.

B.H.: When did this so-called adultery occur?

C.D.: A couple of years after we were married. It ended quickly, though.

B.H.: And then what? Could I get a chronology?

C.D.: Eve got married . . . but we stayed friends. We became even closer, actually. We always had *girls' night out* a couple of nights a week back then. Still do.

B.H.: Where do you go?

C.D.: A honky-tonk. A country dancing bar.

B.H.: Do you dance?

C.D.: Sometimes. Eve is the real dancer, though. Watching her is a treat. She and her partners enter nationwide competitions. It's poetry in motion—the turns, the loops. People leave the floor to watch them.

B.H.: What did Rick have to say about your *girls' night out* when you were married?

C.D.: He said he'd kill me if I ever cheated on him.

B.H.: Did you?

ARCHIBALD SHAW:

I object. Could I have a word with my client?

STENOGRAPHER'S NOTE:

(Miss Davis and Mr. Shaw leave the room.)

"Cantrice, remember what we went over," said Shaw, once they were out in the corridor. "Don't offer any more information than what they ask. Take your time. 'Yes' or 'No' answers are fine. Don't let them rattle you, as in that 'impotence/sterility' question. They try to aggravate you. They hope you'll lose your composure and say something you ordinarily wouldn't."

STENOGRAPHER:

    I'm ready, Mr. Hurley.

B.H.:   Was his liaison with Eve Angel his only infidelity you know about?

C.D.:   No. He had any number of motorcycle girls . . . I mean, No. Just No.

B.H.:   Anyone in particular?

C.D.:   How would I know their names? They were low-class sluts.

B.H.:   Did you ever videotape those occasions?

C.D.:   [No response.]

B.H.:   Would you *please* answer the question, Miss Davis?

C.D.:   I didn't think you wanted an answer. No.

B.H.:   Is "No" your answer?

C.D.:   Yes.

B.H.:   Do you know where Mr. Ricker is now?

C.D.:   In a mental hospital?

B.H.:   How did you find out?

C.D.:   I'm afraid of him. I ask around.

B.H.:   Do you think Ricker would harm you if he were released from jail?

C.D.:   Absolutely.

B.H.:   Why?

C.D.:   Wouldn't you, if somebody locked you up for five years?

B.H.:   I hereby conclude this deposition.

ARCHIBALD SHAW:

    I would like to indicate that it is now five o'clock.

(Whereupon the deposition
was concluded at 5:00 P.M.)

"Who was that sonofabitch?" asked Cantrice as she and Shaw left Hurley's office.

"I vaguely remember him from your first restraining orders against Rick," replied Shaw. "From way, way back. And then perhaps . . . um, he might have been around for the trial. But he didn't last long with the firm representing Rick, as I recall. He had his own ideas about how the case should proceed. He didn't want to follow the lead counsel's direction, so they canned him.

"Now he thinks he'll come back to haunt us. Well, Archibald Shaw has news for him."

Chapter 10

"Larkin, come with me," shouted a guard at the open cell door. "You have a meeting with your caseworker." The old man was alone in the cell. Earlier in the day, Ricker had been taken out to serve on a work detail.

Caseworker? thought Larkin. What now? What do I need with a caseworker? I'm here on a probate matter. A divorce. Why do they treat me like a criminal?

"They say you're not eating," said the small, fussy man from behind his flimsy desk. He was in his early thirties with a shiny forehead and bad skin. Larkin had seen him elsewhere in the prison recruiting candidates for A.A. meetings and religious services. They were in a room on the tier reserved for private conferences—lawyers, quasi-official visits. It had a phone, a desk, two plastic chairs, a wastebasket, nothing else. "They say you're on a hunger strike."

The old man shrugged absently.

"The County is concerned about you," asserted the young man. "About all of our inmates, of course, but in particular about intelligent, white-collar offenders like yourself. You're already in the protective custody section of this prison, but if you engage in a hunger strike, or any other act of disobedience around here—I'm telling you this for your own good, you know—Administration gets upset." He stared at Larkin aggressively, tapping his ballpoint pen on the table for emphasis. "They may want to place you somewhere else. In psychiatric evaluation, for example, or the infirmary ward, both of which are in *maximum security*. Am I getting through to you?"

The old man straightened up. I can't offend this little jerk, he thought with a twinge of panic; I can't risk letting him, with whatever power he has in here, undermine me from behind the scenes with some in-jail consequences, some version of the Army's *failure to obey a lawful order.* I can't risk having my status, like Ricker's, to go from *civil* to *criminal* for who-knows-why?

"I'm sorry," Larkin replied, wondering if he should add the word "sir." He decided against it. "I've always been a poor eater, even on the outside."

The caseworker seemed placated. The pen tapping stopped. "How are you sleeping? How do you get along with the other inmates? Your *cellmate?*"

"I'm sleeping fine," responded Larkin. "I can't explain it. The worse things get, the better I sleep. They took everything I own, and there's nothing I can do about it. Nothing. And so I sleep as much as I can. Sleep is my *only* refuge, as a matter of fact. But they wake us up at 5:00 A.M.; I'd sleep longer if they'd let me. . . ."

The caseworker cut the old man off. "And what about your *cellmate?* Do you get along with him?"

"Ricker?" replied Larkin. "Sure. Why not? He's a lot like me. Led a law-abiding life. Had money. Then a woman did him in. Lawyers, courts did him in. Never had a criminal record, he tells me. . . ."

Again the caseworker cut him off. "What are *his* plans when he gets out? Does he share them with you?"

Larkin watched the young man suspiciously. This man doesn't care about me; why did he call me in here? What does he really want? To find out, Larkin decided to play Ricker's *pecking order* game. According to the rules, those who talk first, or freely, are dismissed as inferior.

In the uncomfortable silence that followed, the caseworker's high forehead grew shinier; his small, dark eyes darted. "Tell me," he asked, tapping his pen on the desk once again, "has Mr. Ricker made any threatening remarks about his wife in your presence. In other words, Mr. Larkin, do you think Mr. Ricker would harm his wife if he were released?

"By the way," added the caseworker, "anything you tell us will go a long way toward improving your status around here . . . um, such as our finding more comfortable surroundings for you. . . ."

Bingo, thought Larkin, trying not to smile. "Harm his wife? I doubt it. He just wants to get out. Get out and get on with his life."

Chapter II

Ever since she received the subpoena from Hurley for her deposition, Eve Angel had trouble sleeping— indeed, the night before her appearance she hardly slept at all. Her uneasiness stemmed from her divided loyalties: support for her best friend, Cantrice; fair play for an already-betrayed Rick. Her dilemma was not eased by Shaw, who told her—warned her, actually—that he'd be there only to protect Cantrice's interests, not necessarily hers. She could ask him occasional questions, he said (less than reassuringly), but she should not expect him to shield her from the opposing counsel's legitimate *right to know*.

She arrived early for the deposition, wearing a pastel blouse, pleated skirt, and low boots of soft leather. Her blouse had subtle piping suggesting a western yoke, and her boots, too fragile for chores, were probably chosen for comfort—dancing, on another occasion—but under these circumstances, for the reassurance that familiar clothing often brings.

Eve Angel had straight, shiny, straw-colored hair turned in at the shoulders. Her eyes, similarly a straw-colored light brown, were spaced far apart on her small, flat face, giving her an expression of openness, honesty. This was not lost on Hurley, as he watched her delve into an over-the-shoulder burlap handbag of Navaho design and come up with a pair of oversized reading glasses.

"I only use them for fine print," she said, noting the dozens of documents spread out over the table. With her glasses on, she had an owlish look.

This woman could be a treasure, thought Hurley, fleetingly. He turned to the court stenographer. "Would you swear the witness?" he asked.

STENOGRAPHER:
> Do you swear that the testimony you are about to give will be the truth, the whole truth, and nothing but the truth, so help you, God?

E.W.: Yes, I do.

COUNSEL FOR
THE DEFENSE, BRIAN HURLEY:
> Please state your name for the record.

E.W.: Eve Angel Welz.

B.H.: How long have you known Denton Ricker?

E.W.: Let me see . . . he was married for five or. . . .

B.H.: Let me rephrase the question. When did you first meet Mr. Ricker?

E.W.: Around the time of his wedding.

B.H.: Do you mean to tell me that you didn't meet your best friend's fiancee until the wedding?

E.W.: Cantrice kept him pretty much to herself . . . and, I guess they were married fairly quickly. Not that she had to. She wasn't pregnant or anything.

B.H.: Could you describe him?

E.W.: He liked horses better than people.

B.H.: Could you clarify that answer?

E.W.: He was hard to talk to. Quiet. Aloof. Businesslike.

B.H.: What about his hobby, motorcycling?

E.W.: [Smiling.] He did it, but I don't think he enjoyed it very much.

B.H.: What makes you say that?

E.W.: [Still smiling.] Everyone thought he was such a macho guy with a noisy motorcycle, but the Rick I knew was happiest behind the wheel of a big car, listening to his favorite cassettes on the stereo.

B.H.: What were his favorites?

E.W. [No response.]

B.H.: It's not important, Miss Welz. I was just curious. You don't have to answer if you'd be uncomfortable doing so.

E.W.: Thank you. It is personal. I would be uncomfortable answering.

B.H.: Did he ever flirt with you? Make a pass?

E.W.: Yes.

B.H.: Could you elaborate?

E.W.: We had a brief affair.

B.H.: Yes. Please go on.

E.W.: Cantrice knew. She put me up to it, actually. They were crazy kids. We were all crazy and stupid. Drugs, sex, rock and roll—it was still the Age of Aquarius for us. We were like flower children. No consequences. If it felt good, we did it. But I am still puzzled. Cantrice was so possessive, jealous . . . and then that.

B.H.: Then what happened?

E.W.: I started falling for Rick, so I ended it. Cantrice was my friend. I owed it to her to be sane. To have some perspective.

B.H.: How did Ricker take it? Breaking up?

E.W.: I think he was hurt. In fact, I know he was. But he accepted my decision to end it in much the same manner as he did when it began. In some ways he was like a little boy. He sort of . . . just went along . . . as if he didn't know the rules. But I can't speak for him. Sorry.

B.H.: After the affair, then what?

E.W. Nothing. If their marriage was lousy, that was their

business. I married Stewie. But I stayed friends with Cantrice ... we just kept away from the old stuff. We avoided mentioning it, too.

B.H.: Do you see Cantrice regularly?

E.W. Yes. We go dancing together at least once a week.

B.H.: Does Stewie, your husband, approve? Does he accompany you?

E.W.: I don't live with Stewie anymore ... we're separated.

B.H.: I'm confused. Are you divorced? What are the terms of your separation?

E.W.: I don't know. He walked out on me a couple of years ago. We weren't getting along too well, and ... he decided to leave. There were no kids involved, so no big deal, right?

B.H.: Do you hear from him? Where is he now?

E.W.: The last I heard, he was in Casper, Wyoming. In with some oil field people. But I have no details.

B.H.: Let's move on to another subject. When did you last see Denton Ricker?

E.W.: I visited him in jail.

B.H.: What was the purpose of that visit?

E.W.: His aunt had died. I wanted to tell him, and perhaps comfort him in his loss.

B.H.: Did you?

E.W.: He knew. He had sent her a Christmas card, and it came back "deceased."

B.H.: Have you spoken to him since then?

E.W.: No.

B.H.: I may be stepping out of line by asking this question ... but what are your feelings toward Mr. Ricker?

E.W.: I don't understand.

B.H.: Well, Miss Welz, do you love him?

Eve Angel inhaled quickly with an audible gasp and her eyes filled up. "Let's recess for ten minutes," said Hurley, taking a box of Kleenex from the credenza behind him and placing it on the table near her.

Everyone, their eyes on Eve Angel, remained motionless. After a few moments she looked up and smiled. "I'm sorry," she said, "let's continue. I'm okay," then added, "I didn't sleep much last night. I'm nervous, upset."

E.W.:   I'm sorry. Let's continue. I'm O.K. I didn't sleep much last night. I'm nervous. Upset.

B.H.:   [To stenographer] Is that on the record?

STENO.:

        Yes, Mr. Hurley.

B.H.:   Just a few more questions, Miss Welz. Do you think Mr. Ricker would harm your friend Cantrice if he were released from prison?

E.W.:   [Shrugging.] I have no idea about that . . . sorry.

B.H.:   Did you ever see him hit her?

ARCHIBALD SHAW:

        She testified four years ago under oath, Counselor, that she did.

B.H.:   I've never been able to find that testimony on the record, Mr. Shaw. So, with your permission. . . . Did you ever see him hit her, Miss Welz?

E.W.:   I saw her in tears. Hysterical. It was upsetting. I tried to put it out of my mind. Perhaps I succeeded. Those days are a blur to me now.

Chapter 12

Ricker was called into court on a *habeas corpus* warrant, the legal justification for bringing inmates before a judge, the ticket to ride the never-ending court/prison shuttle. (If you miss one, don't worry; another will be along shortly.) He wore a blue scrub uniform. The ritual was always the same:

He sat up on a high bench while guards—transporting officers, this time—cuffed him at the wrists and ankles. Later, with the same guards on either side, Ricker shuffled, chains clattering, along corridors toward the impenetrable hydraulic exit doors. The officer who controlled these doors from within a bulletproof cage kept them waiting. Presently, he looked Ricker over, checked his papers, and then, with a nod to the guards, pushed the button energizing the noisy mechanism. Once through, Ricker waited once again while the guards accompanying him, who weren't allowed to carry firearms within the prison, took turns retrieving their guns from security lockers in a vault beside the main entrance. Finally, they led Ricker to what formerly had been called a paddywagon but was now referred to by the more politically-correct designation: van. "Watch your head," they always say. It means, "Get in."

These vans are the same size and shape as those used by air-courier delivery services, but with modifications for a vastly different payload. The freight compartment, the body of the truck, is fitted out with an inner cage. The prisoners sit on wooden planks along the sides of this cage.

Ricker had always gotten carsick easily, but on these trips, with inmates often smoking in the dark, confined area, his nausea was especially severe. It's punishment. It's what jail is all about, he thought, so why complain? The drivers will still make hairpin turns, jackrabbit starts, and screeching halts, totally indifferent to the cargo in back. (Or was there some deliberate aggression here?) Ricker wondered if civilians seeing these vans on the road had any idea of the suffering of the human beings caged inside them.

Not only were prisoners cuffed at the hands and feet; two or three men were often shackled together. On this trip, an especially crowded one, Ricker found himself sitting in the middle of a string of three men (the worst arrangement, with each of the others chained to him pulling in opposite directions at every swerve along the way). He sat on the hard bench, head in his hands, elbows on his knees. Cutting into his knees, as the trip wore on. He relieved his pain by moaning. "Tell that wimp to shut up," said a teenage voice somewhere in the semi-darkness. No one came to Ricker's defense.

In court, on a bench outside the courtroom, he was told by the young public defender assigned to his case, that evidence had been gathered against him in prison. "They want to give it to a grand jury," added the lawyer, a recent graduate from a predominantly Jewish law school in New York. The young man was obviously an intellectual, out of place among men in handcuffs but sent down by his elders to cut his teeth in the real world. "The grand jury decides whether or not there is sufficient evidence for a trial. They could have a time-consuming jury trial, or simply a hearing before a judge."

This kid couldn't care less about me, thought Ricker, as the young lawyer went on and on in nasal tones. Taking my case will bring him nothing: no money, no interesting legal insight, and no respect from his peers. "What are *they* charging me with?" Ricker asked, running his hands through his thick, dark hair with frustration and dismay.

"I've seen some of the affidavits," replied the young lawyer, glancing quickly at his wristwatch. "There's an incriminating letter. They have the names of people with whom you conspired."

"Conspired?" gasped Ricker, incredulous.

The young lawyer seemed unimpressed with his client's naiveté—the feigned naiveté of hardened criminals, he thought, suppressing a smile but smirking, nonetheless. "To murder your ex-wife, of course. If they make their charges stick it could mean another five, ten years behind bars."

"You've got to be kidding," groaned Ricker. "What letter? Who are these people? I never conspired with anybody. I don't want to harm Cantrice, and if I did, I certainly wouldn't tell any of these jailbirds about it. I just want to do my last year and get out."

The lawyer droned on, chanting almost: "Granted, these inmates are not very reliable witnesses. Their credibility would certainly be challenged by me or whoever is chosen to represent you, but anything can happen when you go to trial. Conspiracy trials, in particular, never go as planned. When you get in front of a jury your whole case could turn on some unexpected testimony—from your ex-wife, for instance—an emotional appeal from a tormented woman. A woman living in constant fear."

"Are you trying to head me in some direction?" asked Ricker, dreading the answer.

"I'd go for a plea bargain," the young lawyer responded. "If we waive the jury trial and simply appear before a judge . . . well, he just might be more lenient . . . um, more than might; he's certain to be. I guarantee it. I see probation. Close monitoring for a year or two. You certainly have no objection to that, do you?"

"You guarantee probation for a year or two?" asked Ricker. "When does this hearing take place?"

"We can do it this morning," said the smiling lawyer, opening his slim, Italian leather briefcase. "I have the papers right here for you to sign."

Chapter 13

After Ricker had signed all the documents that his young, court-appointed lawyer had put before him, cooperated with everyone, and, in turn, received everyone's smiles, their best wishes—blessings, even—he was brought down to the basement of the courthouse to languish in a holding cell until the judgment against him, the plea bargain that he had made, could be translated into a document that the sheriff's department could implement.

There is a holding cell in every courthouse, in most every police station. It's called the "tank." You can spend a few hours there, or you can spend most of the day. You can have company —rough young men, for the most part, who may or may not be amusing—or you can be alone.

Ricker was in with a group of rowdy teenagers who were trying to impress one another. Their leader was snorting sugar from the small paper packets that accompany take-out coffee. He held his clenched fist vertically, then carefully tapped out a small amount of ordinary sugar from the torn-off corner of one of the packets onto the fleshy area between the knuckles of his thumb and forefinger. His friends watched with admiration as he inhaled the granules into his nose. These youngsters did not seem inconvenienced by jail. Indeed, they appeared to be as comfortable there as in their former schoolyards, playgrounds— at worst, detention halls.

More than that. Jail gave them status. It promoted them— something their schools were reluctant to do. It earned them respect from their peers and reputations as more worldly, adult, in-the-know about important subjects. Not math or geography, but what really matters: sex, cars, drugs, and quick money.

Finally, Ricker's name was called. Transporting officers led him from the cell to a high bench for the familiar shackling process:

Handcuffs. The universal symbol of subjugation. The guards at each facility have their own sets, which only their keys fit. When a man is picked up, the facility set is exchanged for those of the transporting officers. At their destination the same officers recover their cuffs, and the prisoners are given over to the new authorities for reshackling with new ones. A constant exchange—uncuffing, recuffing.

This process is done carefully, efficiently, professionally. The familiar sound of chains. A soft sound, actually. Not like the rolling and latching of heavy steel doors that give the "slammer" its name. Chains are like the tide moving a slope of pebbles along the sand. A series of soft clicks as the links pass over one another.

Later, from an entrance in the basement of the courthouse, overhead steel garage doors opened and Ricker's van emerged. On a routine trip like this, the drivers might make half a dozen stops—courthouses, police stations, jails—picking up and dropping off prisoners along the way. In vans with no windows except in the driver's compartment, if you want to see out you have to settle for an obstructed view: the backs of guards—their heads, their hats. Around and beyond that, the tops of trees or telephone wires are all that's visible, so craning your neck accomplishes little. Where are they headed, you wonder? How long will it take? You seldom bother to ask. You're cattle back there. They've got a manifest somewhere, and your name is on it.

The officers up front—drivers, deputies, guards (all designations apply)—receive radio messages continuously. Like fighter pilots, they often change course, swooping down on some police station for a last-minute detainee here, or snatching up some defendant whose case took a turn for the worse there, or delivering some poor soul elsewhere for whom a judge, having weighed the options—the street, a prison cell—made the comfortable choice. Society's thumbs are happiest when pointing down, anyway.

Lakewood State Hospital for the Criminally Insane made its presence known to Ricker from the start, from the moment he stepped out of the van, squinting and blinking, into daylight and was led through Gothic arches into the ancient building.

A sense of doom and foreboding made this place much scarier to him than any of the jails they had moved him to, and through, in his last four years. Why? He looked around the lobby for clues. Industrial furniture: Formica, plastic, and chrome. A receptionist's counter. A narrow, high-ceilinged, fluorescent-lit hallway leading back into the entrails of the building, and there, at the end of the hall, a heavy iron door. His eyes kept returning to that tunnel-like passageway . . . to that impenetrable door.

And the smell. For some reason Ricker thought of animals in a veterinarian's waiting room. Sick or wounded creatures in similar lobbies leaving clues for those who would come later. Small creatures in a panic leaving traces of urine, feces, blood, vomit—bodily secretions never fully masked by disinfectant. Odors still perceptible on some level to those who followed.

Ricker likewise sensed the grim procession of those before him. On some subconscious level he felt their presence. In the silence he heard their screams. The cries of the mentally deranged. Lunatics in straitjackets.

He fought off the irresistible urge to imitate them. To go berserk. To give in to hysteria. To let out screams of his own.

Befoul his pants. Drool. Lapse into convulsions and seizures and eventually into some infantile state. Some involuntary state. Some vegetative state.

The two guards, one on each side of Ricker, led him down the narrow corridor toward the metal door. Here they stopped before a glass-shielded video camera and waited. "They'll let us in, in a minute or two," one of the guards said. "They're sending someone down for us now."

Standing in front of the locked door, Ricker felt faint. His knees felt weak. Part of him yearned to collapse. Let them carry me in, he thought. Let them drag my limp body in.

Suddenly he felt like vomiting. A strange taste in his mouth—coppery, like bile or ipecac—accompanied by a wave of nausea. Water formed copiously in his mouth, and, without warning, in his bowels as well.

They converged upon him—men in white coats with syringes. They knew what they were doing. They knew what they had to do. They eased his pain.

Chapter 14

Except for a small window, Ricker's cell had no bars. It was in a new wing of the old hospital. The prison disguised as a hospital. Doctors had a hand in naming things here. They brought their own brand of reality to this place: candy on receptionists' desks, framed posters on walls, flowers in vases, pretty names for ugly things.

Ricker's cell, called a "room" here, had walls of cream-colored tile and a floor and ceiling of concrete painted pale green. The window consisted of plastic panes set into a thick metal grid through which escape would be impossible. The solid steel door contained two openings with hinged metal flaps that could be closed and latched from the outside. He had a single, bunk-type bed with a pale green rubber mattress and matching rubber pillow.

At no time during his stay at Lakewood did Ricker meet anyone criminally insane; nobody threatened him; he saw no violence, no brutality. Nor did he see men with grotesque physical deformities and the psychopathic behavioral symptoms he imagined to accompany such afflictions. He looked closely at his fellow inmates for signs of their particular mental derangement:

cannibalism, infanticide, sadism, serial killing. . . . He expected to find the stuff of nightmares; he did not get what he expected.

Instead, he saw hordes of alcoholics, with and without shakes and tremors, and drug addicts, burned-out cases with symptoms of withdrawal although they were long past anything that could be considered a withdrawal period.

He saw men with runny noses, skin rashes, speech impediments. Blind and half-blind. Crippled and half-crippled. Half-cured AIDS patients. Every degree of retardation imaginable. Palsy. Senile dementia. Things he had no name for. Every one of these men showed signs of some mental defect but, thought Ricker, so did most of the inmates and many of the guards at every other prison he'd ever been in, albeit to a lesser extent. And furthermore, he mused, so did most of the bums on skid row, who by some quirk of fate just didn't *happen* to be in jail at that particular moment. And while we're at it, he speculated further, why not include everybody on the poor side of town? When times are bad and money is scarce, can mental problems be far behind?

Did that mean all down-and-outs were mentally defective, all derelicts crazy to some extent? He had a tattoo, a full beard, and a biker's bad attitude to go with them. Some considered him violent. In spite of Gulbrandsen's kind words, wasn't he the quintessential loser? Wasn't he just as crazy as everyone else in this place? Lying on the long bench beside the door to his psychiatrist's office, using his Bible for a pillow, he thought the answer to both questions might very well be "Yes."

"You are here for ninety days' psychiatric evaluation," said Dr. Randerath, once his patient was seated in the chair beside his desk, "during which time those in charge hope to determine where to send you for the balance of your sentence."

The doctor's office was located in the old part of the hospital, the grim part, the part housing therapy rooms, unused rooms, mysterious unmarked rooms. Rooms with inner soundproof doors. In one room, a table girded with leather straps next to an ancient wooden console from which medusa-like electrodes emanated. In another room (behind drawn amber shades), a cabinet containing cold stainless steel instruments near one wall—in the center, a porcelain, barbershop-like chair above a floor drain.

Inmates (they were called "patients" here) waited on benches beside certain doors in the dimly-lit corridor. Eventually their doctors would open these doors and summon them in.

"My sentence!" snapped Ricker, from his chair beside the doctor's desk. "Probation, you mean."

Maintaining eye contact, the doctor said nothing.

"Evaluation for what? Conspiracy? Is that what they're charging me with? Conspiracy to harm my wife? Bullshit! I made a plea bargain. I have my attorney's guarantee. The sentence is *probation*."

Randerath turned to the slim folder on his desk. He was an Indian from India, with grayish, tan-colored skin. His thick, straight hair was black and shiny, his dark eyes intense—in a way, hypnotic (silent movies, the eyes of Valentino came to mind). He wore a tweed jacket with elbow patches in style of a country gentleman. In general, thought Ricker, his appearance is quite pleasant. He imagined the doctor's wife: blond, slightly taller than her husband (in heels); their large house filled with kids, an English nanny; a mud room with soccer balls, ski boots, and riding helmets; two Volvos in the circular driveway.

"I can't seem to find your court records," said Randerath, in a slightly British accent, "which is indeed unfortunate, since I would like to respond, with appropriate cognizance, to your concerns: the charges against you, the nature of your offense, and the sentence, if any, imposed. Anyway, I shall make every effort to obtain your records before our next meeting, which is *shed'yuled* [his pronunciation] for next Tuesday. Your sessions with me, every Tuesday and Thursday, will last one hour and fifteen minutes and commence promptly at 1:30 P.M. A *shed'yule* confirming this should be posted in the cafeteria. [They call the chow hall a 'cafeteria,' here.] By way of introduction, is there anything further you'd like to say or ask me at this time?"

"I told you I had my attorney's guarantee that my plea bargain would result in probation. I had a court-appointed lawyer, Doctor, who guaranteed leniency for me. Do you know what 'probation' means? It means I get out. I want out. I want fucking out!"

"Perhaps they merely want you here for a psychiatric evaluation before releasing you, Mr. Ricker. Before releasing you back into society?"

Chapter 15

"We still can't seem to locate your court records," Randerath said when, at their next session, Ricker was seated in his chair beside the doctor's desk.

"I trusted this Jewish lawyer."

"Go on," suggested Randerath.

"He talked me into a plea bargain to get me out of jail. He gave me his word and I trusted him. Why did I trust him? Let me tell you why:

"I once had a Jewish girlfriend. I believe in Fate, by the way. So I believed that Fate sent me this Jewish girlfriend for some reason, for some purpose. And sure enough, a few weeks later, she took me to her Jewish synagogue. It was on a High Holy Day, a fast day, and she wanted company, so I went with her. I was flabbergasted by the experience.

"They're a lot like Catholics, by the way, with their rituals. The music. The tabernacle. The rabbi and the congregation saying lines from their Day of Atonement service, in turn. But it wasn't *how* they said it, but *what* they said that got to me.

"They were atoning for their sins of the past year. Sins mentioned in their prayer books. Sins actually *spelled out* in black and white in their prayer books! Sins in which they may have cheated people. Shortchanged them. Sins in which they may have sold defective merchandise, or treated their rich sick patients better than their poor sick patients. Or the sin of having defended their poor clients with less enthusiasm than they would their rich clients. . . .

"Anyway, I was impressed by the *humanity* of these words and everybody's concern, not for themselves, but for their fellow human beings. I walked out of there with new feelings for the worthiness of mankind. New respect for the dignity and impor-tance of every one of us here on earth no matter how wretched. I was in a state of grace that took a long time wearing off. . . .

"So when this Jewish lawyer was sent to represent me, I said to myself: Why was it that I met this girl who took me to a Jewish house of worship? Was Fate preparing me for something down the road?—namely, this lawyer with his plea bargain!

"And so I trusted him. I thought he was sent to help me. I signed his fucking documents."

Chapter 16

At their next session, it was Randerath who spoke first: "Once again Mr. Ricker, I am distressed to inform you that we still haven't found your court records. Because of circumstances beyond your control—beyond mine, too—we are once again forced to proceed in the dark, if you will, regarding your prospects."

Both men sat, for a considerable length of time, in the silence that followed. A minute. A long minute of silence. Then another. Finally, an endless five minutes had elapsed, both men staring at each other with Ricker turning away first, for the most part. But every so often, Ricker would maintain eye contact and it would be Randerath who turned away first. Then, according to Randerath's ticking clock on the other side of the room, ten minutes had gone by. Then fifteen.

"Is this bullshit, or what?" Ricker finally said.

Still nothing from Randerath.

"Are you playing some sort of shrink game with me?"

"Not at all," Randerath replied. "What might you expect me to say?—to have said?"

"How about questioning me? Ask me about my childhood. Get a picture of my life."

"Would you like to tell me about yourself?" asked the doctor.

Ricker frowned. "Actually, I wouldn't tell you shit. I don't know you. I don't think I trust you."

"Do you consider me your enemy? How do you see me?"

Ricker sat up straight in his flimsy plastic chair: "I see you as a person with power over me. You can write a good report about me, or not. If I rub you the wrong way, you might fuck me. [Ricker decided a little candor, even false candor, might be appropriate at that point in his conversation. Acknowledge my position as weak, he thought, but my mental state, strong.]

"Anyway," he continued, "why should I trust you? Who are you working for? me or the State? They're the ones who are paying you. What standing could I possibly have around here? [His objective: to appear capable of understanding his predicament—i.e., reality, a commodity in short supply among the insane. Will these sessions be inner dialog, second-guessing, and head games like this from now on? he mused (not entirely displeased by the prospect.)]"

"One of the tasks assigned to me here at the hospital," explained Randerath, never once looking away from his patient, "is the psychiatric evaluation of those admitted from the criminal justice system. I am required to address a number of categories in a protocol given to me by the court, and I try to do so with the utmost scientific objectivity. This means to me, Mr. Ricker, that neither your interests nor those of the State shall deter me from conducting myself professionally and ethically."

"What are those protocol categories, if I may ask?" asked Ricker, who wasn't sure he even knew what a "protocol" was. "Could they be trying to weasel out of my plea bargain? Could they be trying to get you to give them some reason—any reason—to keep me locked up?"

Randerath again smiled. He was obviously enjoying this exchange. "Confidentiality prevents me from discussing my duties with patients in this institution, but candidly, Mr. Ricker,

I don't reveal my treatment mode with my private patients either, and they do pay their own bills. Actually, the doctor/patient relationship that obtains outside prison doesn't necessarily apply here, but let me assure you, Mr. Ricker, that I'm scrupulously vigilant about what I perceive to be 'patients' rights.' I took an oath as a physician; I won't do the State's bidding if it runs counter to your best interests. When I get your court documents—if I ever do (the doctor shrugged and shook his head, woefully)—you can be sure I'll evaluate your situation with the utmost professional diligence."

"They framed me with some garbage about a 'conspiracy' to harm my wife," declared Ricker, hoping, by providing his side of the story first, to anticipate and counterbalance the specious affidavits he imagined to be in among the court records destined to find their way to Randerath. "They want you to justify their bogus case by discovering some sort of violent streak in me. They're looking for hidden anger and plans for revenge."

"That may very well be part of your *legal* dilemma," said Randerath, his gaze benign, compassionate, "but as far as I'm concerned, you're starting with a clean slate in here. I'll consult your case history, of course, but I see the blind acceptance of it as cheating both of us, especially me. I see science as inquiry without prejudice—letting the chips fall where they may, as you Americans like to say—and, to me, good science is its own reward."

Ricker left the interview elated, though doubts remained. The lost files. The confidential protocol. His conclusion: Randerath was merely another part of a System determined to categorize him as a danger to society and bond him to the criminal justice system for the rest of his life. And yet, on some level he was pleased with the session. Why?

For one thing, he had the first opportunity in more than four years to talk to someone in authority who could respond rationally. And now—especially now, surrounded by genuine loonies—he was close to overjoyed by that twice-a-week prospect. Here, in a sea of blank stares, pained expressions, and angry grimaces, he found himself sporting an ear-to-ear smile.

Chapter 17

The fact that this was no ordinary prison but a mentally-oriented one revealed itself to Ricker in many ways, all of which he found troubling. Instead of having access to basic necessities, here he received a foot locker with only a blanket, towel, change of uniform, underwear, and toilet paper. That was it. None of the so-called "canteen" items: health and beauty aids, junk food, or housekeeping articles to which he had been accustomed. His toothbrush, toothpaste, and soap were kept in his cubbyhole near the bathroom (used by others? he wondered) and dispensed to him by an attendant. They called the guards here "attendants."

Two periods of so-called "recreation" took place in the day room following the noon and evening meals. Ricker inquired about weightlifting and basketball, or even the possibility of walking in the yard. "Pumping iron?" responded the slim, neatly-dressed attendant, looking him up and down. "Take my advice. Ask for *medication*. Relax and enjoy life a little."

During their twice-a-day indoor recreation periods, zombie-like inmates stared blankly at the loud, non-stop TV (cartoons and MTV almost exclusively). But what really fascinated Ricker were the smokers. In any prison, almost everyone smokes, guards included, and this place was no exception. But here, most inmates were too poor to afford cigarettes. Here they had to roll their own.

They'd spread out their paraphernalia on cafeteria tables in the day room. Some rolled by hand, but most used small rolling machines, devices that looked like tiny conveyer belts—small frames with rollers. A rubber belt wove its way around these rollers and, when properly heaped with tobacco, would, if all went well, discharge something resembling a cigarette. Actually, it took quite a knack to produce a smokable product, a knack that Ricker never quite mastered. Licking and hand-doctoring his imperfect specimens, he'd wonder what went wrong. . . .

Like the others, he'd sit before his pale blue canister of Bugler tobacco. He'd lick his paper as they did and insert it into his machine. He'd put his heap of tobacco on the belt and allow the paper to encircle it, to pack it into a cylindrical shape. But somehow what emerged always seemed flawed: mutilated, wrinkled, torn, and with strands of tobacco spilling from the ends.

Meanwhile, the smokers rolled on, often stockpiling thirty or more masterpieces to take back to their rooms, a ready arsenal for friends who knew exactly where to go for a smoke. But when these two activities were combined, rolling along with smoking, a truly fascinating dimension to this ritual emerged: it became a self-contained, self-sustaining, self-gratifying process.

If, for instance, a patient produced an exceptionally fine product, he just might choose to put it to the test. After admiring it for a while—at arm's length, if his eyesight were failing—he'd go over to The Machine for lighting it up. Matches and cigarette lighters were contraband, forbidden within the hospital, which furnished a device, The Machine, a black box with a coil inside, to give the patient his light.

Arriving at The Machine, the man would, most likely, stop and stare at his cigarette—examine each end carefully, since not only are no two cigarettes alike, neither are each of the two ends equally suitable for lighting. After choosing the more appropriate of the ends, he would insert it into a hole in the side of The Machine and press a button. An electrical current would then heat an inner wire coil and ignite the tip of the cigarette. Then, back at his seat once again, the smoker would embark on the business at hand, the very serious business of "smoking."

This was not something he did while he was doing something else. This was the activity itself. To Ricker there was poetry in what he saw:

> A deep drag, a few seconds' wait,
> and then the slow exhale—
> nose, mouth, or an easy combination of both.
> Ah, the smoke from deep within.
> His smoke.
> A bit of a miracle: fire, light, heat, taste . . . satisfaction.
> Memories of his youth,
> the cigarettes of days gone by:
> pool halls, street corners, the Army,
> cocktails . . . sex.
> A life measured in cigarettes.
> The cigarettes of days gone by.

Ricker watched the smoker smoke—stared, actually. These inmates didn't seem to mind, or perhaps they didn't even notice his eyes on them. Anyway, he'd think: they're fair game, better than TV. His own private show: live but not unpredictable—no script but not improvisational; dull, but somehow compelling.

With time, the denouement would occur—the smoker would approach a crossroads: To snuff or not to snuff. He'd frown—a troubled man regarding a barely holdable cigarette butt with dismay. Deep lines would crease his classic brow. Wrinkles, like those of Robert Frost (a mark of character) would appear.

To snuff or not to snuff.

If snuffing were the verdict, the smoker would carefully pinch the burning embers, peel off and discard the paper, and put all salvageable shreds of tobacco back into his Bugler can for another time. Sitting in a haze of smoke (a haze in his mind too, perhaps), he'd remain motionless. But wait!—he just might do something unexpected. Time permitting, he just might light up once again.

The smoke in the day room, in the new section of the hospital, was re-circulated in a ventilation system that included cells, common rooms, and administrative offices. It took in no fresh air from the outside. In this facility no windows could be opened; you were doomed to breathe the same air for months— who knows?—even for years. If one person had a cold or the flu, everyone got it, and the last man to get it might, after a few weeks, reinfect everyone else all over again with a new, mutant strain of the virus.

The doctor assigned to "sick call," a man in his seventies, perhaps late seventies, presided over his endless procession of runny noses with what seemed, at first glance, to be a *sensible detachment* from the tedious complaints of his patients. But upon closer examination: detachment—yes; sensible—hardly. "Where am I?" would better describe this old relic. Senile dementia would describe him better still. "Nurse . . . nurse. What are these . . . m-m-mental cases doing wandering about in *m-my* waiting room? Nurse . . . nurse."

Chapter 18

Since his last session with Randerath, on Thursday of the previous week, Ricker had seen his mood deteriorate from some misbegotten version of satisfaction with his therapist to one reflecting reality. The grim reality of prison life. Weekend visitors for some—but not for him—played a part. And the too-perfect summer weather played a part as well.

Looking out through the metal-caged plastic window in his room, he saw high, wispy clouds and blue sky. Not a tentative, pastel tint, either, but a solid chemical blue—acrylic, almost, in its strength of color. Deep blue holding its own against the variegated greens of the tall pine forest that rose up beyond the hospital grounds. An irreplaceable summer day, lost to him in prison.

A day on horseback of years past, he thought. A day to ride for miles across fields and along trails. To ride aimlessly, without map or compass. "Give me back that day and I'll ask for nothing more," he whispered, as a prayer to God. "That day on horseback is all I ask. Nothing more."

"Your prayers have been answered," said an attendant at Ricker's open door.

Startled, Ricker turned from the window.

"Your court documents have been found," announced the attendant. "They came in this morning."

By the following Tuesday, desperate for his session with Randerath, Ricker sat nervously on the arm rest of the bench beside the doctor's door. Randerath opened it promptly at 1:30. "Keeping patients waiting is a game I don't play," he said, smiling cordially.

When they were both seated, the doctor continued: "Eureka! We are finally in possession of your court documents. They turned up in the Merrimac County Commissioner's office, of all places, while the esteemed administrator was on vacation in Alaska."

"Are we having fun yet?" said Ricker, staring, with a sense of dread, at the suddenly bulging file folder on Randerath's desk.

"Bravo, Mr. Ricker. You've caught your doctor committing gratuitous sarcasm. I commend you for it. But getting back to the court records . . . *conspiracy to commit a felonious assault.* It seems that you waived a jury trial in order to go before Judge Allissa, who, under sentencing guidelines enacted by the Massachusetts Legislature last year, was required to give you a minimum of ten years in state and county facilities, with no parole eligibility for five years."

When Ricker heard these words he became acutely aware of his stomach and the fact that his lunch was not the least bit digested. It was just as he ate it, garbage, sitting there in tiny, chewed-up globs, mixing together but not going anywhere. He thought he could taste parts of it. The oilier parts.

Beads of perspiration formed on his forehead, and a ringing in his ears grew louder and louder. At the same time, Randerath's voice was getting fainter. The doctor's lips were moving but no sound was coming out.

Randerath eased his unconscious patient to the floor and called for an attendant by pushing a small button on the far side of his desk. After Ricker had been given an injection, he was taken in a wheelchair, head bobbing on his chest, back to the new wing of the hospital—back to his room.

There's no way I can do that kind of time, he thought, when he regained consciousness . . . though, all along, he knew they would give up on him, sell him out, betray him. He knew he'd be breathing jailhouse air for the rest of his life.

He knew he would never again smell hay, leather saddlery, liniment, creosote, woodstoves, apples rotting on the ground . . . manure. The stuff of his life. The stuff that gave him dignity.

Manure, he thought. If I could just muck out a stall full of it . . . or brush down the horse that left it. If I could just have that horse's blanket, the ranker the better. If only I could wrap myself in that horse's blanket, go to sleep smelling that horse . . . ah, what sweet dreams . . . what peaceful dreams. . . ."

His wish list. His Rosary.

His illusion. Prayers, once comforting, he realized now, were nothing more than a mockery of hope, a narcotic to mask unspeakable pain.

Indeed, Ricker was one of those men who found "doing time" unspeakably painful. He could never give in to the routine of jail, never accept institutionalization as a way of life. For many convicts, jail becomes home. They make their surroundings their own. They accumulate heavy blankets, untorn sheets, and goosedown pillows. They separate their laundry into whites and colors and criticize those who don't. They seem to know the rules—complain if things are not as they should be. They insist on their rights.

Ricker was not one of these men. He never complained about anything. The arbitrariness of guards never bothered him. He kept his eye on the outside. He could endure any pain with his wrap-up date in mind, and now, with that expectation blown to smithereens, his despair was overwhelming. As the day wore on, he lay in his bed wrapped in a blanket, the picture of the quintessential mental patient: shivering slightly, praying for death, pondering the details of suicide.

The setting sun projected his window and its grid of bars onto the wall above him where it reddened, then weakened, then disappeared entirely. Ricker's stomach pain persisted; nausea came and went in waves, but he suppressed the urge to vomit, to see the blood he knew would be there. The sinking feeling of dread and despair he remembered upon entering the Lakewood Hospital for the Criminally Insane returned: the taste of vomit in his mouth and the sour smell of nervous sweat from his armpits.

Before the evening meal, a nurse came around with a cart. Now Ricker would be included in *medication*. Now he would join the others, nine out of ten in this place, who took some type of drug four times a day. A fifth in the middle of the night for those needing it. He swallowed the contents of a tiny plastic vial of liquid that tasted like maraschino cherry syrup.

Within seconds his stomach settled. His throat relaxed. The metallic taste was masked by the syrup and never returned. Even the ominous recollection of his anxiety disappeared. The heavy cloud of doom and foreboding had evaporated into thin air.

Chapter 19

At 1:30 Randerath opened his door, and a languid Ricker slouched into his small, impersonal office. Impersonal in that no family photographs were on display, none of the clues that patients seek out so desperately for insights into their psychiatrist's private life. Except for an oriental rug on the floor, and a Roman-numeraled wind-up clock on a side table, it could have been the office of any therapist on Lakewood's staff.

Ricker had always imagined a psychiatrist's desk to be somewhat messy but not chaotic. That message would tell the patient that, yes, while our lives are never totally neat and orderly, we still try to keep them under control. Randerath's desk was pristine. Its surface held only a pad of paper and a ballpoint pen. On one occasion, however, an ivory-handled silver letter opener lay beside the paper. On the side facing Ricker.

"Apart from bodily functions," asked Ricker, dropping noisily, recklessly into his chair, "what do inmates do in prison that's exactly the same as if they were doing it on the outside?"

Ricker's eyes strayed from the letter opener to the doctor's loudly ticking clock while the man behind the desk pondered the question.

"Sports, TV . . . masturbation?"

"Maybe basketball for brief moments," said Ricker, embarrassed by Randerath's candor. "TV will get you only part way. For me it's reading. When I get into a book, I'm there. Total escape. It doesn't matter where I am physically; the story sets the stage, and I'm a rapt audience. The best escape, of course, is sleep. If I sleep eight hours a day, I've reduced a ten-year sentence by three years and four months. I'd love to sleep twelve hours a day. Thorazine helps."

Ricker's eyes were back on the letter opener as he spoke. It was obviously there for a purpose. Had a trap been set to entice him? Were guards stationed behind some two-way mirror ready to pounce—or, worse, to film the episode for a soon-to-be-convened grand jury?

As if on some unspoken cue, Ricker reached for the dagger. (For what is a letter opener but a modified dagger?) The handle felt so good, fit so perfectly in his grasp. He had no choice but to take it and then plunge it repeatedly into the doctor's chest.

Randerath put up no resistance. His body seemed to be beckoning to the weapon, charming it in some hypnotic way. Luring it to strike home.

I am living up to the expectations of this place, thought Ricker. They want criminally insane; well, who am I to deny them?

At that point Ricker woke up in his bunk. Thank God it was only a dream, he thought. He had fallen asleep with his clothes on and was drenched in sweat. He had no clean uniforms to change into. He smelled vile from old and new perspiration and unlaundered clothes.

"Have you had any dreams lately?" asked Randerath.

"None that I can remember," responded Ricker, his appearance slightly unkempt. Lately, he had abandoned all attempts to impress his doctor; indeed, his attitude was becoming one of hostility.

"This place is something I'm dreaming up, isn't it? It can't be real, devised by civilized men in these enlightened times? We've come a long way since the days of the *noble savage*, haven't we, Doctor? We've progressed to dungeons, and inquisitions, and the House of Lords!—to civilized behavior—haven't we, Doctor?"

Randerath knew the pitfalls implicit in his patient's rhetorical outburst. He had a feeling wits were being matched and had no intention of coming up short. Answering one question with another, a psychiatrist's mainstay, seemed appropriate: "What about your tattoo? Tell me about *it*. Do you regret *it*?"

Back in college . . . Gulbrandsen . . . something about an ally crossed Ricker's mind. "My tattoo?" Then he remembered: "It's my totem for life."

Noble savages and now totems, thought Randerath, wondering what will come next?

". . . and I will take it to the grave."

Randerath's face dropped. "Don't you realize how lucky you are? Not only do you have a totem, you have a strong one. Your bird can soar. It has no claws, but it can speak. Why do you not appreciate this gift?"

Ricker shrugged.

"If you could fly," ventured Randerath, "would you see it differently, then?"

"Of course. Do you have that kind of magic?"

"Try," suggested the doctor. "Run over to that wall and fly over it."

Ricker ran toward the prison's high brick wall. He willed himself over it, and, as he knew he would, started gaining altitude. Just as he was about to clear the parapet, he lost speed, went into a stall, fell toward the ground. Good news: he woke before he landed.

"Yes, I have had a dream, since you ask," conceded Ricker. "Just the other night. We were to have a foot race, you and I, and if I won you'd grant me my freedom. You spotted me half a lap on a quarter-mile oval cinder track. You know the kind. With bleachers on two sides and a football field in the center.

"I had to beat you for only 220 yards, but you had to run the whole 440. Even so, every time I looked back you were a little closer. Gaining. All action froze when I looked, as if the race were a series of still pictures. But each one showed you getting nearer, closing the gap."

The loudly ticking clock indicated that the session was over.

"Did I catch up?" the doctor asked, rising.

"No," said Ricker, also rising. "I don't think so. It was like one of those infinity paradoxes. Each time I'd look, I'd find that you shortened the distance between us by half. The way I see it, you'd never quite reach me."

"Does that mean you won your freedom?" asked the doctor, opening the door.

Ricker gasped. Beyond the door was an upper-story, sky-scraper view of nothing but sky. No ledge. No balcony. A howling wind and endless, cloudless blue.

Chapter 20

A check for ten thousand dollars!—a moment's elation,
then lingering skepticism, even for Jay Arsenault, a man
two weeks behind in his rent. In a plain envelope, unac-
companied by a cover letter, it was made payable to the *Justice
Denied Hotline* and bore the company name "Ponti" on top, with
a signature—an illegible scrawl—on the bottom. Few clues to go
on, thought Jay; a quid pro quo, but for what?

Eleven years had elapsed since Jay began practicing law, a
rollercoaster career lately in decline. At his pinnacle, hosting a
men's rights talk show from Chicago, Jay planned to ride the
crest of a Men's Rights Movement, ride it to fame and fortune.
Now memories of that experience had an unreal quality for him,
as if they happened to somebody else—which, in a way, they did.
The young, dynamic, albeit controversial lawyer of those days,
giving way, through a series of setbacks, to the current Jay Arsenault: a droopy-eyed, underpaid, public defender who picked up
work from the bulletin board of the second-rate law school from
which he graduated.

Jay tucked the check in among the deposit slips in the back of his checkbook. He'd cash it at the next opportunity. Maybe. Perhaps answers would be forthcoming in the interim.

They weren't. The check cleared—he had called his bank to inquire. "Whose check is it?" he asked the manager.

"Don't *you* know?" she responded.

After hearing Jay's explanation, she offered to help. Ten minutes later she called back. "Ponti Importing," she said. "Located in Chelsea. But don't tell anybody I told you."

An on-line search provided further answers: Ponti Importing Corporation, President/CEO: Ernesto Ponti, Annual Gross Sales 106.5 million, Number of employees worldwide: 1225. . . .

Corporate litigation? wondered Jay, or (worldwide?) a Sicilian connection?—echoes from his past, perhaps—from his days at Hallsmith and Ingoldsby, his former employer, a law firm that did not turn away clients with ties to Organized Crime. He immediately regretted cashing the check. And then, two uneasy weeks later, at 8:45 P.M., the phone on his bedside table began to ring.

The caller on his private line—a woman, a friend of a friend from Jay's talk-show days—apologized for using her connections to acquire his unlisted number, apologized further for calling at such an odd hour. She mentioned Ponti and Yes, she said, she had sent the check. Could they meet? She'd come by for him. Could she pick him up the following morning at his apartment?

Since law school, Jay had lived in the Dorchester section of Boston, a blue collar neighborhood of endless three-family tenements, his apartment little more than a sleeping room: a refrigerator for milk, beer, and some bottled water, a bed in the opposite corner, and, in the middle, on a coffee table, his telephone answering machine:

The Justice Denied Hotline.

Back in his early years, Jay saw himself as the Ralph Nader of the Men's Rights Movement, doing for men what Nader did for consumers. Day-old beard, rolled up sleeves, fighting a crusade from the trenches. Lately, though, his *Hotline* phone seldom rang, and when it did, the callers seemed to have every reason but the correct one for calling. Few were bona fide victims of inequitable divorce judgments, few were seeking the one thing, Jay, a men's rights lawyer, was willing to fight for on their behalf: fair play in court. Of those warranting a return call, most seemed to be felons. Pathetic cases when you dig beneath the surface, he thought, but too demanding, too exhausting for him to pursue. Society had written off these violent men, and an increasingly cynical Jay Arsenault likewise found himself running out of patience with their plights, the trouble that seemed to follow them around like a bad penny.

The next morning a little after ten, a vintage black Lincoln Town Car, chauffeured, pulled up at Jay's front stairs. It attracted considerable attention. The woman in the back seat introduced herself as Sally St. Germain, Ernest Ponti's secretary. Aide-de-camp. More, perhaps. Details, she assured him, would come with time.

She had the plain, uncomplicated appearance that made guessing her age difficult: maybe thirty-five, maybe a decade younger. Her wavy, shoulder-length, jet black hair—anthracitic in its unforgiving blackness—provided a startling contrast to the delicate whiteness of her skin. Her clear blue eyes, without excessive make-up, drew you in comfortably.

Red was her color, but she seemed to get it slightly wrong. Her lipstick seemed too intense, and the crimson of her plastic earrings, matching bracelet, and sporty shoes, Jay thought, might be somewhat inappropriate for a woman of her age, her professional status. He waited for a glimpse of her left hand. Red nail polish, and, to his disappointment, the thin gold ring.

As they drove away, she began her explanation: "Ernest can use all the help he can get. He's seventy-two years old. Too old for the trouble facing him.

"This is one of his private cars," she confided, the hint of a blush sweeping across her youthfully chubby, porcelain-like face. "I get to use it during working hours . . . well, all the time actually, except weekends. Stanley," she said, introducing her chauffeur, "I'd like you to meet Jay Arsenault. One of my fellow

Frenchmen . . . and," she added, "from what I hear, an honest lawyer."

Sally smoothed down her mid-length black and white cotton print dress as she twisted sideways to face Jay on the awkward back seat. "Since Ernest's wife died about ten years ago, after a long bout with leukemia, he's been seeing the same woman. He won't marry her—or anybody, for that matter—but in Massachusetts after ten years, wouldn't they be considered married, in the eyes of the court, as far as his property was concerned?" She looked at Jay for his legal comment.

"In fact," he offered, smiling agreeably at the woman next to him, "according to recent judgments, after a decade, if they were to separate, the division of property is not only the same as if they were *legally* married, it is the same as if their marriage were *long-term*, and that means she gets half of everything in his estate."

Jay's spirits rose as he spoke. Was this elation because of her? he wondered, some favorable chemistry, or should he attribute it to the check for a clean ten grand, money without ties to the underworld? "Massachusetts has a law on the books regarding divorce settlements, but there's ample leeway built in to reflect society's ever-changing attitudes. Right now this state is a no-man's-land for men."

"What do you mean, 'leeway'?" she asked.

"How the pie gets divided up is simply left to the discretion of the presiding judge."

"What about appeals. A higher court? A different judge?" asked Sally.

"Your boss obviously has the money for it, but do you think he has the stomach for years of aggravation?"

Sally shrugged with a goofy face. (Jay would be seeing that gesture in his mind for years to come. That childlike shrug, that corkscrew smile.)

"Mmm . . . I guess not," she conceded. "Anyway, with the ten-year mark approaching, Ernest's daughters, both with grown children of their own, are worried. They see their dad's girlfriend as having designs on his money, indeed ready to cash in on her investment."

"She gave the old man the best years of her life, she'll tell the court," said Jay, leaning back, crossing his legs. . . .

Sally, who had maintained constant eye contact to that point, turned away reflectively. As she did, Jay, in a split-second of insight, caught an overview of himself and the young woman sitting next to him. He saw himself leaning back, crossing his legs, checking out his crease, his brown, not-quite-matching socks; but this time the thirty-seven-year-old bachelor, who had always been self-conscious in close quarters with women, found himself actually enjoying the experience—comfortable, mobilized, ready for any test and fairly sure he'd pass it. "I've heard that argument a time or two," he added, once again drawing her attention. "With a good lawyer, she'll win her case. She'll write her own ticket."

"Mmm . . . just as I thought," said Sally, noting his smile and returning it. They were approaching Ponti's property now, a block-long factory building enclosed by a high, well-maintained, wrought-iron fence. "That's why I . . . er, and the others, the daughters—and Ernest as well, although he won't admit it— need your advice so badly, your assistance, perhaps."

As the car drove through the main gate, a uniformed guard gave them a smile and a salute with a touch of his cap. Stanley pulled up to the imposing building, stopped at a wide granite staircase flanked by two lions sejant, and opened the car door for Sally. At the top of the stairs, Jay did the same with the multi-paned, heavily varnished oak doors of the executive entrance to Ponti's main plant and corporate headquarters.

Entering the marble, high-ceilinged, executive lobby was like stepping into an ornate Renaissance jewel box. The only windows were small stained-glass door panels depicting nineteenth century scenes of labor and commerce. Their footsteps echoed on burnished green marble. Polished marble columns rose to the ceiling. Jay looked up. No Michelangelo fresco, but gold leaf moldings, filigree vaultings, and a magnificent brass chandelier substituted nicely. Brightly lit, it appeared to Jay to be hiding angels among its twinkling points of light. Palestrina. The Missa Brevis, the only cassette in his stereo for the past month, began running through his mind. He watched as Sally pushed a mother-of-pearl button. A whirling sound followed, and he noticed that above the elevator door the arrow on a brass dial began to sweep slowly counterclockwise.

Riding up, they faced a gleaming brass gate as the old-fashioned open-faced elevator provided snapshot glimpses of the activities on each floor: warehouse and food-packing operations on the first six, three more of administrative offices, and at the top, the executive suites. Remaining seated, Ponti greeted them from behind a cluttered desk in his palatial, oak-paneled office, a small white Maltese dog in his lap.

"I have lawyers coming out of my ears," said the short, robust man who looked more like sixty than someone about to turn seventy-three. His hair was gray, shiny, and thick, styled with a wave in front, reminiscent of some bygone era—the days before hair spray, the Wildroot Creme Oil days. "They all say I have nothing to worry about," he added, smiling, revealing teeth that appeared near-perfect in a non-artificial way. "But Sally, here . . . well, she sees problems. She can't seem to relax and enjoy all the money I'm paying her. She's a nervous Nellie, Mr. Arsenault. By the way, did she tell you what she does for me here?"

Apparently, over the years, as Ponti took less and less interest in the daily operation of his importing and food-processing empire, Sally had taken on more and more of the responsibility for running it. Simply by working cooperatively with his department heads, through consensus rather than by exerting authority, she put together a management team in which every-one compromised his or her personal autonomy for the good of the company. No arm-twisting was needed; her lack of ego set the tone—in a way, coaxed her managers and foremen into considering the needs of other departments, needs often in conflict with their own.

Lately, Ponti had branched out—against his will but on Sally's insistence—into institutional food distribution: supplying restaurants, company cafeterias, hospitals, nursing homes—any food service operation—with all their requirements from storage and preparation to serving, clean-up, and waste disposal.

"I'm too old for this aggravation," said Ponti, the smile gone. "What do I need the money for? My *fiancee?* My grandchildren?"

"How about for yourself!" proclaimed Sally.

After a moment's thought, Ponti shrugged. "Do what you think best," he said to her; then, as an aside to Jay, added: "She will anyway, you know."

Later, leaving the building, Jay and Sally were once again alone on the elevator. "What's my assignment?" he asked, as she pushed a well-worn "L" button. Thumping noises followed, and then, as they descended, chain could be heard piling up below them. "How do you see me helping the old man?"

"His girlfriend's name is Laura Tonzillo. A child bride the first time around."

"First time around?"

"There's been no second time . . . yet," explained Sally. "Laura lost a premature baby, then went into a career in modeling, TV commercials—glitzy stuff—and, of course . . . the affairs. She's had her share of them over the years. Who knows—maybe still . . . ? Perhaps you could turn up something to disqualify her?" Sally looked up at Jay with a half-smile, hopefully.

"We'll never know if we don't try," he responded, touching the top of her arm. "At least you'll be able to live with your conscience, knowing you gave it a shot, that you made an effort to help your . . . er, boss. By the way, what's your personal relationship with Ponti? I don't mean to be rude, but how does protecting the old man against a palimony lawsuit creep into . . . um." He fumbled for words. ". . . into your job description?"

"I constantly wonder about that myself, Mr. Arsenault—all the time, in the middle of the night, even. My job, the business part, centers around money, and with a man such as Ponti, the line between business money and personal money isn't very distinct. Especially at his age. He gets confused . . . I get confused."

Jay floundered on: "But . . . um, you seem to be involved in the *intimate* aspects of this situation? I'm willing to look into it, by the way. But I always like to know what drives people to do things. You, for instance . . . your stake . . . *personally*, I mean."

"I don't understand." she said, her usual response in awkward situations. When backed into corners she had learned to let others say the difficult words; there will always be time to add your part later. Experience had taught her that while others speak, you have a golden opportunity to relax and fashion an unhurried response.

They walked across the lobby toward the large front doors. Her chauffeur, Stanley, cigarette in hand, waited just outside. "I'm a married woman, *personally*. Otherwise, I'm driven by my concern for Ponti."

"But your concern for the old man, is it . . . um, for an employer? A father figure? A friend?" Jay felt uncomfortable questioning her, but he was conducting an investigation, was he not? Investigators snoop, they're curious—it's their prerogative.

Sally smiled with relief. "Actually, my father and Ernest were childhood friends. They grew up in an immigrant neighbor-hood—in Boston's West End—then both joined the Army during the Second World War. They served together. When my dad was killed, Ernest vowed to help me. He stood by his word, hired me out of high school. I owe a lot to the man."

"I'm sorry to hear about your father," said Jay, again touching her arm. "Forgive my intrusiveness. I'll start formulating a game plan for Ponti right away. I'll call you at the end of the week for particulars: social security numbers, addresses, other details. I charge $250 a day, and, if I'm through before your ten thousand is used up, I'll return what's left. Fair enough?"

"Fair enough," she said, her smile flashing. She extended her hand. "Stanley will drive you back to town. If you'll excuse me,

I'm way behind in my work upstairs. But I'll be waiting for your call, Jay. And thank you. Thanks for your concern."

After their handshake, Jay got into the front seat of the limousine. "Some gal," he said as they drove toward the gate.

"Some gal," repeated Stanley, glancing over.

"What's her husband like?"

Stanley's eyes were back on the road. "He reminds me of a Protestant pastor . . . in some ways. I don't think he works. . . ." They drove on in silence. "But I'm not sure . . . um, if he works . . . for a living . . . or what?"

"What about Ponti's girlfriend, Laura Tonzillo?" asked Jay, changing an apparently difficult subject for Stanley.

"I've known her for ten years," replied the chauffeur. "She's never said 'hello,' 'goodby,' or 'how are you?' to me . . . ever."

Chapter 21

L aura Tonzillo was an only child, although her extended
family was a large one. Nine aunts and uncles, and
endless cousins, lately with spouses and children of
their own. A formidable group—some close, all devoted. That
was their code, their bond; they stuck together, especially when
one of their own was in need. Laura was in need. A forty-two-
year-old divorcee facing life alone—and then, miraculously,
there was Ponti! Her savior . . . almost. So he wouldn't remarry;
perhaps, with time, he'd change his mind. The family took the
old man to its bosom. That was ten years ago; he'd been there
ever since.

Christmas. Easter. Thanksgiving. Enormous feasts brought
them all together. Liquor first, then wine—but from beginning
to end, all manner of food; each family member arriving with his
or her specialty: aunts with lasagna, eggplant Parmigiana; uncles
with roasts: beef, pork, veal, or lamb, swimming in tomato
sauce; cousins with pickled peppers, stuffed peppers, stuffed
mushrooms, pasta, antipasti. They knew the strength of food,
the miracles it could perform. Their spouses could be here

today, gone tomorrow, but their food and their family, never failing them, would live on forever.

In the steamy kitchen, they all pitched in, smiling, laughing, telling jokes, telling family stories—legends passed down for generations—about children, now grown, or about old-timers, now dead. They filled Ponti in on their family secrets (well, sort of—it's all fiction these fables, these acts of heroism, of derring-do, of monumental audacity!—as if consistency in the retelling of their versions could make a dubious event credible). But so what? The spirit of joy and celebration was what counted, anyway, and that was always in abundance.

Ponti was in heaven. A king. The family's former patriarch, Arthur Tonzillo, an aging lawyer, abdicated eagerly. Ponti became the new focus of respect (well, sort of—in-law acceptance was the best he could hope for). But to all appearances, he was becoming almost one of the family. The mourning period for a lost wife was behind him; the time for dwelling in the past was coming to an end.

He had an army of adoring adopted family members surrounding him now. Waiting on him. Attending to his every need. "Thank you, Uncle Ernesto," the young girls, opening their gifts, would squeal on his lap. (The older ones would tuck their hundreds away discreetly; send him a thank-you note later.)

And so ten years flew by. Happy years, he'd have to admit. As man and wife, he and Laura traveled to the capitals of Europe on lavish vacations, or spent quiet months in the small fishing village near Porto Ercole, where Ponti's father was born. On the heels of interminable winter vacations in the Caribbean with golf and sailing came endless travels abroad on business: visits to food processing and packing plants; but, more important, to the villas of their owners—leisurely visits to renew acquaintances, to fulfill the social amenities required when dealing with Europeans. The "Signora," bedecked in jewelry from countless duty-free shops, played her part, but the name on her passport remained *Laura Tonzillo*.

"Where will you be staying?" or "How long will you be in this country?" customs agents asked.

"How should I know?" she'd snap, with a shrug. "Ask my husband."

Back in Boston, their social life would continue. They'd entertain lavishly from his opulent Beacon Hill townhouse, and then all summer long and into the fall from his sprawling Whale Rock estate overlooking Cape Cod Bay. Eager members of Laura's family added new enthusiasm to the festivities—new inspiration, new spirit, their own brand of style, to what had existed before, to the ever-diminishing circle of Ponti's friends.

Alas, old friends gone without explanation. Where is so-and-so? Ponti would ask on occasion, looking around the room with a sinking feeling at the absence of a former golf partner, or someone who had helped his daughters—people who shared a big chunk of his past, who suffered along with him, for years, at his wife's bedside.

Where were they now? he wondered. Dying off? Moving to Florida? Or were they simply abandoning their old friend, distancing themselves out of an unwillingness to cope with so many unfamiliar faces? Fresh faces?

Meanwhile, rejuvenated by his new, stimulating source of energy, Ponti tried hard not to mourn their absence. "You have a new lease on life," members of Laura's family told him. They put an *Italian Stallion* bumper sticker on his Cadillac. "You're as young as you feel. . . ."

Chapter 22

While still a student in law school, Arthur Tonzillo had the good fortune to be introduced to the most powerful mayor in the history of Boston. This occurred well before Mayor Curley's troubles in Federal Court as a defendant on mail fraud charges, before his incarceration and subsequent pardon by President Truman. The young Tonzillo was drawn to the Mayor, and, in spite of the demands of his studies, never missed an opportunity to lend a hand around City Hall. When it came time to pass the bar exam, the Mayor placed the all-important call. Later, he told the fledgling lawyer to specialize in labor relations, that some day he'd be called upon to repay kindness with kindness, in the spirit of Irish good will. Politicians—thought Tonzillo, trying to keep a straight face—what would we ever do without them?

To a Boston lawyer, ties to Beacon Hill, to the State House, mean influence in court—ultimately, the license to print money. Tonzillo nurtured those ties, strengthened that influence, and along with the money came a city at his feet, under his thumb. But on holidays, feast days, his interest lay only in his family— gathering them around him, allowing them to share his bounty.

Regardless of the venue, no matter who was nominal host at family feasts, Arthur Tonzillo would always take his place at the head of the table, followed by his wealthy younger brother Dominic, a contractor, an owner of real estate and a builder of homes—later, buildings, and, later still, shopping malls. Then came the sons of these men: Arthur had three, his brother four, most of whom worked in construction—worked, for the most part, for Dominic. Arthur's youngest, however, was the exception. Stephen chose Harvard. As an undergraduate: the humanities. For a career, his dad's: law.

Proud of the young man's accomplishments, Arthur Tonzillo, thinking *dynasty*, continued to cultivate his political connections—minimum effort for maximum return, he'd tell his son: appearances with enthusiasm and a hefty check at First Communions and fund-raisers, and attendance with sympathy and floral arrangements at wakes and funerals (signing the guestbook, in every instance, an absolute must).

"I want to get married," Laura, a freshman drama major at U-Mass, Boston, told her uncle Arthur at one of the large, family gatherings at Dominic's house. She waited until the powerful lawyer had finished the first few courses of the all-day meal and had gone out onto the porch for some fresh air to revive his appetite. His brother's estate on thirty-two acres west of Boston was considered rural when purchased; later, with Boston bulging outward, it was, to Dominic's chagrin, becoming suburban chic. The ambitious contractor had once envisioned a Tonzillo compound: his house surrounded by the homes of his children and their families—and, as well, their dogs, goats, chickens, cars, and trucks. They had room for everything, had they not? and enough money to buy it all? But the town was changing. Volvos. School budgets. Grumblings about zoning, trucks on lawns, construction equipment stored willy-nilly. . . .

"But you're still a child," replied her uncle Arthur, sitting in a comfortable rocking chair, sipping a glass of Dominic's homemade red wine. His teenage niece stood facing him in a pretty pink party frock. She had the beauty common to every Tonzillo woman—their vivacious spirit as girls, their charm and grace into old age.

"As you well know, I'm in college," she said, going over to him and kissing him on the cheek. "Thanks to you for paying my tuition. But I think it's time for me to grow up and quit school."

She went back to the porch railing, and, with a pirouette, turned to face her uncle, giving him the trademark Tonzillo smile: irresistible, radiant. "He's a Jewish boy . . . he teaches high school, but his family has money."

"Let him buy you a house, then, and you may marry in the Church," said the cocky lawyer. "And bring me a plate of your mother's stuffed mushrooms . . . and another glass of wine."

Beaming, she again kissed him on the cheek, and ran into the house.

Sidney Chafitz bought the house for his young bride, but a justice-of-the-peace conducted the short marriage ceremony, and Uncle Arthur toasted the happiness of the newlyweds with the bridegroom's cheap wine. "*Aceto,*" he said raising his glass high. Family members giggled. It's pronounced ah-chay'-toe, and it means "vinegar."

Sidney was always up early for school and corrected papers into the night. "I'll teach them truth through fiction," he often said, regarding his lit. course. "Midwesterners like Mark Twain, defining America from its heartland. Jews with pictures of immigrant life in crowded cities. Blacks looking into the human soul . . . seeing pain. American Indians from the Southwest, the fabric of their culture . . . torn.

"If my students want non-fiction they can go elsewhere. Footnotes and self-serving lies, so-called facts to further ambitious frauds—you won't get that in any of my courses," he'd add.

"Why aren't I pregnant?" she'd add in response, first subtly, so as not to offend, but later with increasing impatience, stridently, bitterly . . . accusingly.

Laura, too beautiful to wither away in domestic obscurity, but somehow beyond her acting-class schoolmates, was encouraged by friends and family alike to make something of her good looks—to go into modeling, to do TV commercials.

It started slowly, innocently: the agency, the glossy eight-by-ten head shots, the résumé. The cattle calls. The auditions. The call-backs. The shoots. The late nights, then overnights. Finally, those occasional week-ends away from home. Sidney, unable to sleep, would be feigning it when she came in before dawn—gorgeous, her make-up still on, her smoky perfume—heady, intoxicating. She'd slip into her side of the bed, careful not to disturb him. When he got up to use the bathroom—heart pounding, stomach in knots—he'd chew a Valium or two. Wash it down with mouthwash. On his return, she'd be the one feigning sleep.

Then came her pregnancy. "Is it his?" someone in her family asked at their next get-together.

"Of course not," she replied, in Sidney's presence. Later, especially in his presence.

Later still, staring at him, she'd bring up the subject, even among their friends, who, smiling boldly, would move to her side and also stare.

"She wants a divorce," said Arthur Tonzillo, ushering Sidney into his spacious corner office in a new high-rise building in Boston. The Tonzillos occupied a whole floor—one of the top floors. Maybe more than one. "How much do you want to give her?"

Sidney, who was making $15,900 a year, offered half. "Fair enough," said Arthur, quickly shaking hands as he led the nervous young man to the cluster of elevator doors. "Come in on Friday to sign the papers . . . and by the way, Sidney," he added, "it would certainly be better if you stayed away from the house . . . um, from now on."

On Friday, the young schoolteacher arrived to find one of Dominic's sons in the office. Arthur's nephew wore his construction worker clothes: boots, canvas trousers, denim jacket. "Let's drink a toast to our amicable agreement," said Arthur, uncorking a bottle of expensive red wine.

Reading the agreement he was to sign, Sidney noticed that his house was to be given over to his wife debt-free, and, in the interim, he would be required to make the mortgage and tax payments to the bank. He also noticed a clause requiring that he maintain a million dollars worth of life insurance naming Laura as beneficiary. He balked. Muttered something about a lawyer.

Arthur smiled. "That's an unnecessary expense I had hoped to save you. We wanted this to run smoothly, didn't we, Nunzio?"

At that point, his rugged young nephew turned from the window, from the spectacular view extending from the Bunker Hill Monument and "Old Ironsides" in Charlestown, to include the entire harbor, Logan Airport, the harbor islands, and, in the distance, Nantasket Beach, Minot Light, and, beyond that, nothing but ocean extending all the way to Europe. Nunzio shook off his faraway, dazed look, and put down his wineglass. Approaching Sidney, he grabbed the nervous schoolteacher by both lapels and spit a whole mouthful of wine into his face.

"Check this out with one of your kosher lawyers," said Arthur, pushing the document toward him. "Then bring it back signed and notarized. And for your sake, the sooner the better."

Chapter 23

After her deposition, Eve Angel, her eyes still red from crying, unexpectedly found Cantrice in Hurley's waiting room.

"I couldn't resist meeting you here," said Cantrice, with a conspiratorial wink—then, looking at Eve Angel closely, added: "Was it terrible?"

Before her friend could answer, Cantrice continued in a loud voice: "I'm sorry you had to go through such an ordeal. Rick's lawyer is ruthless. He has no consideration for a person's feelings."

Hurley's receptionist looked up, startled.

"I don't mind," said Eve Angel, irritably. "They do what they do. How can I blame that fellow for serving his client's interests?"

"When it's against *my* interests, you can blame him plenty," snapped Cantrice. "Everybody's turning on me, Eve, don't you be one of them. Nobody's perfect, don't forget—not me, and not you either."

They rode down the elevator in silence. Finally Eve Angel spoke: "I just have one question for you. It came up at my deposition, but it's been bothering me for a long time, actually. I hope you won't think I'm turning on you if I ask it."

Cantrice knew. Knew immediately what it would be. Eve Angel had given her a free ride for years—never challenging, never confronting her. Perhaps all that was about to come to an end.

Friends make small sacrifices for each other; best friends do more.

They suspend judgment. They choke down their own values, those bred in their bones. God knows, they often pay the price: sleepless nights, anxious days. Worse.

"So what's the big question you've been saving up for me?" Cantrice finally ventured.

They had left Hurley's office building and were in the parking lot now—scanning it for their separate cars. "It's nothing," said Eve Angel, spotting her faded, ten-year-old Bonneville. She headed toward it. "I've gone this long . . . I guess it's not that important."

"No, I want to know," insisted Cantrice, at her heels. "I've got plans for the future, and they include you. I've got to know what's bothering you."

"I'd just like to know one thing," said Eve Angel, turning to face her friend. "Did Rick ever hit you? I know he was violent. Loud, sometimes. Profane. I witnessed a tantrum or two myself. But we claimed more than that . . . we claimed he hit you with a beer bottle or something . . . did he?"

Cantrice hesitated. How many times had she imagined her friend asking that very question? Heard it voiced, even—in her dreams. But it never came. Not until now. "Do you know what being *abusive* means in a marriage, Eve? Being intimidated on a daily basis by an inconsiderate bully with tattoos and a motorcycle. Even with my mother around as an eyewitness in case anything happened. It was frightening."

"But he didn't actually do it, did he?" replied Eve Angel. She knew the answer, of course. Knew it now—too late. A man's life in ruins. "He never *physically* hit you?"

Cantrice, sensing a way out of her dilemma, replied cautiously: "Mental abuse is just as bad, you know. Worse! It was like living with a *time bomb*. He could blow up any minute and kill me. I had to do what I did." Her voice gained in pitch and intensity. "I couldn't, for my own safety, just wait there for him to explode, could I? You wouldn't want me to have waited until it was too late? Until I was a victim?"

"But we *lied* in court," maintained Eve Angel.

"Everybody lies in court." exclaimed Cantrice. "You don't think court is a place where anybody tells the truth, do you?"

Cantrice had played a trump card. Played it inadvertently, but realized nonetheless, the moment the words were out, that no rebuttal would be forthcoming; her friend had been stopped cold. Waiting for the response she knew would never come, the answer for which there was no answer, she stared at the little blond woman who stood silently before her. Then with confidence—smugness, even—she continued:

"Those who lie convincingly in court are the only winners. Those who blush and stammer . . . well, Eve, they deserve what they get. Lying is a way of life in court; certainly you knew that. Cops lie. Lawyers lie their heads off. Everybody lies. Everybody!

"We did what we had to do. We didn't enjoy it . . . but we got the job done. Now, Eve," she added, putting both her hands on her friend's shoulders, "you're supposed to be loyal to me—by my side, to comfort me, support me. How can we go away together, to Florida, if you're not on my side?"

Chapter 24

When an attendant told Ricker to get into a clean uniform, that he had a visitor, he assumed it to be just another dream. His dreams had become particularly vivid lately, as Randerath had predicted. "The more you listen to the voice of your subconscious," the doctor had told him, "the more it will speak to you. Put a pad of paper next to your bed and the floodgates will open. Ignore that inner voice and it will turn its tiny back on you and become mute."

A man waiting in the hospital's small conference room got up when Ricker appeared at the open door. "Brian Hurley," he said, extending his hand. "Remember me?"

Ricker's puzzled expression prompted Hurley to continue. "I was a lawyer who worked behind the scenes, mostly, with the team representing you in the early stages of your difficulties with your ex-wife, Cantrice. My firm took me off your case without explanation, but I was troubled by it then, and it nags me to this day; in fact, the more I think about it, the angrier I get."

Still reeling from his latest betrayal, the plea bargain that promised probation but delivered an unspeakably harsh sentence, Ricker regarded the tall, redheaded man with suspicion. How many times had these people approached him over the years with their *deals*, dangling hope before him like a hypnotist's watch? Later, he'd find out what they took from him. Later, he'd find out the price he'd have to pay.

Hurley fit the description Ricker had learned to distrust: pleasant smile, cool demeanor, wearing what looked like an off-the-rack suit from some mall, a suit that he might very well have picked out, tried on, bought, and worn home, all in less than an hour—perfect fit, too. Cop clothes, Ricker couldn't help thinking.

"I'm no longer with the firm," confided Hurley, who had been fired under contentious circumstances—a common scenario in his profession: egos clash, feathers get ruffled, doors slam. I've had some free time lately, and I thought I'd offer you my services on a *pro bono* basis if you're interested."

Ricker, who was studying the soft-spoken, personable young man for any signs of recognition (and still not finding any), thanked him guardedly, conceding to himself that perhaps he might not be a cop after all. "Isn't it too late? Didn't Archibald Shaw finish me off . . . permanently?" Ricker slumped deeper into his plastic chair across the small conference table from Hurley. Was this conversation lapsing into theater of the absurd? *Pro bono; is he serious?—I couldn't pay anyway!*

"It's never too late, as long as you have the spirit to fight," responded Hurley. "But here's why I'm here: You were obviously victimized from the start by a phony 209A protective order—framed, if you will, by your ex-wife, Cantrice. Did you know that her lawyer, Archibald Shaw, was her legal guardian as a child? He put unlimited resources into her case, not only to win in court, but—I hate to admit it, Mr. Ricker—to gain influence with *my* former law firm as well, the people who were representing *you!*"

Ricker found himself hanging onto Hurley's every word. Something about the lawyer, or his voice, had a seductive quality. Convincing. In a way, hypnotic. He found his resistance to the man melting away.

"Remembering back, a number of things stuck in my craw," continued Hurley. "Shaw mounted too strenuous an effort for such flimsy litigation. He had few facts but managed to generate a mountain of documents: motions, affidavits, complaints—all spurious, all garbage. It all added up to nothing, and, as one of your attorneys, I had intended to refute the whole kit and caboodle. At that point, my firm pulled me off your case and, shortly thereafter, told me to clean out my desk.

"Neither side attempted even a semblance of fair play; on the contrary, they blurred the distinction between civil and criminal complaints against you to such an extent that the judges you faced, in your brief, hurried moments before them, never really had an opportunity to challenge what little evidence they did have. Their heads were spinning. You're lucky they didn't give you 'life without parole'!"

Hurley smiled, waiting for Ricker's response. There was none. He forged ahead anyway. "As you probably know, it was the non-criminal prisoners in the Soviet Union who got sent to Siberia. The felons there were no problem; their crimes were blamed on vodka, and moreover, who really cared? It was the civil cases that got psychological evaluations, tranquilizers, electroshock therapy, even lobotomies. Although you're no dissident or threat to the state, the circumstances are not dissimilar." Then, as if to say "I rest my case," Hurley dropped his hands to the table, folded them, and looked up at Ricker.

Hearing his old, half-forgotten suspicions voiced so aptly by this man, Ricker was becoming alert. Chemicals were waging war within his body—adrenaline, Thorazine—conflicting signals at nerve endings in his brain. Lightheaded, he sat up in his seat, his thoughts racing ahead: Justice? Fair play? Vindication? Freedom! And yet he had been down this road so many times before, and it had always led to betrayal. "The last man they sent sold me out," he said weakly, after keeping Hurley fidgeting in his chair. "Promising me one thing . . . then, after I signed his papers, delivering something else."

"Bait and switch?" asked Hurley.

"Can we appeal? Sue for malpractice?"

"It's too late for an appeal," explained Hurley. "Malpractice judgments are seldom imposed on court-appointed public servants, so we're out of luck there. But I came here hoping to clear you from a different angle."

Ricker's raised eyebrow urged him on.

"Discredit their *assault with a dangerous weapon* finding, the original and obviously trumped-up charges upon which your ex-wife had you jailed; after that, we can cast doubt on their allegations that you conspired with other inmates to harm her when you got out."

"Okay," said Ricker. "Assuming I go along with your program, how would you proceed?"

Hurley relaxed on his side of the conference table. He produced a yellow legal pad from his large, suitcase-like briefcase and a ballpoint pen from the inner pocket of his suit jacket. His smile seemed sincere. "First of all, did you write a threatening letter to your ex-wife recently?"

"Of course not," responded Ricker.

"I didn't think so, but did they show you a letter allegedly written by you in which you threatened to feed her body parts to her cat? I believe it was unsigned."

"They showed me some bogus letter. It's all part of their frameup. They've been pulling this crap on me for years. I can't believe these asinine courts take them seriously." Ricker was getting worked up. The chemical mix, he thought. This is no time to lose it.

"Did you ever threaten your ex-wife using those words—you know—about the cat?"

"Yes."

"Where? When? Under what circumstances?"

"I had just gotten back from a weekend in Laconia, New Hampshire," explained Ricker. "A motorcycle rally. I found that she had changed the locks on the doors. My keys wouldn't fit. She locked me out of my own house!

"There was a cat's dish beside the back door. I threw it through a window. That's when I said those words about feeding her to her cat. Anyway, the cops came down the driveway about then, blue lights flashing. They arrested me."

"Did they hear you threaten your wife?"

"No. They arrived after that." Then he cast an angry glance at Hurley. "Hey, wait a minute. Did I say something inappropriate? She locks me out of my house. The house my grandfather built . . . on land that had been in my family for generations . . . and you're bent out of shape because I have harsh words for her?"

"A lie detector would prove you threatened her, Mr. Ricker. I just want to make sure the threat didn't come from the letter they claim you wrote."

Ricker shook his head in dismay. "I made the cat threat again, in court," he admitted, slouching back guiltily into his seat. "In fact, from then on whenever I'd see the bitch, I'd make meowing noises."

"Whatever," responded Hurley, dismissing the remark with a wave of his hand. "But let's get back to the letter. Did you examine it closely?"

"Sure, but it was phony from the get-go. Any moron could see that."

"Well, Mr. Ricker," proclaimed Hurley, "It was not introduced into the court record as an *exhibit*, nor was it mentioned orally. Your fingerprints are now, incidentally, all over it."

"Shit," groaned Ricker. "Those bastards. What can we do?"

"Your ninety-day evaluation period ends soon," said the lawyer, taking off his jacket and hanging it on the back of his plastic chair. He wore suspenders, a current trend; all lawyers were sporting them at the time. Rolling up his sleeves, he continued: "I'll file a motion for a hearing to reopen your case based on *new evidence*. Meanwhile, I'll have my experts talk to the people here at the hospital for an objective reading of your mental state. Then we'll 'habe' you into court and challenge everything in the court record.

"We'll start with the original *assault with a deadly weapon* charges—a beer bottle, if I'm not mistaken—and go on from there. Your outbursts in court. The criminalization of the civil complaint against you. And most recently, the threatening letter, the so-called conspiracy with other inmates, and the plea bargain that landed you here.

"At the very least, I'll put an end to this psychiatric evaluation charade. Who knows what they might be planning if they think you won't be represented by competent counsel. They might even try to have your case heard *ex-parte*—behind closed doors, with those representing you, *guardians ad litem* [court-appointed spokesmen for children or mental incompetents], allowing the prosecution to accuse you of posing a danger to society and/or to yourself and permitting them to recommend institutionalization of some sort as being in *your* best interest, especially since you seem to have no family or friends to come forward on your behalf."

Suddenly, thoughts of his Aunt Grace crossed Ricker's mind. *How can you help me? You can't even help yourself,* she had said to him. And it was true. True then and true now.

Except now there was this man. This new man holding out hope for him. Asking for his approval to step in and protect him from those who would lock him away for the rest of his life *for his own good!* What are my choices? he thought, knowing full well that he had none.

"Here's what I want you to do:" he said, standing, facing Hurley. "I want you to subpoena my last lawyer. Find out who he is and depose him. Ask him, under oath, if he didn't *guarantee* me probation. I want you to look the bastard straight in the eye and make him answer. I want the System to account for itself. For its bullshit!"

Affecting a kindly smile, Hurley, without words, seemed to shrug off Ricker's suggestion.

"I'm tired of this brother-lawyer crap. I want you to nail that bastard. I want out of here. I want fucking out, get it? I want to walk out scot-free. If you can't do that, then get the hell out of my face." Ricker headed for the door.

"That's my objective, Ricker," said Hurley, making no attempt to stop the angry young man. After Ricker, turning at the door, ambled back to his seat, Hurley proceeded calmly:

"You can't come at them with guns blazing or they'll shut you down fast. I intend to start slowly. I'll recommend that your drugs be discontinued. They may fight me on this, but if they do, it will tell us where this place stands for objectivity. We'll put them to the test. We'll fight our way up the ladder one rung at a time. The higher we go, the more they'll have to take us seriously. We'll get their attention, Mr. Ricker, eventually . . . trust me."

Sensing Ricker's tacit approval, Hurley continued: "First, to get a handle on your early problems, your *assault with a deadly weapon* charges, I'll need some *discovery*—evidence, depositions. From your ex-wife, for instance, and her friend Eve Angel. But for your current dilemma, what about fellow prisoners? Do any cellmates come to mind who might have incriminated you?"

Ricker thought for a moment. "They put a divorce case in with me on the fourth floor of the Middlesex County House of Correction. He kept asking me questions about prison, about the *pecking order*, and, of course, the usual: how long is your sentence, and what's it for? I don't know if this could relate to the conspiracy frame-up that landed me here, but at one point they took him out for interrogation. When he returned he said they asked about *me*."

"What was his name? What did they ask?"

"Ben Larkin. He wouldn't talk about their questions. I had once advised him never to get involved telling tales between prisoners and administration, and he reminded me of my own words. He clammed up on me. Anyway, I knew how he felt, and so I left him alone."

Chapter 25

"This Larkin meant me no harm; I'm sure of it," continued Ricker, rising from his seat to pace the sparsely-furnished, cinderblock conference room in the new wing at Lakewood. Every so often guards would peek in at them through the small square window in the door; neither man took umbrage. "He seemed like an ethical old guy; his divorce just got out of hand, and the court locked him away."

"I'd like to find out what they asked him," mused Hurley, "and his responses as well. He could have been a 'plant,' not from divorce court at all, or even an inmate, but an informer sent to spy on you." Hurley doubted it, but then again he knew Archibald Shaw and the warden were friends. Also, with Shaw and Ricker's ex-wife, Cantrice, spending such inordinate amounts of time and money to keep this man locked up . . . well, anything seemed possible.

"Can you think of anyone else to add to our deposition list?" asked Hurley. "Someone with facts to bolster your case?"

"A friend from high school, Rene Dakota, comes to mind," replied Ricker, back at his seat again. "Rene, whose legal name might still be Descoteux, owns a beauty salon in Boston.

Cantrice had her hair done there. I think he'd be honest, and, because of the nature of his business, he knows a ton of gossip. Some of it might even be useful, if only to discredit my ex-wife."

Hurley jotted down the name. "Now what about Eve Angel? If we depose her, do you think she might change her testimony—you know, about you striking your wife?"

"Forget it! I don't want a deposition from her." Ricker folded his arms across his chest. "I don't want Eve Angel to face perjury charges. I'll do my time if need be. Let her alone."

"There won't be any perjury charges; there never are," said Hurley, dismayed at Ricker's sudden intransigence. "Judges will never punish a woman for lying, Mr. Ricker, didn't you know that? It's a woman's husband or boyfriend that keeps her honest. It's knowing that sooner or later her man will get out of jail— and then what?—that keeps her honest, not some absurd prospect of perjury charges."

"I don't care," insisted Ricker. "Keep her out of it. She has enough to worry about. Her husband recently left for Wyoming. Her life will be difficult alone. I don't want to add to her problems."

"But Eve Angel testified that she saw you assault your wife. She was the prosecution's only eyewitness. She sent you away, Mr. Ricker. Why are you protecting her?"

"Did you hear her testify against me? I didn't."

Hurley, who had gone over to the window, turned and stared directly at the man he came to help. "Granted, most of her testimony came from interrogatories and sworn affidavits, but somewhere along the line she went to court; some judge heard her words."

"Well, I didn't," said Ricker, leaning back in his chair, his arms still crossed on his chest. "I don't give a damn about *some judge*; she never appeared at the trial, so, as far as I'm concerned, she's just another pawn in this scam of theirs. They manipulated her, exploited her loyalty to Cantrice to get what they wanted. She's as much a victim in this thing as I am."

Hurley sat back down with a sigh. Exasperated or satisfied, he seemed placated, at least, by Ricker's response. "What if I depose her and *not* ask her anything about her testimony? Try to find out—let's say—how she feels about you. A character witness. *That* couldn't hurt, could it?"

Chapter 26

"It seems that they want me to reduce or eliminate your medication," noted Randerath, looking at new documents in one of Ricker's two file folders, the fatter, unmarked one. The other, the one marked "Confidential," had been pushed aside and remained unopened.

"Will you?" asked Ricker, with the hint of a smile. There was hidden irony here. Of course Randerath would initiate his drug withdrawal, but some game had to be played out first.

"Do you want me to?"

"Yes . . . of course I do."

Randerath's smile faded. "I could fight it on professional grounds," he said, closing the file folder with an air of finality. "As your physician, I have ample latitude in this matter. You were in a state of extreme anxiety when you got here. I think *we* have that condition under control, but relapses are the rule; the dependency/infantilism syndrome constitutes an irresistible cycle. What are your thoughts?"

Sensing, with uneasiness, that the game had ended, Ricker was pleased nonetheless at being consulted in his own case. He thought the "we" as used by Randerath was not the nurses' condescending "we" when doting over a patient but rather the voice of the hospital verbalized by a spokesman as to a colleague. Ricker took it as a validation of himself as a person, as evidence that Randerath didn't see him as some psychotic *vegetable*.

"I was in shock at the severity of my sentence . . . [Suddenly he was aware, as he spoke, that his words had none of the *head games* self-consciousness he remembered from his first encounters with Randerath. Had he broken through some psychological barrier? Transcended some limits to his personality and emerged on the other side? Not *pecking order* techniques, either, but natural, spontaneous responses.] . . . and the unfairness of the System. I think anybody would be a little depressed and anxious under the circumstances."

"I agree," acknowledged Randerath, "and I'm prepared to acquiesce to the wishes of your attorney. I'll order a reduction of your medication incrementally over the next seventy-two hours and, if circumstances don't indicate otherwise, eliminate it entirely after that. Is that agreeable to you?"

Ricker was grinning broadly as he left Randerath's office. If this were a dream, now would be about the time he'd wake up.

Chapter 27

From a grab-bag of civvies in a closet in the hospital's administration building, the authorities at Lakewood came up with some clothes for Ricker to wear to court. He would respond to his *habeas corpus* warrant by appearing clean-shaven, with his hair neatly trimmed, wearing a freshly-ironed sport coat and a tie. It would be the first time in more than four years the young man had worn anything decent.

Proper attire brought thoughts of his Aunt Grace—regrets over unattained respectability, his unfulfilled destiny, the gentleman's life denied him—thoughts he would not allow to dampen his mood. His image in the receptionist's small mirror smiled back at him. Even the hospital staff seemed to share his euphoria.

Nonetheless, processing-out still had that old familiar feeling: handcuffs and leg irons. "We'll be stopping in Walpole for some long-term prisoners," said one of the drivers. "Don't talk to them or have anything to do with them."

At Walpole, a maximum security state prison—the toughest Massachusetts has to offer—Ricker's van was forced to wait in a sweltering parking area. Half an hour went by, maybe more.

The drivers didn't care, they had air conditioning in their sealed-off compartment. Leaving their motor running, they'd occasionally get out and walk over to other vans, chat with other drivers.

In the cage in the back of his van—an oven—Ricker lay drenched in sweat. He lay, as best he could, on his narrow wooden bench. He would have preferred the floor, but it smelled strongly of urine. Finally, three guards approached the van with two heavily-shackled men, whom they put in with Ricker. The men, in their twenties, one white, the other black, were chained together. Both wore tee shirts and faded denim jeans.

They seemed to have a devil-may-care attitude toward their impending journey. The pair joked with each other in hushed tones but made no effort to communicate with Ricker. They had been called into court after the discovery of some very old warrants on minor offenses that would not affect their life sentences one way or the other.

During the ride to the Merrimac County Courthouse, Ricker remained bent over in his usual mode on these trips: his head cradled in his hands, his elbows on his knees. He kept his eyes closed, braced himself against swerves, and resigned himself to the discomfort that seemed to increase with every endless mile.

From the corner of his eye he saw one of the two young lifers from Walpole take a tiny key from his mouth and begin to jiggle it in the other man's handcuffs. The cuffs seemed reluctant to open, but the man persisted, smiling and unhurried at his task. Ricker gave no indication that he had seen anything.

The ride had more than its share of sharp corners, turns that drove Ricker's head deeper between his legs. The next time he had a chance to look over at the young men, one was totally free of handcuffs and leg irons. Oh, God! he thought, these guys are trouble, and I'm right here in the middle of it. If one of them gets a guard's gun we might all be killed.

In prison, Ricker had learned never to trust anyone, especially inmates. They were totally selfish. They had the morality of the street, which is to say none at all. Guards, at least, were consistent in their warehousing of people; they went by the rule book; if it didn't say it, they didn't do it. Anyway, given a choice in a gunfight, there was no doubt in Ricker's mind: he'd side with the guards. Especially now that Hurley held out some hope for him. But even if he could remain uninvolved, then what? He could not envision a single scenario that would improve his situation.

As the van approached Merrimac County, Ricker became more and more anxious. The lifers had draped their chains across their wrists and ankles in such a way as to appear to be locked up normally. Anyone looking in would see nothing out of the ordinary, nothing suspicious.

Ricker didn't know whether he wanted them to get out first or, whether he'd be safer if he were the first to leave. In situations where everyone is headed for the same destination, very often the ones who stand up first are the first to be let out.

When the rear door opened, Ricker was summoned by name. On his way out he glanced back at the others. Their shackles were firmly in place for all to see; no longer draped slackly, but taut and secure. Locked up tight.

Could I have been imagining the whole thing, he thought? Should I mention it to the guard bringing me into the building? Ricker certainly knew never to rat out, snitch on, or squeal on fellow prisoners, that the penalty for such betrayal could very well be death. He'd heard of instances where inmates, waiting in line for chow, had their throats cut with filed-down license plates; or, weightlifting, had heavy barbells dropped across their necks in plain view of dozens of men, all of whom claimed to have seen nothing. There was a code, and it was strictly enforced.

But what about the innocent guards? If they were killed it would be their families who would suffer. Could he do anything to help these men? wondered Ricker. Could he warn them, somehow, so they might be a tiny bit more vigilant? Just a split-second of heightened awareness might give them the slim edge that could save their lives, and nobody would be the wiser. Who would suspect him of having said anything if a guard was a little less indifferent in his monotonous routine? "I think those guys from Walpole can take off their cuffs," he said to the guard once they were inside the courthouse.

"Impossible," the guard replied. "Prisoners try to wriggle out of them all the time, but they never succeed. I know sometimes it looks like they do, but don't worry, they're just wasting their time."

Chapter 28

Neither Brian Hurley nor Archibald Shaw was in court when Ricker was brought before the judge hearing his case—a woman this time. He had never seen her before. This was Superior Court. All his charges were criminal now. District attorneys of this political party or that, elected by the people, were conducting the prosecution. The heavy hand of power politics was clenched into a fist against him now.

Hurley's motion to revisit his case had been denied. The *new evidence* promised by Hurley never materialized. Now Ricker would be forced to serve out, unchallenged, whatever sentence they imposed. His psychiatric evaluation—whatever that told them—unchallenged. His plea bargain—unchallenged. Now he was back to Square One. He saw himself at the mercy of the System, now. A System that wanted him behind bars for the rest of his life.

Looking up at the black-robed figure behind the bench, he wondered: could this woman have any compassion for me? No, he concluded. She'd surely side with the consensus of previous judges, with the good-old-boy lawyers, with the ex-wife. She herself looked like a middle-aged housewife, albeit one with a gavel, a black robe, and the power to punish strangers. Strangers like him.

She was no doubt well-qualified—overqualified, in all probability—for the routine cases she'd be facing. Degrees from Wellesley, Radcliffe, Sarah Lawrence—doctorates, post-doctorates, clerkships with notables: potential Supreme Court candidates. Perhaps she'd be one herself some day. And what was he? A throwaway. Expendable. Not worth the effort—any effort.

Psychiatrists and penal authorities had filed reports and affidavits with the court. These and other documents were passed down to the four lawyers arguing Ricker's case—two for the defendant, two for the Commonwealth of Massachusetts—discussed among them in hushed tones, passed over to the clerk, and then, once again, with an air of finality this time, passed back up to the judge. The lawyers then approached the bench, where they continued in whispers, some gesturing, some merely nodding. Some occasionally turning part way around to glance over their eyeglasses at Ricker. Finally, heads nodded, and, in a concluding flurry of activity, the clerk affixed his stamp, and the judge her signature, to whatever rulings had been made; while the lawyers, returning to their table, gathered their papers, closed their bulging brief cases with audible snaps and clicks, and left the courtroom together.

Ricker tried desperately to read his fate in the eyes, the demeanor, of the judge, who by now was on to other matters. New players had entered the courtroom; new lawyers were opening briefcases; new documents were being handed out. Ricker stood up defiantly. "What about me?" he shouted as loudly as he could.

All heads turned. The newcomers, seeing a man in handcuffs, affected expressions of disgust. The guard moved quickly, placing himself between Ricker and the others. He spun his prisoner around toward a door beside the dock, through which he pushed Ricker, while managing, all the while, to create as little disturbance as possible. Suddenly they were in the back hall; the door had been closed with hardly a click; the crisis averted.

The guard (obviously well practiced at that maneuver) turned to Ricker. "We'll go back to Walpole when they're through with those other two monkeys." Smiling benevolently as he spoke, he gently prodded his prisoner toward the elevator for the return trip to the basement.

Chapter 29

The guard who brought Ricker downstairs did not mention his outburst to anyone along the way. Apparently, such displays were common occurrences around there. As they neared the holding cells, Ricker saw the guard from Lakewood, the one to whom he confided about the cuffs. Could this man have said anything to the two "lifers?" Could he have confronted them? Questioned them? Searched them? Was Ricker's betrayal exposed? As if his plight weren't futile enough, serving time among killers doing multiple life sentences would, if he were deemed a traitor, be disastrous.

Alone in his holding cell, Ricker wondered if things in his life could get any worse. As the physical manifestations of his despair and depression returned—the headache, the knot in his gut—he wished he were back at Lakewood, wished he had never left, had never heard of Hurley. He would gladly return as one of Randerath's relapsed, hopeless cases. One of the majority needing attention, care, comfort—one of the failures. He longed for some Thorazine. For the death penalty. For a lethal injection.

Ah, lethal injection. The words sounded so inviting to him. The prospect so tantalizing. Massachusetts has no death penalty. Those self-righteous sons-of-bitches, thought Ricker. Hypocrites. Take Texas. For all their free-wheeling, frontier justice, they have lethal injection for capital punishment. If only he could go to Texas and volunteer for "death row."

Sitting on the wooden bench, his head in his hands, Ricker suddenly longed to cry. To sob like a baby until exhausted. No, not like a baby. Like the parent of a dead baby.

When was the last time he had given in to tears? He couldn't remember. In his childhood, certainly, in the arms of his Aunt Grace, but that memory had long since faded. And what about now? Why was he incapable of crying now? Could the legend be true, he wondered?—the legend that claimed if you couldn't cry, you had no soul. Had he sold his soul to Satan at some time?—or times, even?—during his reckless years? He was sure he had, somehow. In fact, he'd never been surer about anything in his life.

Just then, he heard the sound of others approaching from upstairs. It was the pair from Walpole. The guards accompanying them debated between themselves whether or not to put them in with Ricker or assign them a different cell. They were all put together.

Ricker was forced to share his bench—eventually, crowded off it—but subtly, without eye contact, without violence. Relieved, he sat on the other side of the cell, on the floor. It was obvious: the lifers meant him no harm.

Shifts changed. Vans came and went. Finally, only one van was left and one pair of drivers. The court was waiting for a Spanish-language interpreter who, because of a scheduling mix-up, had been assigned to a different jurisdiction. The hearing for a Latino defendant who understood no English was being delayed until another interpreter could be found and brought in to assist the man, and it was almost 6:00 P.M. before the case was heard. It took less than five minutes for a decision to be rendered: the Spanish-speaking prisoner was sentenced to the Northstone Correctional Facility, brought back downstairs, shackled to Ricker, and finally they all departed, without supper, and, for Ricker, without hope.

Chapter 30

High intensity orange halogen floodlights illuminated the Northstone Correctional Facility. The barbed wire fences. The ancient grey stone buildings with vertical black bars across endless rows of windows. The other structures: garages with enormous doors, factory-like buildings with tall smokestacks and loading docks, nondescript sheds, and corrugated metal Quonset huts. Amber sulfurous light gave an other-worldly look to this prisonscape, like the lifeless surface of Mars, or like Germany during the War: the barracks, the incinerators, the railroad sidings, the cattle cars. . . .

And the shadows were equally troubling: angles cut out willy-nilly from brick, dangerous black rectangular zones. Voids. And the background noise—constant, all night long— the drone of machinery: generators, transformers, ventilation. And the smells: hydraulic fluid, diesel fuel, spent diesel, the lowest octanes.

At Northstone's back door, the drivers opened the cage and asked Ricker and the man shackled to him to step outside. They wanted only the Latino prisoner, planned to separate him from Ricker at the first opportunity; but as soon as the two left the van, the lifers from Walpole came storming out behind them, and there was gunfire. Screams, gunfire, profanity, and more gunfire. Then moaning. Then nothing.

Ricker, thrown to the ground, wasn't sure if he had been hit. His distress, he thought, might come from being pinned under a fat man (a guard?), who was gurgling, bleeding, possibly dying there, right on top of him. He could feel something sticky, like not-so-warm blood, oozing down his neck. Could it be his own, he wondered? Quick wounds brought no pain—he knew that—endorphins, or something, blocked it. You'd have to put your hand to the spot; if it came up bloody . . . well.

The Latino prisoner was trying hysterically to free himself from Ricker, pulling the chain that bound them together. Let the bastard pull, thought Ricker; he'll get nothing from me. I'm dead meat. Finally, voices came running out of the Northstone lockup, voices shouting conflicting commands, voices betraying panic and ineptitude.

At the scene, guards and administrators gave first aid to the wounded transporting officers, one of whom was lifted carefully from where he lay on top of Ricker. They removed the Latino man's cuffs, recuffed him, and brought him inside.

Sirens approached, dozens of them—interminably, and eventually sirens left, although fewer, it seemed. A lone ambulance took away the two wounded guards. Someone asked if Ricker were dead. Someone else said, "If he isn't, are you going to call another ambulance for him? Let's save the state some money and let the scumbag croak."

A shoe—the toe of a shoe—prodded gingerly at Ricker's head, as if to examine it, but at a distance. "I think this guy's alive," the first voice said.

"I still say, 'leave him,'" said the second voice. "Let's let the M.E. deal with him later. That is, if he's still alive by then, which I hope he isn't." The voices made their way back into the building.

Slowly, Ricker moved a hand to his eyes to clear the sticky blood from his eyelids. A few feet from his face he could see part of the face of one of the lifers; the other part, along with most of the man's head, had been blown off. The remains of the second man, his tee shirt in bloody shreds, lay next to the body of his dead companion.

The sight made Ricker queasy: brain tissue that only moments before had been capable of thought were splattered everywhere, while his own brain tissue—not so different— continued to function, continued trying to process what he had just witnessed, or worse, continued on to the next step: contemplating the future, the years he faced behind bars. Perhaps these men were not so bad off, after all, he concluded. At least now they were free. Without court orders. Without lawyers. At least now they could feel no pain.

After the wounded guards had been taken to the hospital, all activity stopped. The scene, as if frozen in time, awaited the arrival of the Merrimac County Medical Examiner. He would take charge. His signature alone would legitimize anything and everything done there that night. He would have sole authority to examine and release the bodies of the prisoners (including Ricker?), and authorize a hearse from the morgue to come for them. Meanwhile, everyone waited. Two-way radios that had been chattering, grew still. Voices could be heard inside the prison office, while outside there was an uneasy silence.

Ricker could see a County Sheriff's cruiser near him, blue lights flashing, driver's side door open. The only sound was an occasional radio transmission from somewhere close by.

The decision was his: run for it, or accept his fate at the hands of the System, a fate that in all probability would result in his being locked away from society forever. His Aunt Grace had told him how Fate or God sometimes intervenes at crucial moments. If you're blessed with such an opportunity, the old woman had said, take it. Take it, and acknowledge it later; show some gratitude for your gift, or you may never get another. Was this open car door such an opportunity? If he ignored this offering, would he ever get another?

Ricker stood up and ran to the cruiser, got in, closed the door, and turned the key. A grinding noise startled him; the engine had been left running. What a waste of gas, he thought, smiling. Why is it that cops have no qualms about wasting taxpayers' money? He shifted into *drive* and sped down the hill to the access road. A distracted guard at a sentry station half turned toward him, saw the blue lights, and casually, as if after the fact, waved him through.

Chapter 31

Ricker, a mile or two down the road, and in unfamiliar territory, was speeding along at seventy miles an hour when he noticed a white Camaro pull over. It dawned on him that his cruiser's blue lights were on and that the driver of the sports car expected to be given a speeding ticket. Ricker pulled in behind the car and, pacing himself with the special rhythm required of this ritual, slowly approached the driver's open window. Two teenage boys sat nervously in the front seat.

"I'm not going to give you boys a ticket," he said, walking the thin line between having to pass himself off as a friendly cop, or alienating them as an authoritarian bully. "You have the right to refuse, but I've just been involved in a nasty bit of police business and I could use a ride to the hospital. To Boston. Are you boys interested? I just spoke to headquarters, and the chief doesn't want me driving if I can avoid it."

"We'll take you, sir," replied the older of the two, the one who wasn't driving. "Kevin and I would love to do it. More than anything—right, Kevin?"

Ricker grabbed a Sheriff's Department windbreaker and a staticy two-way police radio from the front seat of the cruiser.

Waving the other boy into the back seat, he got in next to Kevin, and off they sped.

"How fast should we go, sir?" asked the boy in back, leaning over. "Seventy? Eighty? You name it. Now that we're on *police business* and don't have to worry about getting a ticket."

"We're doing just fine, son," said Ricker, noting that the 60 miles per hour at which they traveled was perfect for that stretch of road. He didn't want to get chatty with these kids. What he knew of the *pecking order* required him to maintain his dominant position by saying as little as possible. He decided to adopt the image of a high-echelon plainclothes detective surviving heroic duty at an unusually brutal crime scene:

His coolness, as a result of years of experience under fire, would allow him a little modesty. He'd let the rookies go for celebrity status—getting in front of the TV lights when they came on. (First the equipment trucks arrive and set up, next the *on camera* people—the so-called *talent*, get their noses powdered—and then it's *show time*. Fifteen minutes later they've sped away without a trace. See you at eleven!)

When it became his turn to be interviewed, he'd give a reluctant, noncommittal response and then slip off, bruised and bloodied, into the shadows to fight another day. His performance would be like *method acting*. If it worked he could become the character whose part he was playing. It might not only save his life now, he mused, it might open up possibilities for the way he could survive in the future. It was dress rehearsal time, and his audience was a couple of dumb teenagers.

He'd allow the strain of his job to wrinkle the corners of his eyes. Harden them a bit—but not too much. He'd come across as no-stranger-to-suffering, his own as well as that of others. He turned down the squelch on his two-way radio. His part of the job was done, the dangerous, tough part. Now the paper-pushers could come in and mop things up. He'd check in later, in the morning. File his report then. The Chief would probably want to debrief him anyway:

—So . . . what do you think? How was Ricker tied into this gunplay?

—I don't think he was part of it, Chief. He tried to warn a guard.

—Really? Then he knew . . . beforehand, even.

—Um, well . . . I guess.

—Then, Detective, wouldn't you say he was an accessory? An accessory before the fact?

The boy in the back seat kept leaning over, kept asking questions of Ricker: "Why don't you monitor your radio, sir? Why don't you call in your position? Your destination?"

His patience running out, Ricker finally spoke. "Kevin, would you like to answer your friend's question? Why don't we tell headquarters where we are?"

Kevin thought a while—a long while—much to Ricker's satisfaction. The longer the better.

"So the crooks won't listen in and ambush us?" the youngster finally replied, without taking his eyes off the road.

Ricker smiled. These kids must be sent from heaven, he thought. "No, boys, the reason that I couldn't care less about my radio is simply because I'm too tired to bother listening to a bunch of second-shift rookies exchange ten-fours. I'd rather listen to Frank Sinatra.

"By the way," he added. "do either of you boys know who Frank Sinatra is?"

"Is he the police chief?" ventured Kevin, glancing over.

They reached Mass General Hospital without incident. "Why don't you boys stop by the station tomorrow morning?" suggested Ricker, taking off his blood-caked sport coat. "About 10:30 would be good. If I'm not mistaken, you'll both be entitled to some well-deserved congratulations from the Chief of Police."

Slipping into the police windbreaker, Ricker grabbed his two-way radio and headed for the men's room, throwing his sport coat into a trash receptacle along the way.

In the mirror of the brightly lit room he saw a wounded man. His hair was matted with dry brown blood. Caked and cracking blood streaked his throat and blotted his shirt and tie. While he was washing up, a security guard came into the bathroom. He noticed Ricker and hesitated for a moment as if weighing some decision in his mind.

Chapter 32

His decision made, the hospital security guard headed straight for Ricker. "Why don't you use the employees' locker room?" the man suggested, with the eager-to-please expression of a public servant ready for retirement. "It's much more comfortable. You can even take a shower there. I'll get you a towel and some soap."

The offer sounded good to the bloodied veteran. Feeling increasingly comfortable in his new persona, Ricker thought that maybe the time had come for him to relax and accept the blandishments of a grateful citizenry, although, he conceded, it is always more to accommodate an adoring public than it is for their own self-indulgence that heroes accept such hospitality.

And so, feigning a slight limp, he accompanied the guard toward the employees' basement locker room.

"Looks like you've had a tough night," said the security guard, glancing at the matted blood in Ricker's hair and on his clothes. "If you need medical attention, you've come to the right place."

"I'll be fine," said Ricker, determined to budget his words. He did not intend to curry favor from this man. In fact, just the opposite. A little unintentional rudeness might go a long way. Silence would once again be his source of power. He'd let the older man do all the talking, ask the questions, feel awkward, grovel for answers.

"It's mostly ambulance drivers and E.M.T.s that use this place," said the security guard, leading Ricker into the locker room. "Some of them have their own locks for these lockers, but for the most part, everyone leaves their stuff out in the open. We're a pretty honest bunch of guys. I've been here twenty-nine years and haven't heard of a single case of anything missing. But it never hurts to be careful, so you might want to keep an eye on your valuables: your wallet, your gun. . . . I've got to get going, but enjoy your shower. I might catch up with you later."

"Thanks," said Ricker, glad to see the last of the man in uniform.

Chapter 33

Just after midnight, as Ricker headed to the showers with his soap and towel, the locker room suddenly became crowded, noisy. Must be a shift change, he thought. A few people showered, some shaved. Some only changed without showering, from uniforms to civvies or vice-versa.

Worried that the kids who drove him in from Northstone might have learned he was an escapee and reported his where-abouts to the authorities, Ricker changed his mind and decided not to take a shower after all, although he longed for one. Then he noticed an ambulance driver hanging a garment bag in an open locker across from his. After the man had taken off his uniform and entered the shower room, Ricker quickly fin-ished dressing, took the man's belongings, and rushed from the building.

At North Station, an Amtrak terminal a block or two from Mass General Hospital, Ricker found a stall in the men's room and opened the garment bag. The clothing inside fit him perfectly, and a wallet in one of the shoes at the bottom of the bag contained more than $350 in cash.

When he left the station, he felt transformed mentally as well as physically—well-dressed, pleasant in appearance, and self-assured. His step, tentative at first, took on confidence with every stride. Perhaps, he thought, his luck had finally changed. "Thank you, thank you, thank you," he whispered to no one in particular. Show gratitude for your gifts, his aunt had advised him as a child. To God? To Fate? She didn't say. It seemed to make no difference to her; the act of acknowledging one's good fortune was what counted, she said.

Thank you. Thank you. Thank you.

Walking out into the cool predawn air, Ricker could smell the harbor nearby. Salt, seaweed, or perhaps rotting marine life. The ocean. Above him, an elevated train screeched, entering the wide curve at North Station, the Boston Garden "T" stop. Sirens approached. Ricker hardly gave them a thought. Somehow, he expected them to be ambulances headed for Mass General, and they were.

Thank you. Thank you. Thank you.

He began walking in the opposite direction, away from the hospital, toward the waterfront. To where the land would end and the water and sky would begin. Toward the eastern horizon, now slightly different from the rest of the mostly starless city sky. Slightly brighter in some barely discernible way. A feeling, rather than anything his naked eye could perceive with certainty.

He headed to where the land would end and the water and sky would begin. The promise of dawn was calling him. And as he walked, something else urged him on. It was his ally. His totem. The bird on his breast.

Chapter 34

Graffiti artists had vandalized the sign. Did it say *"Fairy To Gay*haven?" Ricker, weary from a night without sleep, couldn't be sure. The faded, battered sign on a half-demolished pier was his only clue that the Bayhaven Ferry had ever existed. But where was it now?

Walking the busy, mid-morning streets searching for the ferry, Ricker mingled inconspicuously with the end-of-the-summer crowd, the tourists for whom Boston is a favorite destination. He went first to the Rowes Wharf, the "T" Wharf section of Boston's North End, to where passenger ships once docked. Here he saw stockbrokers with briefcases walking from the harbor-view condominiums where they lived to the high-rise office buildings where they worked.

Boston's waterfront was in the hands of the developers now —the gentrifiers. Commercial maritime interests had been displaced to other sites along the coast or disappeared altogether. Container vessels still had a terminal in Charlestown, and oil and gas farms still remained along the inner harbor in Chelsea, but the truly unprofitable, the marginal operations, like the Bayhaven Ferry, were scattered willy-nilly. A money-losing venture by any standards, the ferry, Ricker learned from an old ex-longshoreman loitering in the area, clung to life from the *other* side of the harbor, the low-rent side of the Callahan Tunnel, from the section of East Boston that was destined for the "wrecking ball." It and its neighbors, according to the former longshoreman, would soon become part of Logan Airport.

But the Boston side, Ricker noted, was a different story entirely—it was in the midst of a Renaissance. The restoration of this stretch of harborside real estate had, in effect, transformed it back in time. Cobblestones and gaslights, as they did in the nineteenth century, once again lined the piers and foggy back streets of this seaport city. It was Dickens. It was London. It was *Currier & Ives*.

It was money in the bank for the upscale, world-class hotels towering above the foggy coastline. Interconnected by waterfront pavilions, they provided their patrons with all the amenities: *al fresco* dining during the summer or, inside, vast seafood restaurants with fishnets and lobster pots adorning the walls and ceilings, with seaview tables facing the busy harbor, facing the endless, restless Atlantic, facing East Boston and the current home of the Bayhaven Ferry.

The dilapidated ferry was of the old style, not one of the bus-like craft currently in use for hauling people and cars as quickly as possible. Ricker made his way up gangplanks and along companionways to the large cabin on the top deck of the antiquated vessel. The drafty cabin was totally enclosed by windows—not aluminum sliders, but rigid wooden panels of small panes held in with putty and a crust of numerous coats of peeling paint: red over white over red again. Many of the panes were broken or missing altogether. If I want fresh air, he thought, I'll sit near one of these.

But once outside the harbor, on the open, chill September sea, those thoughts quickly vanished. The ship made slow progress against the white-capped ocean chop. Ricker watched droplets of sea spray coalesce on the windows and then run down in tiny streams. He was glad to be inside. He stretched out on a deck chair on the sunny side of the mostly deserted cabin and, comforted by the throbbing of propellers far below him, fell into a deep, untroubled sleep.

Chapter 35

Bay Haven had undergone its share of transformations over its three-hundred-year history. Abandoned as a whaling port in the nineteenth century, it was rediscovered by artists and writers in the twentieth. It was isolated enough to be an enclave, a sanctuary, the perfect environment to nourish the creative spirit. Inevitably, the best-kept secret in Greenwich Village became a popular destination. Free-thinkers, avant-guardists, bohemians of every variety soon flocked to its shores, its isolated dunes and, later, to the bars, galleries, playhouses, and motels built to accommodate them. Recently, in its current incarnation, it had become the refuge of choice for gays. The laissez-faire spirit still persisted, and the money-making enterprises flourished—the hawkers and gawkers were everywhere. Welcome, fellows, to paradise.

Ricker found a pay phone in the ferry terminal and looked up "consignment shops" in the local yellow pages. Three were listed.

"Neil's Clothing—New & Used" was not far from the center of town, on a back street that seemed more residential than commercial. A beauty parlor and bicycle rental shop (closed for the season) were on either side of Neil's, with apartments upstairs. A tiny bell jingled when Ricker opened the door.

"I'd like something dignified, high-class, a bit matronly, if you know what I mean," he said.

Neil returned from the back room with a tweed suit: jacket, skirt, and frilly white blouse. Simple. Elegant. The jacket and blouse fit perfectly; the skirt was too large. "No problem," he said leading Ricker to the triptych mirrors in the back of his shop.

Ricker held the skirt in place over his jockey shorts while Neil put pins in for alterations. "I'll need some lingerie, I suppose," queried Ricker. As if in response, Neil lifted the skirt. The man wearing it had an undeniable erection.

Suddenly the nervous tension between them disappeared, replaced by another kind of tension—the playful, careless, relaxed kind. The sexual kind. "You'll excuse me," said Ricker. "I've never been in a skirt before. . . . My own, that is."

"How do you like the feeling?" asked Neil, fussing around the hem, the waistband, taking measurements, making tiny markings with a soaplike chalk, losing no opportunity to brush up against the bulge in Ricker's shorts. It was a game they both seemed to enjoy.

Just then the jingling door announced the entrance of a man of indeterminate middle-age, delicately built—dressed in casual but stylish summer clothes. His appearance was reminiscent of Truman Capote. "I hope I'm not interrupting anything," he said. He waited for the sarcasm of his remark to sink in. "I see my coat is still in the window. Any bites? Any teeny nibbles at least?"

"Not a one, Leslie," responded Neil. "Too early in the season for a fur coat. But we did try, didn't we?"

"Yes, we did, and thank you," said Leslie, smiling thinly. "But as you know, I'll be leaving today, tomorrow at the latest, for my annual migration, so I'll take it along with me now. Unless . . . um, your friend here might be interested?"

"How much?" asked Ricker.

"A genuine Persian lamb in impeccable condition should fetch at least $500, but rather than *schlep* it all the way to the Coast, I'll let you have it for $175."

Neil who was asking $100, half of which would have gone to him, changed the subject to underwear. "I can't sell it used," he said. "The Commonwealth of Massachusetts has a law against merchants selling used undies. But Leslie might have some to throw into the bargain."

Leslie lived in a one-room garden apartment on the other side of town. Ricker put on a pair of soft goatskin gloves before getting into the man's car, which was already packed for his cross-country trip.

"So you want to be a woman," said Leslie, glancing over as he drove. "Do you know where to begin?"

"I'd like to *look* like one, at least."

"Then you're wasting your time; you might as well be a Martian in drag. A macho guy like you will never bring it off. Pad your hips, toss your hair—you're nowhere!"

Back at his gloomy, barren apartment, Leslie regarded his guest from over the rim of the plastic tumbler of sherry he was sipping. Ricker slouched on the sofa across from him with a can of room-temperature beer. Neither spoke.

The long silence was finally broken by Leslie. "You're ready, aren't you?" he said, never once losing eye contact with his guest.

"How did you know? How did you do it?"

"Take off your gloves, my darling," said Leslie. " . . . and tell me why you want to be a woman."

Chapter 36

Ricker decided to settle in Cambridge—the People's Republic of Cambridge, as it was called by conservatives. Granted, city administration tended toward the liberal, the permissive—they had no choice with universities and their students, faculty, and infrastructure bordering on and often co-mingling with rundown blue-collar neighborhoods and the diverse inhabitants they'd bring to the mix. Street people. Drugs. Indeed, such a demographic mélange made it impossible for the city to please everybody, so they tolerated most everything. Ricker became invisible here. He traveled by bicycle or public transportation, shopped through classified ads, and resorted to bulletin boards to meet more complicated needs.

The fall passed slowly for Ricker. The winter. Months seemed like years. Hardly thirty-six, Ricker looked a weary ten, fifteen years older. His pudgy weightlifter's physique was going to flab, drooping into a pear-shaped combination of haggard and obese—a body in decline. The city was taking its toll on his face as well—the contours sagging, rearranging themselves into jowls and folds with loose skin around his eyelids and throat. His complexion had become pasty, blemished. Bad food, missed meals, too much booze, and little or no exercise left him flaccid, weak, unhealthy-looking. I'm on the road to the graveyard, he thought, staring at his face in the mirror—a stranger's face, the face of an old man. . . .

. . . or an old woman, he mused. A bag lady! Handicapped. Crippled.

Arming himself with an array of cosmetics, Ricker sat before his mirror. He knew what he had to do, and glamour was not his objective. On the contrary, his plan was to use makeup to heighten his wrinkles, accentuate flaws, add deformities.

Four years in prison teaches a man patience, a lesson Ricker had no choice but to learn. Serving time on phony, trumped-up charges adds another element: bitterness—enough bitterness to last a lifetime on the outside; indeed, many lifetimes, he thought, as he slowly plucked out his facial hair with tweezers, as he applied his makeup, as he fashioned his unsettling disguise.

On the street, eyes turned away. His old woman's trembling hands faltered convincingly; his infirmities seemed to give him new, unlimited freedom. He could, he had no doubt, move unchallenged toward any objective, any target.

Later that night, with sleet turning to driving rain, as one of society's unseen discards, Ricker sought shelter on Warranton Street, among Boston's off-Broadway playhouses. He smiled contentedly. Layered in coats and sweaters, he was warm and dry. He looked around the deserted back alley in which he stood: dumpsters. . . . Overflowing dumpsters. Trash.

What first attracted him was the sound. Masked by rain, the vague choral notes blended with the hiss of car tires on wet pavement. Enchanted, Ricker pursued slowly. A choir. The hint of a choir—elsewhere, but nearby—a church, a theatre—rehearsing, stopping, starting, fading out, then in. Thin choral notes amid the hiss of car tires in the rain.

Ricker followed the sound to a pile of discarded scenery. A heap beside a dumpster. The music came from an imitation crystal ball, an overly large glass sphere glued to a plastic pedestal. It had been buried among stage settings. Props. Carry-

ing it back with him on the Red Line to Cambridge, Ricker
attracted little attention. Except for a nine- or ten-year-old boy
staring at him from across the aisle, nobody on the near-empty
train gave him a second glance.

"Are you a fortune-teller?" asked the youngster, moving to
the seat beside him.

Ricker smiled down at the boy.

"Tell my fortune," he asked.

Ricker looked over at the child's mother. With a clarity of
vision that surprised him, he saw an older-than-her-years
divorced school teacher: no money—no prospects for any—
many left-wing friends, all in public sector jobs: psychological
services, halfway houses, battered-women's shelters, counseling;
or no jobs at all: welfare programs, assistance, handouts. "What
would you like to know?" whispered Ricker, in the weak, cracking voice of an old lady, a voice that somehow flowed from him
naturally, without his even trying. "One question. Choose it
carefully."

"Who will I marry?" asked the boy, without hesitation.

Ricker was in no hurry to respond. When he felt ready, he
leaned down to the youngster, and the words emerged as if on
their own: "Somebody like your mom," he said in a hushed,
rasping voice, "a woman who would share her last scrap of food
with a needy stranger. A woman who will some day break
your heart."

Back at his room, Ricker placed the crystal ball on top of the
high wardrobe his landlady had provided in lieu of a closet.
Occasionally, it seemed to emit faint music—nothing tangible,
though. Nothing traceable. When the sound of steam escaping
from his radiator stopped, *it* would continue on. If only I could
write music, he thought. If only I could preserve these melodies
for another time, for tomorrow . . . voices, choirs, choral works
fully scored.

Chapter 37

Ricker, after his escape, tried to suppress his strongest urge: to return to familiar surroundings, to visit the people and places he had yearned to see for so long. An unnecessary precaution. The judge assigned the task of signing warrants for his arrest was puzzled: two-and-a-half years for violation of a restraining order, another two-and-a-half on and over (not to run concurrently) for domestic abuse—five years— four served with parole denied? It didn't add up. Then again, in many cases the real facts never come out in court, never appear on the record. Lawyers agree to the sentence as a result of their mutual assessment of the circumstances and their consensus as to the best remedy—best for the victim or his or her family, that is, to satisfy their perception of appropriate retribution; or, best for society, to appease its righteous indignation, regardless of what the letter of the law happens to say.

And so the judge, who hadn't seen the latest rulings, those arising from Ricker's plea bargain, signed the district attorney's warrants. But then, with second thoughts on the matter— nagging doubts from years on the bench—he modified his orders; he removed the open-ended provisions; in effect, he allowed the warrants to expire after eighteen months. As a result, federal authorities ignored them totally—no action would be taken in neighboring states; and local authorities, North Shore communities in Merrimac County, put the matter of capturing Denton Ricker on their lowest priority status—which is to say, they would make no effort whatsoever to pursue him. If he committed subsequent crimes, if he were arrested for anything, the warrants would be triggered; otherwise, he was virtually a free man.

But Ricker didn't know that. He saw himself as a fugitive; at times, a romantic figure—Robin Hood, Pretty Boy Floyd, a desperado in a western movie. At other times he saw himself merely as a hunted animal. Living by his wits. His agenda—one word: survival.

Then, by accident, in the Boston Public Library, he discovered the literature and websites of a growing subculture. People like himself—out West for the most part, or down South—but in New England, too. In New Hampshire, the *Live Free or Die* state. Some of their numbers called themselves *survivalists*, wore camouflage, fired live ammunition. Others were members of *white supremacist* groups, Christian cults. They were all joined by a common thread. Hate.

They spoke Ricker's language. Curious, he reached out to them. But when they returned the favor, he stepped back. He saw them pursuing him as dope-pushers would, offering him their irresistible prize, their panacea for society's ills, their prescription that would set him right. But it was not *what* they offered but *they themselves* that Ricker found most troubling. Every one of them was fatally flawed. Every one a loser. Every one of them known to the police. The FBI. On lists. In databases.

Worse. Every one of them a possible undercover cop.

Which is not to say he eschewed their philosophies, entirely. He didn't. With a discerning eye he accepted parts of what they espoused. The anti-government, anarchistic, survivalist parts. *Governments cannot give you freedom—you're born with that—they can only take it from you*, their literature proclaimed. He agreed. The rules he had been brought up with had failed him; now he had to find new rules to obey, or perhaps to make up his own rules as he went along.

He had a good start. His first rule: survival.

With his first winter as a fugitive behind him, and well into the spring, his athletic physique was returning. He was exercising, jogging, acting as his own drill-instructor. Punishing himself. And his self-discipline was paying off. His energy was returning. His confidence.

He decided to make contact with his past; a risky step, but he felt ready to take it. Entering the back room of Rene Dakota's Newbury Street salon through the rear delivery entrance, he waited among shelves of hair dyes and shampoos at a table where employees ate their lunch. Finally Rene appeared. "Come back at nine," said the busy young man, startled to see his friend. Then hugging Ricker, added emotionally, "my last customer should be through by then. We've got years of catching up to do."

Clean shaven, in a bow tie, seersucker suit, and penny loafers, Ricker walked out into the sunshine of a perfect spring afternoon. He felt comfortable in Boston's fashionable Back Bay, where he easily joined the ebb and flow of the stylish set on Newbury Street. Relaxed, unhurried, he appeared indistinguishable from the other young men strolling there. Some had beepers, to be sure, some even carried tiny phones, but most, like himself, seemed unconstrained by responsibility, unencumbered by the exigencies of a workaday world.

Ricker passed the time watching fashionable women meander through upscale, toney boutiques holding the shopping bags of other, tonier establishments (their *bona fides*, separating them, the buyers, from others, the mere browsers). He mingled with them as they drifted into art galleries whose guest books hungered for their names (filet mignon to insatiable database appetites). He sat across from them at sidewalk cafes as they read untranslated novels at umbrella'd tables. Aproned young men, at their own pace, would appear with menus. Cappucino?—the list offered dozens of varieties.

Ricker ambled behind women whose strangely uplifting perfume followed in their wakes. Intoxicated by the heady aroma, he'd continue on into the competing fragrances of lush potted gardens overflowing from flower shops onto the sidewalk. A global chic sidewalk. A Boston *arrondissement*. And, in its midst, a man without a country. An émigré. Ricker.

At 9:15 P.M. Rene locked his front door and closed the slats on his venetian blinds. He found two cans of icy beer in his tiny back room refrigerator and handed one to Ricker. "We were different people then . . . and only five years ago," noted Rene, walking out into the shop—turning out some lights, leaving others on. "It seems like five decades, so much has changed."

Rene, at 33, was starting to go bald; indeed, the process was well under way. A particular tragedy for a man working with the hair of others—cutting it, shaping it, coaxing it this way and that—touching it all day long. Caressing it. Alas, for himself, the irony of . . . losing it. And so he ignored his own appearance, pulling his own thick blond side hair back into to a ponytail and securing it with a rubber band, all the while trying to disregard the few unruly strands—all that remained—on top.

"Fill me in," said Ricker, slouching into one of the plush chairs in the salon's waiting area. Draping his legs over an adjacent chair, he turned to address his friend: "What's happened to the old homestead? My lawyers said it was sold at a loss. How could that be?"

"Your parents borrowed heavily to build up the place. Did you know about those debts?"

"Of course," admitted Ricker with a shrug. "When I came back from college I made the monthly payments. But there was enough coming in. . . ."

"Well, Cantrice made very few of those payments," interjected Rene. "She fell behind fast . . . what with legal bills, and your aunt's nursing home . . . anyway, your neighbors, the Ehrlichs, came to the rescue and bought the place."

"Fine rescue," snapped Ricker. "Twenty-five acres of prime land in North Shore *horse country*, worth millions—stolen from me is what it amounts to."

"And don't think for one minute that everyone doesn't know it. The Dowlings settled that land . . . for generations."

"What's it like now?" asked Ricker.

"About the same as when you had it; no improvements, from what I can see. A family, the Dillaways, lease it from Ehrlich, run it as a stable—sort of. A far cry from the way your parents did, though. I'm boarding a lame quarter horse there. I just can't seem to break with the past and move on."

"Take me up there the next time you go," said Ricker. "I know it will kill me to see the place, but it's something I've got to do."

Chapter 38

They went up early on a Sunday with Rene behind the wheel of his ancient, rusty BMW and Rick on the passenger side—ill-at-ease, talkative: "I don't think I could have kept the place going myself. I was considering selling off some of the land."

"What about the *covenants?*" asked Rene.

"You tell me," snapped Ricker.

Rene shrugged. "What about your parents' life insurance?" he asked, glancing over at Ricker. Isolated strands of blond hair from the top of his head danced in the breeze.

"That helped. My share reduced the monthly payments somewhat, but without scheduling shows—all that social, competitive stuff—well, we lost our wealthiest clients. It was all my fault. I had no ambition. For what purpose . . . ? Cantrice?"

They drove in silence, then Rene confided: "You know after you got sent away, a few of us locals tried to give her a hard time. We'd play tricks on her. When they put your aunt in the nursing home we actually vandalized the place. In fact, I think we helped drive your ex-wife into selling. I didn't visit you in jail because I didn't want the police tying you in to our mischief. But we did everything short of burning the house down . . . we even fired off a few shots in her direction. . . ."

Rick smiled, acknowledging without words his friend's gesture of loyalty. Childhood friends can do that. Signals get sent, somehow.

Later, after a few miles in silence, Rick changed the awkward subject. "So what's up with you, Ren? You look about the same as when I left. You never married? And with your Newbury Street gig . . . well, people might think you're *gay?*"

"In a way, I'm married to my business . . . show business," Rene replied, with quick glances toward Rick as he drove. "Show business. That's all hairdressing is, you know. Glitz. Glamour. Playing to people's vanity. Flattering them. Dancing around them, flirting, talking dirty—and dropping names, of course. Important names. I get *invitations* you wouldn't believe! My customers vie for me, like I was some kind of *celebrity!* Everything from gala events, to dinner parties, to romantic one-on-one soirées. . . ."

"'*Gay?*'" Rene smiled. "Did I hear you say '*gay?*'" The young man's smile widened. "Notice how that word sits in the air. Notice how it won't go away no matter how you try to change the subject."

"Were you trying to change the subject?" asked Rick.

"No way," insisted Rene. "Homosexuality is good for the mystique. It's good for business. Mystique is everything on Newbury Street, Rick. It's money in the bank."

"I guess," said Rick, staring down at his thrift-shop cowboy boots, his day-in-the-country boots.

Rene continued: "Anyway, as I said before, my business is show business; it's always being *on*. On stage. An actor—No, a star. A prima donna, even, in front of my captive audience sitting there in curlers. Fast forward. Overdrive. For me it's exhausting, though. I go home totally drained. My horse, Shadow, saves me. Your old stable on my day off, saves me, Rick. They're my only link to sanity."

When they pulled off the main road onto the long drive

leading to what once was his property, Rick felt a wave of depression sweep over him. He could feel chemicals going to work on his stomach, soft tissue beginning to eat itself. "I don't know how much of this I can take," he confided, swallowing the saliva as it formed copiously in his mouth. "I thought I had put it all behind me . . . but you never do, I guess. When something's wrenched from you, I guess you never come to terms with the loss."

They parked in a gravelly strip beside the barn. Except for the horses in their stalls, the place appeared to be totally deserted. Abandoned. Where were the Dillaways? wondered Rick. Who feeds the horses? The only sounds were the chirping of birds in the rafters, and a dog somewhere in the distance, barking.

Shadow, Rene's twenty-five-year-old dappled grey had navicular disease, a progressive form of arthritis affecting the joints in the hoof. "We've tried everything," conceded Rene with a shrug. "She has her good days and her bad ones.

"Where's my *bay-bee?*" he announced in a tiny sing-song voice as they entered the barn. "Where's my *bay-bee?*" One head popped up halfway down the long row of box stalls. Rene unlatched her door and opened it. Unmoving, Shadow looked at him, her head low.

"I guess this is one of her bad ones," he said, slipping the horse's halter over her nose and leading her outside the barn to a row of crossties between posts that held up the low roof. "I was planning to groom her, but on second thought, let's go over to your old orchard and let her graze." The two friends chatted while the horse, unfettered, was allowed to roam in the thick grass among the apple trees.

"I live for moments like this," said Rene, his head pillowed on a long-forgotten cavaletti, a jumping hurdle left to rot beneath the trees. "My soul is here, whatever that means. I'm at peace with myself here. Take this away from me, and my life is garbage. I don't see how you could live all those years in jail, Rick. I would have chosen suicide ten times over. In fact, I'm obsessed with the subject.

"I see all deaths as suicides," he went on to explain, while Rick, lying on his side, listened intently. "I can prove my point by asking this simple question: Do you know how you're going to die?"

"I do," replied Rick, solemnly, "but I don't think everyone else does . . . do they?"

"They do," explained Rene. "They know their vulnerable organs, the diseases to which they're predisposed—in essence, what sooner or later will carry them away. Some of them will take steps to head off the inevitable: they'll jog, watch their diet, quit smoking; but others—a surprisingly large percentage, incidentally—will do nothing. They'll embrace their fate, even hurry it along . . . !"

Lying in the grass, a straw-like blade of it between his teeth, Rick listened as his friend spoke of death. He watched as his childhood chum . . . who would always be a semi-rebellious teenager in his eyes, who owned a mare that he would never put down, never send to the killer's unless or until she could no longer manage to stand up, and who would feed and board her as a pet until that day came . . . went on to speak of death as an angel of mercy.

Chapter 39

Ricker could have taken any boat in the small North Shore harbor, but his eye was on two modest daysailors, seventeen-footers with small cabins, sailable by one person—solo. Since Memorial Day he had been fishing from the breakwater, pulling in stripers and later cooking them over charcoal on a small grill. He allowed the rhythm of the peaceful Cape Ann harbor to wash over him, slow him down as only a large body of water can—flatten out his peaks with its horizon, draw off his heat, impart its own tidal motion to dampen the fast-paced Boston tempo he had arrived with.

He was nearing the end of his first year as a fugitive, a year in which he underwent many changes of guise and garb. At one point in his year-long odyssey, while posing as a fortune-teller, he had met Ben Larkin, a former cellmate of his, a man locked up because of out-of-control divorce proceedings. During their chance encounter at a carnival, Larkin took the opportunity to recommend a lawyer to Ricker, Jay Arsenault, an honest lawyer, according to Larkin. "Call him," he advised the man dressed as a Gypsy, "and when you do, tell him that Ben Larkin sent you."

A few months later Ricker placed the call. And from the call came a meeting, and from the meeting came a deal: Jay's legal services in exchange for a little detective work from Ricker. A little surveillance from an undercover man, a man no stranger to disguise, although, for the Ponti assignment, Jay told him none would be required.

Jay's words cheered him. No disguise. His efforts had not been in vain. His drill-instructor's regimen of exercise and diet, his punishing program of self-discipline had transformed his body as he had hoped it would. He had achieved his goal: athletic respectability. And the reward for his efforts?—the most satisfying reward of all. He could be himself.

One of the two sailboats was taken out on weekend mornings by a middle-aged man in an Australian tennis hat and white shorts. He'd sail only in light breezes and for only two or three hours at a time. The other boat was used more frequently. A couple in their twenties might take it out anytime; they'd wait for moderate to high winds and then practice triangular courses among the lobster pot markers outside the long rip-rap breakwater.

In the middle of June, on a hot Monday morning, Ricker, in Bermuda shorts, John Lennon sunglasses, and a Ski-Nautico tee shirt waited beside his one-man Navy surplus life raft. Activity in the harbor slowed for lunch, continued to slow into the afternoon. Sensing the late-afternoon lull, he slid his rubber raft into the calm water and paddled out toward the two small sailboats. Boarding the more distant one, that of the young couple, he noticed that once-limp flags had begun to move; the water's flat grey surface had picked up streaks of dark-blue ripples. He wasted little time rigging, stuffed his raft into the cabin, and unhooked the mooring. Easing himself comfortably beside the tiller, he slowly pulled in his mainsail. An increasingly brisk southwesterly breeze whipped into it, filled it, and, with a satisfying tug, drew him quickly out of the harbor. Within the hour the breakwater had vanished from sight. His spirits soared as an enormous, unobstructed, neon-red sun set over his stern. Later, under the cover of darkness, he changed course, put the North Star over his left shoulder, and headed for Cape Cod.

The next morning he caught sight of the upper floors of some of Boston's taller buildings and, because of a light, unreliable breeze (he had no motor, no auxiliary power), decided to make the closest landfall available, hoped it would be one of the outer harbor islands between Quincy and Hull. He had a line over the stern trolling for fish and with regularity pulled in striped bass, mackerel, and bluefish. The blues—sharp teeth, nasty dispositions—he cut up for bait; the others he kept marginally alive in a cooler by occasionally splashing in handfuls of icy salt water.

After dropping anchor amid huge boulders at Bumkin Island, just outside Hingham harbor, he launched his tiny raft and paddled the short distance to shore. The island, rising like a half-watermelon out of the water and uninhabited except by rabbits, was once the site of a hospital for casualties of the First World War. Veterans with wounds too grotesque for the delicate eyes of the public would be sent there—to Burrage Hospital, it was called—to isolation.

At the top of the island, Ricker climbed a brickpile—all that was left of the burned-out hospital, and was rewarded with an excellent view: his boat peacefully at anchor, the island shoreline most of the way around, and beyond that the entire bay. His panorama, starting at Pemberton Point on the mainland, the neighboring Coast Guard station, and Fort Revere, continued along the Hull Peninsula, the backside of Nantasket Beach as far as Sunset Point, all close in; then came the Weir River, Land's End, and, in the distance, Hingham Harbor. In the far distance, the Weymouth Back River, the site of the former Hingham Shipyard—a minor shipyard during the Second World War, making small landing craft for beach invasions. Beyond that, on the horizon, loomed the colossus-like crane straddling the Fore River Shipyard in Quincy, a major shipyard recently closed, a builder of heavy cruisers during the War and, later, LP tankers. Finally, closer in again, Peddock's Island and, completing the circuit, the Hull Gut.

Lack of wind locked him on the island. Walking the beach, he discovered a long sandbar facing Sunset Point, a Nantasket bayside outcropping with a sandbar of its own. At low tide the narrow channel between sandbars was almost walkable, easily swimmable. But Ricker chose not to distance himself from his boat; he'd remain on the island and wait for enough wind to get him out of the bay; as soon as it came up, he'd depart. Without an outboard motor the obvious route—the Hull Gut, a direct threshold to the open Atlantic—was closed to him. Even larger vessels under sail were reluctant to use that short but treacherous strait. Changing currents, whirlpools in the onrushing tides, the constant, heavy boat traffic, and of course, for Ricker, the Coast Guard Station nearby, made passage through that channel unthinkable. His plan: broil some of his fish, catch up on sleep, and wait for a stiff wind—then sail back the way he came: along the western, leeward side of Peddock's Island; later he'd turn East, head for Minot's Light and open sea.

Chapter 40

Arthur Tonzillo gave the Fourth of July to Ponti. Although his brother Dominic monopolized the party-giving —Thanksgiving, Christmas, and Easter were always his—other occasions to regale the family might, with sufficient coaxing, be made available. Ponti's estate, acres of oceanfront property on the bayside of Cape Cod just north of the Canal, provided the perfect summer venue. Arthur could hardly refuse such an irresistible invitation; and so, upon Laura's insistence and Dominic's acquiescence (after all, even suburban wooded areas were sweltering in the summer), Ponti was allowed to open his doors to their glittering clan. That was ten years ago. They've been open ever since.

His hospitality did not disappoint them: wine by the case, kegs of beer that were always cold, a charcoal grill that never was, and an endless supply of fireworks. Indeed, that first "Fourth" proved to be just the beginning, the prelude to many summers that began with Memorial Day and didn't end until Labor Day. In between . . . well, the weekends tended to linger on (he'd insist they stay overnight, of course—and then . . . a second night).

Ponti wooed and won his guests from the start. What did they ever do before him? they'd say, or what could they ever conceive of doing without him from now on? they'd think. He was the perfect host, accepting their compliments, believing their words of adoration, taking some unwritten test and passing it with flying colors. Meanwhile, as the decade wore on, Laura, his fiancee, was becoming one of the most important women in the family.

Ricker watched the holiday goings-on from the beach. He was giving sailboat rides to some of the Tonzillo children, teaching others how to sail. Upstairs at Ponti's party, the stranger had become a subject of conversation. They assumed he was a neighbor or the guest of a neighbor for the long Fourth of July weekend. But why not include him in their festivities? some suggested. Why not invite him to their cook-out?

Clean-shaven, dressed in casual sailing clothes: white ducks rolled up at the calves and dockside shoes—he looked like an older-than-most college student, a graduate student, or perhaps a young bachelor in stockbroking, or law. If he had a tale to tell, it would be a pleasant one—carefree moments, few responsibilities.

He zeroed in on Laura. She did not discourage him, but she moved to Ponti's side. It was a game all three seemed, at first, to enjoy.

Two days later Ricker reported to Jay as previously arranged: payphone to payphone.

"I'm getting to know the family well," said Ricker. "They're talkers. Braggers. In fact, you can't shut them up. They hate everybody: Jews, blacks—their golf course humor goes on and on into the night.

"They see Ponti as a senile old fool. A joke."

"Do they have plans for him?" asked Jay. "Are they hatching something tangible?

"Get their game plan."

Chapter 41

Would the summer ever end? thought Ponti. Tonzillo cars and pickup trucks filled his driveway, spilling over onto his lawn—coming and going at all hours, their radios blaring, horns sounding, doors slamming, and tires squealing. Inside, various Tonzillos seemed to be constantly underfoot, and now this stranger, Ricker, had joined their numbers, staying 'till all hours, staying long after their host had gone up to bed, alone.

The old man, often awakened by laughter from the porch below, found his thoughts drifting back to a more tranquil time—an unringing phone, an empty driveway, an early bedtime. He remembered long afternoons with his loved ones. Busy, of course, amid his wife, his daughters, but in those days it was a different sort of busy—not frantic, not the way it had become lately. And the evenings back then were so simple: fresh-picked corn on the cob for supper, a long walk on the beach to watch the sunset, a Scrabble game or two before bedtime, and then sleep—vacation sleep, deep, unbroken, restful sleep. The only sounds: crickets and the pounding surf; and later, pre-dawn birds and the steady, reassuring surf.

Now with Labor Day almost behind him, Ponti felt the satisfaction of having survived his tenth Tonzillo summer. Perhaps his most arduous, but at least the last battle (Labor Day) was ending, and he was left standing. That's some measure of victory for an old man, he concluded.

After most of his holiday guests had left, Ponti sat on his screened-in deck with Arthur Tonzillo, sipping forty-five-year-old Hooper's port, as the shadow from their bluff made its way eastward across the beach toward the sea. They rocked slowly on creaky wicker armchairs and watched the last remaining bathers gathering their things on the darkening beach below, while inside, in the next room, the women did the dishes, straightened up the house, and chatted. On the one hand, they never seemed to run out of things to say; on the other, did they ever really say anything at all? Perhaps serious subjects were hinted at with code words and cues; or could communication be the unspoken kind? The body language of cribmates? An outsider wouldn't have a clue.

Out on the deck, Ponti had a problem to share with his venerable contemporary, his peer, the most formidable member of his new family—perhaps, his ally. "I'm facing a labor dispute, a work stoppage," he confided; then, putting his small dog on the floor and his wineglass on a side table, he turned to Tonzillo as to a priest: "The union wants to close me down. At this point I'm even thinking of selling out, retiring.

"It all started with my secretary, who later became sort of a general manager. She's on the board of directors—in a low-key way, she runs the show. A few years ago she got us into commercial food distribution, which sounded good at the time but required that we hire dozens of drivers, all union. Now they're threatening to strike."

"Fire her first," said Arthur, refilling his glass from the bottle on the floor next to his chair. "Show them who's boss, that you mean business, that you won't take any more of their crap. Show them how tough you still are."

Ponti's face dropped. He looked saddened. Crestfallen. He picked up his dog, who had been sitting at his feet, staring up at him pleadingly. Once again stroking the small white creature in time to the motion of his rocking chair, the old man gathered his thoughts. "Actually, it was an excellent move. We tripled our gross sales in five years. We had been stagnating with imported foods; our market was in decline, drying up. Her idea utilized our resources to their full potential: our plant, our warehouses, our ships, our access to suppliers. But I guess I just wasn't up to it. I wanted to cut back. I was looking toward retirement. She had the energy, the ambition. She made the right choice."

"I've got an idea," said Arthur, slowly rising from his seat, wiping the corners of his mouth with the large white napkin from his lap. He turned at the railing to face his beleaguered host: "How would you like to retire on . . . say, $500,000 a year? First I'll settle your labor problems with a sweetheart deal from the union—I guarantee it. Then I'll get my son Stephen to speak to some Securities and Exchange people—to take the company public. You wind up with fifty-one percent of your stock—still in control—sign a contract for half a mil for life, and then retire or not as you please, without any worries or responsibilities."

Chapter 42

Arthur Tonzillo used all his labor relations connections, called in all the markers he had accumulated for years, for decades. It would be his last request, he promised his union friends. "Have I ever asked for anything *personal* before?" he reminded them. Indeed, representing management, his generosity with company money in settling disputes made skeptics wince. But in difficult negotiations who else could they turn to? He accomplished miracles with his nonchalance, an attitude that infuriated his hard-nosed clients but inspired trust from the unions. He never betrayed that trust. Now he was giving them an opportunity to return the favor.

They wasted little time doing just that. In their new five-year contract, Ponti's workers demanded nothing more than cost-of-living increases. An option for a second five years again held salaries at the cost of living, but, in a vaguely-worded clause, opened the door for discussions of shared health benefit contributions. All in all, a terrible deal for the union, whose rank and file, urged on by their leadership's claims of victory, approved it unanimously. Ponti, incredulous, could breathe easily once again; there would be no strike; his employees would never miss a single day of work.

Shortly afterward, Stephen Tonzillo moved his staff into Ponti's building. As chief financial officer, his office would be located next to Ponti's—between the old man's and that of the woman who acted as general manager.

Daily administrative meetings, normally held in Sally's office, informally, with department heads draped over her furniture and foremen in white uniforms standing against her walls or looking out of her windows, were soon to be convened under vastly different circumstances: the corporation's formal conference room was designated as the new location, minutes were to be taken, and only a small circle of supervisory personnel would be invited to attend. Decisions made at these meetings would then be disseminated along the chain of command for implementation by appropriate departments.

By reducing inefficiency, management hoped, costs would be cut and the company's bottom line strengthened. (So they said in the newly-instituted company bulletins handed out with weekly paychecks.)

Chapter 43

Since his return to Massachusetts from Chicago, where he had hosted a politically-incorrect men's rights talk show, Jay found his former colleagues less than enthusiastic about welcoming him back. Some labeled him a traitor who defamed his home state by calling it a no-man's-land for men, others considered him a show business opportunist, a scandal-monger who betrayed the weaknesses of his former court system for his own self-promoting purposes.

He had envisioned himself returning as a celebrity, in demand as a lawyer for men; instead, he found ruffled feathers every-where.

Trying to pick up the thread of his former law practice, he encountered difficulties at every turn. As a public defender, he was not given a sufficient number of cases to sustain him, and the ones he did get were the most difficult, the most time-consuming. And trying to get docket dates for his hearings also proved no easy task, with court clerks testy, uncooperative, refusing his requests, or ignoring him altogether. Wherever he turned he faced bureaucratic obstacles placed in his path.

"You're down but not quite out," a judge confided. "You'll

have to start from Square One. You'll have to pay your dues all over again . . . I'd give up writing, too, if I were you."

Give up writing? mused Jay with a smile: that may be the least of my problems. Indeed, his subsequent manuscripts proved unpublishable after "The Ceremony," a novel containing anecdotes from his *Justice Denied Hotline*, had failed to live up to expectations. These later works, based, as well, on *Hotline* case histories, sat on and under the desks of dozens of screening editors—triage specialists whose job it was to cull out the unworthy, the inappropriate, the questionable polemics of smart-alec amateurs like himself. Jay understood their dilemma: if his work were given the legitimization that publication provides, the result might be a blow to political correctness, the women's movement, the hard-fought battles that took so many years to win. He imagined their conclusion: nip him in the bud. Slam the door on him, and move a sofa up against it.

But starting his legal career from scratch . . . alas, there must be another way, a better way. Then opportunity beckoned:

On a formal invitation to a recruitment seminar and golf weekend at a posh Catskill resort, a senior partner in the sponsoring law firm added in his own hand: "*Attendance is limited to sixty, for twelve openings, Jay—one is yours for the asking. Call me personally to RSVP.*"

At the welcoming cocktail party, the partner, recognizing Jay, waved to him from amid a circle of men wearing beltless pants and open-collar shirts. Jay, nodding in response, walked on. At the hospitality table, rows of name tags had been arranged alphabetically. Taking his, he hesitated in putting it on. If they want me, they know who I am, a voice inside him whispered. They may want a team player, not a prima donna, countered another inner voice; this may be a test—don't flunk it.

A real voice this time, that of J. J. Entwhistle, an older man in shirtsleeves, bow tie, and vest, intruded on his thoughts: "Fuck the name tag. Everybody knows Jay Arsenault."

"I don't golf, but a job offer. . . ." shrugged Jay.

"The two may go hand in hand," said Entwhistle, a middle-of-the-letterhead trial lawyer who had been with the firm for more than twenty years. "Joining a foursome might be all it takes to convince the big boys that Jay Arsenault is ready to play ball."

Later, after dinner, over open-bar brandy in the resort's opulent lounge, the two men continued their conversation, with the veteran lawyer doing most of the talking:

"We have our world; we're comfortable in it; we're not about to change for you, Jay." Entwhistle, swirling his snifter, occasionally held it up to the dim chandelier light as he spoke. "Our tactics have proven out over time; you may not be comfortable with them, but they work."

Jay put his hardly-touched, eighteen-dollar armagnac down on the table before him. "I'm not comfortable with . . . um, the heavy-handed stuff."

"Somebody has to do it," said Entwhistle, patting down his pockets for the whereabouts of his cigarettes. "The System requires it. Somebody has to be on the top of the food chain, and unfortunately, in this world, it takes strong-arm tactics to put them there. It takes money and political influence to put them there."

The old man fumbled through his pockets with increasing fervor. "Why not have dozens of powerless little ankle-biting firms nipping away at each other, each content with a modest piece of the action, you may ask?"

Jay listened.

"Because the System demands a spokesman, that's why. Someone to represent the *Establishment* point of view." Entwhistle's cigarette search widened. "The System requires someone in charge, a strong man on top. A firm that's not afraid to dictate, to call the shots; but to get there they have to buy influence: politicians who appoint judges, judges who rule for them.

"'Money,' 'political influence,' 'to the winner goes the spoils' —for Christ's sake, Jay!—those aren't pejorative terms. 'A modest piece of the action' is; it means 'a firm without a voice—mute, dumb, inconsequential.'"

Much to Jay's relief, the old curmudgeon finally located his Marlboros in the pocket of the jacket draped over the back of his chair. "Money, political influence . . . the devil's bargain, of course, but the key to success. It's the only concept that works—has for centuries, Jay; other paradigms are written in sand."

Jay went back to his armagnac.

"I was like you when I first started with this outfit," continued Entwhistle, smiling now, amid a cloud of blue smoke. "But I changed. The firm saved my career—in a way, my life. Think about it, Jay; it may save yours."

Fat chance, thought Jay driving home in his rented Taurus, having declined to stay the night. But Ponti's retainer was disappearing fast, and Sally . . . well, somehow the thought of her tapped unlimited energy from within his mind and body; maybe joining Entwhistle's firm wasn't such a bad idea after all. Perhaps my renegade days are over. If I could find a woman like her and settle down, I'd trade my *Hotline* for a set of golf clubs and never look back. Opening the door to his Dorchester apartment, though, the first thing he saw in his darkened living room was the blinking red light of his telephone answering machine:

"*Beep. . . .*"

Then the deep, well-modulated male voice. A voice Jay had never heard before:

"*There's blood on your hands, Jay.*

"*. . . so sanctimonious, and yet, so treacherous. . . .*

"*Who do you think you're fooling? . . .*"

Chapter 44

"Cholera?" said Eve Angel. "I thought that was some medieval plague."

"And what about botulism, the Ebola virus, Dengue Fever?" said Cantrice. "They won't say for sure, claim they're still doing tissue testing, but not only was the coffin closed during the funeral, it was *sealed*—and at the wake there was *no coffin at all!*"

The two friends were seated upstairs in the restaurant section of their favorite honky-tonk. The dancing took place downstairs, on the first floor. Cantrice had waited until after their meal to bring up the subject of her late lawyer, Archibald Shaw. She didn't want to dampen her own appetite as well as Eve Angel's. Now, over coffee and a cigarette, she felt free to speak:

"He'd go into those trendy gourmet stores in Boston for tins of imported fish and other exotic delicacies. The police say that he might have gotten a contaminated one. One that slipped through customs or food inspections. Their excuse is that they can't check out everything."

"What do you mean, excuse?" asked Eve Angel. She didn't smoke, didn't drink before dancing, but sipped a decaf to keep her friend company. "Do you think they're hiding something from you?"

"Of course they are," answered Cantrice with annoyance. "Every time I tell them what mischief Rick's been up to, they give me the run-around. They even claim they have no authority to pick him up. Imagine that! An escapee, and he's allowed his freedom. I heard he once worked as a waiter in a restaurant that Archy frequented. But do you think they investigated? I doubt it."

Eve Angel stared at her friend with concern. "What I'm afraid of, Hon, is that you've been crying 'wolf' so often, if you ever really do need the police they might not come. How many times have you called them in the middle of the night? The strangers you've seen lurking around. After a while they'll become indifferent—they'll think you're paranoid."

"So . . . what do I care what a bunch of lazy cops think?" snapped Cantrice. "There's nothing wrong with anticipating problems, trying to head them off at the pass. Do you want to know how Archy died? Bleeding on the inside, his skin turning black and blue . . . on its own! Worse, but I won't say any more. I don't want to upset you. I only want to protect *us*, as a friend." Cantrice turned away with a sigh. Men at other tables seemed to enjoy observing them—two pretty women engaged in intense conversation; even those escorted managed an occasional glance or two.

"Us?" remarked Eve Angel. "You think I'm in jeopardy, too? Of course you do. Because my testimony helped you and Shaw send him away. But I see it differently, Hon. I visited him in jail. I know him. I know he's not seeking revenge."

"Sure, maybe not against you, Eve. But what about me?" Cantrice swept back a hank of shiny black hair from over her penciled eyebrow. "Did you know a dog on the same floor in Archy's apartment building died of the same thing? The autopsy showed rotting organs, guts disintegrating."

"It sounds horrible," said Eve Angel, reaching over and covering one of Cantrice's hands with one of her own, "only I don't know what to say that will put your mind at ease. I'm worried about you, Hon. Not that Rick's after you, but that you're getting so obsessed with the thought. Maybe you should go down to your mother's in Florida for a vacation. Relax. Get some sun. See things from a new perspective."

"Don't think for one minute that going to Florida or anywhere will save me," said Cantrice, pulling back her hand. "If he wants to get me it won't matter where I am. Look at Archy. Living in a condo with twenty-four-hour security—and the office building where he worked—security and video cameras everywhere. The man was insulated from the outside world. And where is his body now? In quarantine, somewhere? The police won't even say."

"See, you did it again," noted Eve Angel. "I suggested a vacation to relax, and you saw Rick in pursuit. If you could just put him out of your mind, just not fixate on him all the time. . . ."

The music had started. They heard the band warming up as they split their check, and then, descending the back staircase, they could see couples already on the dance floor. But before entering the room, Eve Angel stopped. "I have a plan," she said, blocking Cantrice's path. "Hear me out, Hon. It might just end your Rick problems once and for all."

Chapter 45

"Here's my plan," said Eve Angel, once they were seated downstairs at a secluded table. The cozy ballroom was decorated with wagon wheels and old saddlery. Its barn-board walls were hung with posters of country legends: Loretta Lynn, Willie Nelson, Crystal Gayle, Johnny Cash, George Jones, Merle Haggard. . . . Except for the dance floor and bandstand up front, a bar along one wall, and a pool table in back, the room consisted entirely of small candlelit tables and the flimsy chairs surrounding them.

The band had taken a break while instructors gave a lesson: a line dance in which, it seemed, everyone else in the room was participating. Eve Angel moved the candle away from the center of the table. What she had to say was important; she didn't want anything diverting her friend's attention. "First, let's admit we were wrong to send Rick away. I'll certainly admit that I bore false witness against him. We ask him to forgive us.

"The next thing we do—you do, actually—is get him cleared by the courts and jails and police. After all, he never really committed any crime, right? He's not *guilty* of anything, is he?"

"I don't know," said Cantrice. "Maybe he did something

wrong in prison; his escape, for instance. And now, Archie's death. . . ."

Eve Angel sighed, letting out a long breath of air. "It's up to us—to you, Hon—to get his name cleared. I don't know how much money is left over, but I'd suggest spending it on lawyers. We owe it to Rick. The least we can do is get him his day in court."

"But Eve," protested Cantrice. "Don't you see what that would be *admitting?* That we punished him for nothing. He'd have every right to take his revenge out on us."

"That's just it, Hon. He'd have the *right*, but would he exercise it? I don't think so. If you clear his name he'll respond in kind. With kindness."

"I can't take the chance," said Cantrice. "I don't want to rely on someone's 'maybe' or 'maybe not' kindness toward me. But wait. . . ."

Cantrice smiled, then added, "Let me think it over."

Chapter 46

Eve Angel had her basement fitted out for dancing: shiny hardwood floor, full-length mirrors along one wall, stereo speakers in each corner against the ceiling. A newly-installed phone extension began to ring. "Eve Angel, could you come over?" cried Cantrice. "I don't know what to do. I'm alone and scared. Someone's prowling outside."

"Why don't you call the police?" suggested Eve Angel.

"It's a waste of time," said Cantrice, aiming her remote, clicking off the TV on the other side of her bedroom. "You were right. I ruined it for myself, calling them so often. Lately, it's been taking them a half-hour or more to respond, and last time they never came at all!

"But I'd rather have you," she added. "He'd just disappear into the night if the cops came. But you could talk to him. He'd listen to you. He'd stick around if you were here."

"Wait a minute," cautioned Eve Angel. "Just tell me one thing: did you actually see Rick? Yes or no?" She was cradling the receiver against her neck with a shrugged shoulder, freeing both hands so she could finish polishing the boots she was working on. It was her custom to let all her shoes and boots decline equally lamentably; then, donning a bandanna and rubber gloves, she'd dump the whole lot onto newspapers on her dance floor and polish them en masse.

"I saw a woman," said Cantrice. "I mean I saw someone dressed as a woman who *had* to be him. I ought to know my own husband, don't you think?—no matter how he's dressed."

"What about my plan to clear his name?" Eve Angel reminded her. "If we could offer him hope. Something to allow him to *trust* us. . . ."

"Forget it," interrupted Cantrice. "I thought it over. It's a bad idea. In fact, I think you were much to soft on Stewie. You let him abandon you. Now he's sitting on a ton of oil money. Drives an Eldorado, from what I hear. If you had taken a hard line with him, you might've gotten a chunk of his salary. It may still not be too late. You two are still legally married, aren't you?"

When Eve Angel failed to answer, Cantrice continued: "Forget I said that, Eve. I won't mention Stewie. Just come over. There's something else I have to tell you."

Eve Angel arrived in a hard rain wearing an Australian duster. It was both warm and waterproof. All her coats were long; that was her *style*. She owned no jackets. If you saw a little blond woman in the supermarket in a leotard and a long coat, chances were it would be Eve Angel. Cantrice greeted her at the kitchen door with new concerns:

"I don't know how much more I can take, Eve. Rene, my hairdresser threw me out of his shop this afternoon. Do you remember him?"

Eve Angel shrugged. "Wasn't he a school chum of Rick's?"

"The worst of that bunch. He used to spend his free time hanging around the stable, toadying up to hunt club people who boarded with Rick's parents. Back in those days, he insisted that I come to his place on Newbury Street. I did, of course. They treated me like a prima donna, like one of those TV personalities you see there all the time having their hair done. And since

Rene's salon billed Rick directly . . . well, I'll have to admit, it was delightful while it lasted.

"But after Rick got sent away things cooled off; everything changed. They kept me waiting, sometimes in curlers, even though, by then, I was paying cash. And to make matters worse, Rene started asking me *questions*. Probing. Like an insect with feelers. Like ants who meet each other along a pheromone trail. They start to feel each other all over, you know, for recognition or who knows what?—but if one of those creatures has a wound or sore spot, the others will fixate on it. They will redouble their stroking of that very spot. The irritation will widen the wound, and eventually the friendly probing ritual will kill the poor ant. I learned that in the fifth grade. Funny how you never forget some things.

"Anyway, that's the way I felt about Rene. Always searching for flaws, inconsistencies in what I said, and at the same time, flattering me, cajoling, trying to draw me out. Later, during the trial, there was talk of his testifying on Rick's behalf. . . ."

Cantrice led her friend into the next room, a cozy TV room where the news, without sound, was unfolding on an oversize screen. When they were seated, she continued: "Of course, that was years ago, Eve, water under the dam. And so, today, I thought I'd drop in again. Say 'Hello.' I harbor no grudges. It's a weekday, after all. They don't require reservations on weekday mornings.

"But Rene . . . well, he comes over to me in the waiting room and says, in front of everybody—TV anchor people for all I know—that I'm not welcome there.

"I'm ready to give up, Eve, and it's not just Rene. I sense hostility from everybody in town. I expected it in Rick's old neighborhood; I never felt safe there . . . but here, in a rented condo . . . you'd think. . . ."

Chapter 47

A few weeks after the stalking incident, Cantrice finished liquidating all her assets. Real estate trusts bearing the name "Dowling" had been given over to her by court-appointed *masters*. Their signatures had the weight of the law behind them. Titles to the trusts were negotiable—negotiable to her—so she negotiated them: converted her assets to cash and pocketed the proceeds. Except for a stack of hundreds hidden in her newly-acquired Winnebago, these funds, in the form of CDs, were neatly tucked away in her safe deposit box. Her financial house was in order.

Now all that remained was putting the final pieces of her life in place. Where she'd settle down. And with whom.

Waiting in Eve Angel's kitchen for her friend to finish giving a dance lesson in the basement, she pondered her options. How many times had she left Massachusetts and headed for her mother's place in Florida, only to turn back a couple hundred miles down the road?

Why? Was it the prospect of dealing with Mitzi Davis that deterred her? Even after buying her mother a luxury condo in one of the most desirable retirement communities in Florida,

Cantrice would get no Thank You, didn't really expect one. But how about an invitation to visit?—spend some time out of love, for instance?

Finally, the music coming from the basement stopped. Cantrice rinsed her coffee cup, put it in her friend's dishwasher, and descended the back stairs. "Mom's a problem," she said, after the students left.

"Didn't she invite you down, Hon?" asked Eve Angel, wiping perspiration from her face with a towel. "Or didn't you tell her you're coming . . . regardless?" Eve Angel looked invigorated, flushed—a sharp contrast to her pale, pouting friend.

"'No' to both, for all the difference it makes to Mitzi. She thinks only about herself. You know that, Eve. She's incapable of considering others, even her own daughter. It's not malice, she's just an airhead whose mental age is somewhere around sixteen; she can't help being selfish."

Cantrice looked at herself in Eve Angel's floor-to-ceiling mirrors. She still had those Leslie Caron bangs, the stark beauty of a model—uncomplicated features that never seemed to age: small turned-up nose, tight skin, pixie-cut hairdo—a *je ne sais quoi* mystique that even she couldn't put into words. A lot of good it does me, she thought. I don't want a man . . . but what do I want?

Eve Angel intruded on her thoughts. "So, what do you think she'd do if you simply showed up? She must give some clues about seeing you?"

"She's got a new boyfriend," replied Cantrice. "For all I know she may even be *married* again."

Actually, Mitzi's current beau, an old cowboy retiree, was the most recent in an unbroken string of suitors, fiancees—husbands, even—since Cantrice's father died. If it wasn't this good-ole-boy seeking a warm bed after years of endless prairie wind and cold rain, it would be someone else just like him knocking on her door. Cantrice's mom had kept her beauty and her gentle, helpless grace well into her sixties; her dance card was always full, and her phone never stopped ringing.

Cantrice knew her presence would be an inconvenience, an unwelcome intrusion for her mother, but that told only part of the story. The part that she had trouble admitting, even to herself, was that before long she too would feel ill at ease. Indeed, sooner than "before long" and more than just "ill at ease." In truth, she could hardly abide Mitzi for more than half-hours at a time. If she hadn't left yet, she concluded, perhaps the fault may not lie entirely with her mother.

And what about Eve Angel? Her only friend. How could she leave her behind?

All friendships eventually face a challenge—some dramatic, some subtle, some barely perceptible, even to the parties; these women were at such a crossroads. "Mom's the least of my worries," said Cantrice, up, pacing, nervous about something and not knowing exactly what. "But anyway, I'm going. This time I'm really going to do it, Eve. Florida. It's warm down there now. Not like here. Yecch! How can you stand this place?"

Eve Angel, sitting on one of the folding chairs that lined a wall of her studio, stared at her friend with concern. "Are you okay, Hon?" she asked. "You look pale. Are you all right?"

Cantrice sat down next to her friend and leaned toward her intently: "As all right as you can be in this neck of the woods. Tell you what, Eve, why don't you come along with me? I've got it all planned. There's plenty of room in the RV, and I have enough cash for both of us for a long, long time. We can have some fun. We deserve it. Get your mind off Stewie's side of the bed."

Eve Angel's face dropped. "I know you didn't mean to say that, Hon," she said, holding her anger in check, "but I have no intention of leaving; never did, even for a moment. My life may not be perfect here, but it's not bad either. Anyway, leaving's out of the question. You must know that. Tell me you do."

"I don't. Not by a long shot," replied Cantrice, rising to her feet. "I think I know you, Eve, and I think if the right offer came along—not my offer, but a better one . . . I think you'd take it."

Then touching her friend on the arm in a parting gesture, she added: "But I'll miss you, Eve. More than you'll miss me, I'll miss you. And I'll miss *girls' night out*. And I might even miss Rick. Who knows? Maybe I loved him, or maybe I'll miss him stalking me. [She smiled for the first time that evening.]

"People may not think so, but I have feelings, too, Eve. Maybe that's why I'm leaving. I'm going to start over where people don't know me. I'm not loved around here, so I'm going away. I'm going away to look for love."

Chapter 48

Three weeks of sitting home during what once was *girls' night out* has this cowgirl singin' the blues, thought Eve Angel, smiling. But the truth was no laughing matter. She missed Cantrice. And so, the next day, on her way home from the supermarket, she made a slight detour: on some peculiar impulse, she drove by the absent woman's condo. The "For Rent" sign on the lawn said it all. Her closest—perhaps her only—friend was gone for good.

Maybe Cantrice was right, she thought, continuing on her way home. If the right opportunity came along, maybe I would take it. Pull up stakes myself. Leave it all behind. Laden with grocery bundles, she entered her house.

Then she saw Rick.

He was sitting on her living room sofa.

Eve Angel was frozen at the door, two bundles of groceries in her arms, keys still in her hand. Her pulse quickened as emotions overwhelmed her, conflicting emotions: surprise, shock tinged with fear—fear of fainting. Light-headedness. Why? Out of love? Thoughts flooded in.

"Don't hurt me," she said, her heart pounding. "How did you get in, Rick? What do you want with me? Please tell me."

He stood up facing her with a boyish smile. He was clean-shaven, wearing a sport jacket, no tie, dockside shoes. Although still big and muscular, something about him seemed benign, beaten down, dispirited. As he slowly approached, she sensed no hostility in his demeanor. Her dark emotions faded, but her breathing remained shallow. The fear was gone but something else was still there and, whatever it was, it was strong. Strong and getting stronger.

"Need some help with these?" he said, taking her bundles.

"What are you doing here?" she persisted, nervously following him into the kitchen. "Are you after us, me and Cantrice? She said you were. That scares me, Rick. Tell me, should I be scared? Put those damn groceries down and look at me!"

Eve Angel wished that remark had never left her lips. It sounded like a challenge, an ultimatum. She sounded like Cantrice. She knew her voice had an uncharacteristic aggressive edge—regretted it, but it was too late; the words were out. Meanwhile, his smile fading, Rick appeared to be wounded . . . sad.

"I have no intention of harming either of you," he said, putting her grocery bags on the counter. Then, turning to face her—openly, fully—he added, "I never would . . . I never could, Ange; don't you know that? Don't you know me? We talked about it when you saw me in jail. Don't you remember? You both were the 'bad guys,' not me."

"That was years ago," she replied. "Cantrice said, before she left. . . ."

"I quit. What's the use? I can't change your mind about me. I'm out of here." Rick headed for the door.

"Wait, Rick," she gasped, following him as she spoke. "Maybe you're right. We did perjure ourselves. Maybe the whole thing got away from us back then, but I don't want to make excuses now. Let's close the book on that. Okay? We all suffered, you know—not only you. But I'm willing to put it behind me." She caught the cuff of his jacket, held on to it even after he turned to face her. She felt comfortable holding on to some part of him—if not his hand, at least his sleeve. "Now, what about my question? Were you stalking her?"

"I went by her place . . . once," he admitted, staring at her and hunching his shoulders in exasperation. "I had to reset my clock from the years I lost in jail. I had to see people as they are now, in the present tense, and in their own surroundings—unaware. But I could never harm her, Ange. She's not worth the effort. I couldn't muster enough feeling for her to seek revenge."

Eve Angel became lost in thought. She had asked the right questions, cleared the air. But now what? She looked into his eyes. No. She tried to look, but couldn't. The eyes of a once-lover. The flood of emotions. She'd pass out if she looked; she knew it. Reaching for his hand, she decided to stare at it, instead. Keep her emotions in check. Emotions that could sweep her away if she'd let them.

Their youth: Shy sex, but looking back, overwhelming. Love that she had never felt since. A young girl's love. Summer love.

Their song: "Penny Lane," music that moved you, that followed you around for days. Weeks. Music that haunted your every thought.

And perfume: She used it back then, back in her *flower-child* days. What was the fragrance?—sweeter than patchouli with a robs-your-breath smokiness (a cigarette abandoned for an urgent kiss). And the candles—the only light in the room—lilac, smoky lilac. Could she smell it now? Deja-vu but somehow there, in the kitchen with them, now. Perfume. It was such a part of their ritual in those days, part of their lovemaking . . . their love.

Sensing her confusion, her neediness, perhaps, Rick encircled her small body with his arms. "My little Angel," he murmured into her fresh-scented hair. "My little Angel."

"I believe you, Rick," she said, stepping back to look at him, squeezing his large hand in both of hers now, shaking it slightly, for emphasis. "We were always honest with each other, weren't we? Even when we didn't have to be. More than that, we had love, Rick, a whole summer of it was ours, and then it was over . . . taken from us." She started crying. Slowly at first. I lost my men, she thought. But one came back. The best one came back.

Crying fully now, she brushed her tears into her straw-colored hair with his hand, as if to brush them away, but without letting go of him. "Now it's up to me to clear your name . . . just me alone in this whole wide world to help you, to bring you home." Her body was touching his. She wanted him to hold her once again, to take her in his arms and not let go this time.

"Our love . . . I want it back. I want *you* back," she whispered, her small face brushing his now. Wet against his now. "Come back to me, Rick. We had it once. Let's try for it again. Give your little Angel another chance."

Chapter 49

Returning to his Dorchester apartment before noon on an uneventful Friday, after a week in which he earned hardly enough to pay his rent, Jay noticed a small group gathered in front of his building. As he approached, he saw neighbors milling around the stairs, sitting on the stoop, leaning against cars parked at the curb. His landlady emerged from the group to greet him: "Wouldn't y'know they'd be waitin' across the street, now?" she said in a thick brogue. "I told them you'd been a stranger of late, but for sure they didn't put no faith in me words."

Two plainclothes detectives slowly eased themselves from their unmarked Crown Victoria and approached the small gathering. These people knew what was coming. They had seen it all before. Many times.

"Let's go inside," one of the officers suggested, singling out Jay. They climbed the stairs in silence. Once inside his apartment, the officer continued: "Our warrant says 'conspiracy to commit a crime,' but I've heard it's worse than that."

"What crime? Conspired with whom?" asked Jay. "How much worse?"

"I can't say," said the detective, the talkative one. The other never spoke. "But if I were you I'd plan on jail for the weekend. Maybe longer."

Jay knew he'd get no more from this man. He jotted a few telephone numbers from his address book onto a piece of paper, left his wallet in the freezer, and locked the apartment door. Downstairs in the dimly-lit first floor hallway, he handed the keys to his landlady. "We'll pray for you, Jay," she said, escorting them down the front stairs to the sidewalk.

On the other side of the street, the officers handcuffed Jay, ushered him into the back seat of their cruiser, and then, using a tone of voice and code-like dialog that civilians find difficult to understand and impossible to imitate, the driver reported to headquarters on his radio. The man moved slowly with a relaxed rhythm common to all police officers performing their routine procedures, procedures learned and repeated so often they'd become second-nature. Automatic. A choreography, almost, involving radios, notepads, and gadgets within the car. Movements that play themselves out at their own unrushable pace: Reporting in. Signing off. Checking their wristwatches. Buckling up. Then, pulling away from the curb. Entering the flow of traffic. Disappearing into the ebb and flow of traffic.

The charge, Jay learned from a deputy sheriff at the county jail, was first-degree murder. Archibald Shaw's body had been found decomposing in his Back Bay condominium.

"I insist on a lie detector," cried Jay. "I know nothing about it."

"Would you like to call your lawyer, a colleague, perhaps?" asked the deputy, a dignified man in an immaculate white shirt embellished with gleaming brass emblems. He was booking Jay upstairs, in the administrative offices, not down below in receiving, the conduit through which most convicts pass. "Your arraignment is set for Monday morning."

It was Friday afternoon; who could he call?

His surveillance case came to mind: Ponti. He'd call Sally St. Germain, Ponti's assistant and staff miracle worker.

Sally seemed eager to help, but late, on a sweltering Friday, in the summer. . . . "Well . . . keep your fingers crossed," she cautioned, hanging up on Jay with one hand while dialing one of the most prestigious Boston attorneys with the other. The man, a partner in a law firm doing considerable business with Ponti, was at the Cape on a short errand when Sally's call came through on his private cellular line. Dressed in shorts and sandals, he jotted down her particulars on the back of his shopping list, then dialed a number of his own—one of a couple of dozen programmed into his cellphone. It was to a neighbor, a Superior Court judge whose wife took the call and summoned her husband from his afternoon nap. Presently a document releasing Jay on his own recognizance was faxed from the judge's courthouse office to the penal authorities, whereupon Jay's booking procedure stopped immediately and processing-out began. Within the hour, Jay was in the lobby waiting room, seated in the middle of a row of chairs, his eye on the main entrance.

"I've never been so glad to see anybody in my life," he said, meeting Sally at the door, kissing her tenderly on the cheek. He held her at arm's length, looked into her endless blue eyes for a moment, then drew her close for a prolonged hug.

Eventually, her smile glowing, she squirmed away. "It's nice to be appreciated," she said.

Stanley, Ponti's chauffeur, with his employer's tiny Maltese in his arms, waited by the open limousine door with a handshake for Jay. "You're another sight for sore eyes," said Jay, opening his own door on the other side and climbing into the back seat with Sally.

On the drive back to Boston from the Merrimac County House of Correction, Jay confided his feelings to the woman who had rescued him: "I know I'm in the doghouse in this state because of my Chicago gig, not to mention the *Justice Denied Hotline*, and I know many politicians who want my wrists slapped . . . but to charge me with murder!—I'd say they've gone a tad overboard."

He turned away from her momentarily to stare out of the window. Something at odds with his facile explanation troubled him. He wasn't dealing with Keystone Kops, after all. He wasn't coming back from a kiddie matinee. Along with the echo of his words, he heard heavy steel doors rolling and latching. Slamming. The criminal justice system did it to him before, when he had protested the unfair treatment imposed upon one of his divorce clients. They seemed to be able to do it at will. Perhaps they'd do it again! The thought gave him a sinking feeling. Visceral. Unsettling.

"Who was the victim?" asked Sally.

"Archibald Shaw, a lawyer. I've never even met the man!"

"How did they tie you in?"

"Through Denton Ricker, the fellow I had watching Ponti's beach house. The dead man, Shaw, was Ricker's ex-wife's lawyer in his divorce. The divorce was exceptionally nasty; Ricker, my surveillance guy, even went to jail over it. Moreover, Shaw, who knew the warden, kept hounding the guy, even going so far as to have him charged with serious criminal offenses."

"So you're saying Ricker is a suspect."

"Probably," replied Jay, shrugging. "Since they can't find him, they took me instead. He had plenty of time for mischief, by the way. I didn't keep close tabs on him; in fact, although I still have him working on the Ponti case, I haven't had a report from him for weeks."

"Well . . ." Sally said, turning to face Jay as best she could, "if it's a Ponti report you want, maybe I have something of interest for you." With a gleam in her eye, she went on to explain:

"For the past few weeks Ponti and Laura have been in Italy. They had an audience with the Pope, no less. It was not on their itinerary, which, by the way, I prepared for the old man. He told me all this yesterday morning in a phone call he made from his hotel lobby while Laura was asleep.

"Anyway, His Holiness granted them a special sacrament . . .

when they return to this country, in a week or so, they'll be man and wife."

"Well, that does it, I guess," said Jay with a shrug. "So much for *palimony*. In truth, the Tonzillo investigation was going nowhere. They're an insidious bunch, but they stay within the law."

As his words trailed off, Jay once again became absorbed looking out of his window. Ricker was his problem now. A man to whom he was giving legal assistance in exchange for some harmless surveillance. An easy arrangement, especially with Ricker's fugitive warrants about to expire—but a homicide!— that was another matter entirely.

Jay tried to drive these troubling thoughts from his mind. Concentrating on the view from his window, he saw the lights of Boston. Close in. Reaching skyward. A city side by side with its airport. And, all around him, traffic in gridlock. He saw some drivers desperate to get through the tunnel, while others appeared to be enjoying the leisurely crawl. He saw tourists from different time zones grateful to be on solid ground, sight-seers without a care in the world, looking forward to a weekend along the *Freedom Trail*.

Aware of Sally's eyes on him, he turned to face her once again on the awkward back seat. "I guess all that remains now is to return the balance of your . . . er, Ponti's retainer. As it turns out, I was no help whatsoever—you'll get at least a couple thousand back."

"Forget it, Jay," she said, patting his knee. "From what I can see, you'll need it a lot more than Ponti will. But hold on to your data . . . give me a report, too. Who knows, maybe down the road the information you uncovered about the Tonzillos might prove useful. You can never tell with those characters how things will turn out . . . in the long run."

Surprised that she had touched him—his knee, no less— Jay, averting his eyes, proceeded as though nothing had happened: "I still feel sorry about not helping more. I feel that I disappointed you."

"Do I *look* disappointed?" she said, her smile beaming. "We did the best we could. We took action. We made a sincere effort to help the old man. For my part . . . well, I'm a bit player in somebody else's show, now. The Tonzillos are in charge, now. New Tonzillos appear at the plant every week—every day, even—in positions of authority. Little Tonzillos, big Tonzillos. They could be after my job before long—probably are, as we speak. I have no doubt that my role in Ponti's life is about to come to an end."

They rode in silence. "Did my hand on your knee upset you?" she asked.

"Do I *look* upset?" he replied, grinning broadly.

Chapter 50

Released on his own recognizance, Jay waited for the inevitable—the summons to appear in court. It was not long in coming. His plan: to evaluate the charges against him, then choose appropriate counsel for his defense. Arraignment had been scheduled before a judge unfamiliar to him. Arriving an hour early, he paced the corridor outside the courtroom door.

Eventually, a friendly face approached. It was that of Alfred Candy, a ready-for-retirement assistant district attorney known to insiders as "Sweets." "I won't be prosecuting your case," said the big, grey-haired man, shaking Jay's hand with a kindly smile. "They gave it to Georgene Reilly—she asked for it, actually. In truth, she *begged* for it."

Georgene was an avowed lesbian. A butch. She played the male role in her aggressively active sex life; her frantic, non-stop, non-monogamous sex life. Her reputation as a lawyer, as a professional, was constantly at war with her attempts to be naughty, shocking, defiantly outrageous.

She enjoyed acting-out her persona in Boston bars, the toughest bars, straight or gay—it made no difference to her.

Holding hands with one girl, she couldn't seem to resist catching an eye at another table. If someone unfamiliar happened to walk by, Georgene's gaze would follow—to a point—then she'd toss her head in the opposite direction, a hand through her short, slicked-back red hair. "So what? So I'm promiscuous," she'd whisper, heavily, to her current liaison, reaching between the girl's thighs, "don't tell me it doesn't excite you. That you don't love me for it."

"I simply asked that your case not be given to Georgene," said Sweets, leading Jay into one of the many lawyers' conference rooms on that floor. When they were seated, the old man continued: "I simply asked them: How could a men's rights advocate like you expect fairness from a radical feminist like her? I warned them that it would be a black eye for the Commonwealth, with her catfighting you every step of the way. I asked them to request the Massachusetts Association of District Attorneys to appoint someone else, someone impartial. I asked the Board of Bar Overseers to step in. Everyone turned me down flat on everything.

"Finally, in desperation, I got the court to grant me permission to speak to you first. I told the presiding judge I'd have you in court in time for your arraignment."

Jay said nothing. They had a deal in mind; he'd wait to hear what it was.

"The Commonwealth can't lose on this one, Jay. They want Ricker, but they also want to punish you for your shenanigans in Chicago.

"They think you know of Ricker's whereabouts. That you might have had dealings with him. That you might even be protecting him—a man who admitted to telling other inmates of his plans to harm his ex-wife. Incidentally, they also know you had nothing to do with Shaw's death, Jay, if that's any consolation."

It wasn't, but Jay still said nothing.

"Anyway, from what I hear, the D.A.'s office is prepared to sit back and wait. They'll keep the pressure on you, and wait for Ricker. According to my sources, the police are no hurry to find him. In fact, if you hand him over too soon, you'd ruin their day."

"That isn't what I heard," said Jay. "According to *my* sources, the police are up against a brick wall trying to locate him. They see him as a pro, two steps ahead of them at all times. Making a fool of them. Anyway, if they can take him at will, why do you want me to hand him over?"

The big, grey-haired man shrugged. "What a strange business we're in. Searching for the truth and never finding it, or finding it and twisting it to suit ourselves."

After a long moment of silence, Jay finally spoke: "I have a question for you, Sweets. How do you know Shaw was murdered? Was there a weapon? Signs of a struggle? Anything to link his death to foul play? or to Ricker? . . . or me? . . . or to O.J. Simpson, for that matter?"

Candy smiled. "You're a good lawyer, Jay. And you're right! But the D.A. doesn't care. He doesn't care if Shaw was murdered, or if it was some bad sushi that killed him. Shaw is irrelevant. Punishing you is what's putting a smile on everyone's face around here, nowadays. You know that.

"By the way," continued Candy, "I believe the D.A.'s people when they say they can pick up Ricker any time they want, that they're playing cat-and-mouse with him. Anyway, they're giving you the opportunity to hurry things along. Have him surrender and you're a free man. All charges will be dropped immediately."

"What charges?" asked Jay. "If I'm so damn innocent!"

"I don't have to tell you, Jay. They could come up with any number, starting with Murder One, all the way to conspiracy; even impeding an investigation; even driving with a busted taillight, for God's sake. The list is endless, and you know it. Georgene is bound to get something to stick. I see a one-year investigation with you out on bail, then a trial for a week with or without a jury, and finally, you in the slammer for six months . . . if they haven't taken Ricker in by then. And, as I said before, they're in no great hurry to do that."

Jay put his arm around the older man's shoulders as they began the short walk to the courtroom. "Thanks, Sweets," he said. "I mean it. I appreciate your effort to help me. But here's the way I see it: If I go to trial, I'll win, but my reputation will be ruined in the process. I'll be forced out of Massachusetts. But that doesn't bother me. My career in this state is over, anyway. I see myself back in Chicago. They like me there, at least. I'll do all right there."

Parting at the courtroom door, Sweets continued: "I hear you were offered a job, Jay. Jack Entwhistle's firm. The big boys, biggest in the state. I saw Jack the other day. He said they'd make you a junior partner if you signed on with them."

Jay shrugged.

"Whether you believe it or not, a lot of people around here like you, Jay; you're the only one with the balls to say what has to be said. Anyway, I for one don't want to lose you. This is a good state, it really is, and I see you as a force for making it better.

"I'd surrender Ricker if I were you. And think about Entwhistle. That offer might go a long way toward solving your problems. It would make a lot of people around here very happy."

"I didn't say No," replied Jay, entering the courtroom.

Chapter 51

Soon Ricker began spending his nights at Eve Angel's—not giving up his room in Cambridge, not moving in permanently, but yielding, nonetheless, to the irresistible all-night presence of her body next to his. And then came the predawn phone call. Cantrice. Cantrice from a payphone in Florida. Massachusetts police had approached her asking questions. Ricker's whereabouts. She thought she'd warn her friend . . . just in case.

The best two months of my life, thought Ricker, preparing to distance himself from Eve Angel. Possibly permanently. Possibly never to see her again. Touch her. Smell her perfume. Her soap. Her hair spray. Her hand cream. When she returned from work, she'd find his farewell note.

It doesn't get any better than this—words he thought constantly for two months. He appreciated every minute with her. Every second. *It doesn't get any better than this*. Now those two months would have to sustain him for the rest of his life. Now the hard times would begin. Now he'd pay for his pleasurable moments.

And so he moved back to Cambridge, leaving Eve Angel free of him. Free of *guilt by association* with him.

Three months later, from somewhere in Texas, she dialed his landlady's number:

She had sold her house, she told him, and had left Massachusetts. And, yes, she was married. She had been touring in Texas at the time, competing in the country dancing circuit, which took her out West a lot when a sponsor, a man who owned a number of honky-tonks and a few high-class restaurants as well, spotted her from across the room—picked her out from among dozens of better dancers, from women far prettier than she. She considered herself lucky, she said.

She asked for Rick's blessing. A kind word. Approval. She said she loved him—always would, in a special way—but saw her new life as a chance she couldn't afford to pass up. A chance she had to take.

Which was more painful, Ricker wondered, in the aftermath of the call: being dispossessed by the System, being jailed for four years on trumped-up charges, or losing the woman you love? No contest, came the answer, usually in the middle of a sleepless night—but during the day, as well, pushing its way to the front of his consciousness. Gridlocking him with memories. His one memory. It wouldn't go away:

Eve Angel. She was the dancer, he the rapt audience. It started out that way, at least. She and her partners, practicing for competitions—the loops, the twists and turns, the changes of balance and direction. At other times, without a partner, she'd join line dances—chorus lines on the dance floor, like flocks of starlings in flight, swooping one way then the other, executing intricate choreographies extending, sometimes, to forty or more steps before repeating themselves.

Ricker was content to watch from the sidelines, but then there came that time during a couples' dance, a slow two-step, when she extended her hand to him, pulled him out onto the floor. And following that, the times at home, in the kitchen, when she'd put on a record—Willie, Hank Jr., Emmylou—and lead him down the path she knew so well: her gift to him.

It was Ricker who discovered Western Music Night at a local roadhouse, and it soon became the focus of his week. Looking back, he saw evenings spent there as filled with smiles—his, of course, but Eve Angel's, too, along with a satisfaction he never thought possible. He saw the singers, on stage, in the spotlight, as performers of magic—the songwriters' magic (tunes that would haunt him that night, and for days and nights to come)— and for their part, the dancers, included in that union, privileged to share the experience, the joy handed down to them—to him. Even to him. Eve Angel opened that door, led him through. In his whole life, he had never felt more grateful for anything. Now, these memories fill him with longing. Strong memories: love, music—what could be stronger?

On the heels of her news, her marriage, came his depression—a chemical feeling, he had no doubt. Settling in his most vulnerable organ, his stomach. Soon the blood would make its presence known. Long walks in the cold January air seemed to help. Moving seemed to help.

Halfway across one of the pedestrian walkways on the Longfellow Bridge, by far the most beautiful bridge between Boston and Cambridge, Ricker stopped and stared down at the ice-covered Charles below him. Ninety, one hundred feet to the thin layer of ice. The river's surface was frozen where he stood, frozen all the way up to Harvard College, and, in the opposite direction, as far down as the locks at the Science Museum, where salt water from the ocean, making its way upstream, would melt it.

If he jumped, he'd last no longer than five minutes in the water, he was sure. Hypothermia would finish him off in minutes, seconds. Painlessly, perhaps. The prospect tantalized him. Standing there, chilled to the bone, trembling, the distinction between wet hypothermia vs. dry hypothermia was becoming fuzzy. And the line between the railing and what lay beyond it began to fade. He envisioned the abyss below the bridge disappearing in an instant, along with the weak ice surface; and then, very quickly, the forceful river would consume him, and what lay below the surface of the water would take his breath, his consciousness, his life. . . .

A Boston Police cruiser pulled over to the pedestrian walkway where Ricker stood. Leaning over and rolling down his passenger's window, a young black officer shouted to Ricker. "Jump, you bastard," he said. Then he rolled up his window and drove off.

In a rage, Ricker turned and began walking back to his room in Cambridge. Later, calming down, he realized that the cop might have saved his life. Later still, he sank back into his depression.

During this period—one of isolation, of solitude—Rene's rhetorical question surfaced many times in his mind; indeed, he seldom thought of anything else: Do you know how you're going to die? his friend had asked.

He knew. He had always known. In fact, he knew nothing of the future except one thing. Tomorrow? Next week? Next year? Everything in the future was a big question mark, a complete mystery to him except the only thing he had any control over. His death. The ending of his life. The one thing nobody could prevent him from doing.

Tomorrow? Next week . . . ? But then along came Jay.

As payment for services to clear up his legal difficulties, he agreed to assist Jay with investigating *Justice Denied Hotline* cases. He welcomed the opportunity: performing surveillance—providing truth where before there were only lies, producing facts to level the playing field for those victimized by deception.

He saw Jay as a romantic character, more than just a lawyer or an advocate for a cause. To him, Jay represented Sam Spade, a private eye on a men's rights crusade—Bogart, even—operating out of a shabby room in a rundown neighborhood. Only now, he, Ricker, would be the one doing the investigating, operating under cover, on a mission.

Mulling these thoughts over in his mind, he waited in his room for further word from Jay, whose *Hotline* phone, he discovered, had been disconnected. A bad omen—bad for him, he had no doubt. And what about the Archibald Shaw investigation? Checking the newspapers, he found no mention of the *murder* except on a back page in the Sunday edition of only one paper. Jay's name appeared: former talk-show host . . . flamboyant lawyer once having represented underworld figures. . . .

Underworld figures? What did that mean? wondered Ricker. Did it insinuate that the authorities saw Shaw's death as *mob* related? Unanswered questions, and "no comments" from the police, the article went on to say, shed little light on where the investigation might be going.

It finally arrived along with two other letters at his mail drop, a classified ad dating service in which subscribers, paying by the word, would describe themselves—their appearance and other attributes of fact and fancy—as well as the person sought. To insure privacy, names were forbidden; instead, a code number was assigned to each subscriber. To respond, interested parties would address their letters to the dating service in care of the code number representing that uniquely compatible person out there, that man or woman (and everything in between) who, according to the ad, suited them so perfectly. Ricker portrayed himself as a full-figured Aquarius with Scorpio rising.

Discarding the two other envelopes, he opened the letter from Jay:

> *Dear Ricker,*
>
> *It looks as if I get the last word, since no further contact between us will be possible. Although the police are saying little about Shaw's death—they're calling it a murder, now—behind the scenes, it's you they are really after. Whether you did it or not, let me assure you that NO AMOUNT OF PROOF TO THE CONTRARY will clear you—no alibis, no facts. Nothing will prevent them from prosecuting you for the death of your ex-wife's lawyer.*
>
> *All I can say, in conclusion, is that I wish you luck in a world they told us 'didn't have to be fair' and then went on to prove their point. Too bad the consequences aren't*

cutesy rhetoric. Too bad the boys and girls in charge have the keys to the State House, the courthouse—and, of course, the jailhouse.

 Remember, even if Shaw's death is attributed to forces other than yourself, and the case closed, you will still be in jeopardy. They will not rest until they have you in custody.

Jay

P.S. Eve Angel is dead. She died in childbirth. Some woman from Texas left a message to that effect on my machine. She found my phone number among Eve Angel's papers. I have no further details. Sorry.

J.

P.P.S. After reading this letter, please destroy it.

j.

Chapter 52

Jay arrived early for dinner at Sally's. He wore grey flannels and a blazer, Hush Puppies, no tie. First the amenities, he thought, stopping for the obligatory small talk with her husband, who was gardening in the flowerbeds surrounding their small suburban home. Presently, Sally's beaming face appeared at the screen door. "Would you guys like something to drink?" she asked.

Was the smile for him? wondered Jay. Deprive your husband of it, and then what? Divorce time? Give it to another man, and it's surely quits. What man could sustain the loss of a smile like that and still stay married?

They took their glasses of cold beer around to the flagstoned back patio and settled at a redwood picnic table within reach of a just-lit charcoal grill. Sally's husband had made the small back yard into a refuge: quiet, cool, shady, and private. Those approaching from the busy street wouldn't have a clue that such a delightful sanctuary was tucked away back there.

Sipping in silence, they watched chickadees and sparrows getting a last go at Sally's birdfeeder, followed by squirrels gorging themselves for the night, dropping seeds for mourning doves who, according to Sally, would feed until no sunlight remained.

"I love those doves," she said. "I know they're second cousins to pigeons—trash birds, pests, some say—but their relaxing cooing is music to my ears. Their call reminds me of the all-night *whoos* of winter owls: deep-chested, with long, silent intervals in between that keep you waiting."

Jay tried to imagine the pre-dawn North Shore woods of his youth, tried to remember what sounds broke that misty silence.

Sally, pointing to the doves with her glass, continued: "See how they move in slow, composed circles on the ground—like mother hens, calmly—no heads flicking, no eyes darting. They have a soothing effect on me; along with the cooing . . . well, it's just the thing after a hard day at the office."

"Why do you put up with the squirrels?" asked Jay, noting that one of them had draped itself around the birdfeeder—had monopolized it for the last five minutes, depleting its contents, driving away tiny sparrows and finches who might have had nests of young to feed for the night.

Sally's husband entered the conversation for the first time. A tall, gangly man with salt-and-pepper hair, he looked boyishly handsome. Indeed, he had been a drama major in college and still auditioned for parts at the town's community playhouse. His roles: urban gentlemen, charming aristocrats, cosmopolitan boulevardiers.

"I had similar concerns," he said, defensively, but with a touch of arrogance. "I once got out an old air rifle that could hardly launch a BB to the end of this patio. . . ." Turning toward Sally, he waited for her to continue the story, as she had apparently done in the past.

"He didn't really hurt the little fellas," she said, "but he didn't scare them away, either. If he happened to hit one, it would scamper around confused and upset. Then it would just stand there, on its two tiny hind feet, and look around [were her eyes filling?], as if trying to relate bird feeders to pain."

Her husband finished the story: "A failed experiment quickly abandoned. I threw away the gun, though my own guilt feelings were harder to get rid of. I'd say no one of Nature's creatures is more deserving than any other—don't forget, we're talking seeds here, not predation." Then gesturing toward the squirrel, he added: "They've forgiven me, by the way. I can be working close to the feeder, and they simply ignore me. Even the blue-jays—Cyanocitta is their genus, a great name don't you think? In Italian it means BLUE CITY. In Latin, maybe the same. Anyway, if a cat's in the neighborhood, the jays have a fit . . . but they're quiet when I'm around."

After a long silence, Jay turned to Sally: "Speaking of pre-dation, what's up at work? Is Ponti still there? Did they fire him yet?"

"After the Tonzillos got rid of me," she said, putting down her hardly-touched glass, "from what I hear, things got a bit ugly. I told most of the department heads, good friends of mine, to stay the course, not do anything foolish like force a show-down, not hurt their careers over a bunch of johnny-come-latelys; but, on some level, war had been declared. Unspoken, maybe, but from the reports I got—and I got calls every day—there was a lot of bad blood between the old guard and the new.

"As for Ernest, I don't know what to say, I feel so upset. And it's not just that they took his company; he was ready to retire, anyway. It was *how* they did it. Stripping the man of his dignity. Reducing him to. . . ." Sally shrugged. "Now he's alone. An old man, alone."

Sally's husband, rising from his place at the picnic table, checked his wristwatch. "If you'll excuse me, Jay, as Sally knows, I have an engagement elsewhere this evening, and I won't be joining you both for dinner. It was a pleasure meeting you, though. I wish you luck in your men's rights endeavors."

After he left, Sally continued with her story: "To explain how they ousted the old man, I have to go back to the period right after the labor strike was settled. Back then, when the Tonzillos arranged for Ponti, the *company*, to go public, they issued Ponti the *man*, and his wife, Laura, fifty-one percent of the stock: twenty-five-point-five percent each, that is. That's the way Stephen Tonzillo, Laura's cousin, had arranged it. His father, Arthur, the brains behind the scheme, is now CEO. At the first stockholder's meeting the Tonzillos took over. Ponti's people couldn't muster even thirty percent of the voting stock. Laura voted with her family; that finished off their marriage . . . and her husband was forced to clean out his desk.

"Laura had been staying at their Beacon Hill townhouse, but with the summer approaching she really wanted to be at the Cape, at Whale Rock . . . but I'm getting ahead of myself . . . where was I?"

"You had him cleaning out his desk," offered Jay.

"I mean *literally*," she explained, shaking her head. "Just picture the old man going, for the last time, to the company he built: the business, the building, the people . . . the memories. Entering his marble lobby, going up his brass elevator . . . the elevator he loved. . . ." Tears formed in her large blue eyes— unstoppable, this time. She rushed into the house, leaving Jay alone at the table.

Suddenly grackles. Black, shiny, iridescent purple-green, yellow-eyed: a dozen ganged-up on the birdfeeder and the grassless earth below it, while an equal number, albeit duller, grey-eyed, brownish blackbirds, occupied the fringes of the lawn. An omen, Jay thought with dismay. Bad luck. Death.

But his anxiety at their abrupt appearance and aggressive behavior soon vanished as the yellow-eyed, iridescent birds began to seek out and feed the duller ones. No matter where a small, dull bird would go, a shiny one would always find it. Find it and feed it.

Sally finally returned, damp and red around the eyes, cheeks, and nose. "I'm sorry," she said [She had missed the grackle invasion; they disappeared as quickly as they arrived.]. "Ponti knew my father. I've worked with him for so many years. How could they do that to a harmless old man? . . . and it was all so fucking legal!

"Anyway, while he's cleaning out his desk, he's served with restraining orders by a deputy from Cape Cod, who had been tipped off that he would be there. So the Tonzillos not only took away his business, they kicked him out of his house, his family house in Whale Rock, where he lived for over a quarter of a century, where he brought up his kids. . . .

"His daughters' height markings were on the wall in the kitchen. He showed me. He couldn't stop bragging about his girls. On their birthdays he'd go through the ritual of recording their year's growth with marks on the wall, along with their names and ages—Katie 4 . . . Peggy Ann. . . ." Sally's face, normally cream-colored like translucent porcelain, had become raw and swollen; her eyelids pink, puffy as a prizefighter's, her nose stuffed.

"I was afraid something like that would happen, you know," she added, hoarsely. "That's why I hired you in the first place. I tried to head it off. . . ." Once again she began to falter.

Jay feared more tears. Torn between guilt for failing her—and what?—tenderness, affection—he longed to hold her, to comfort her. Impossible, of course, under the circumstances . . . or was it? She had once touched his knee; did *that* mean anything? Running a hand through his short, dark hair, he opted for restraint, prudence. "And I was no help whatsoever. I took your ten thousand and did nothing. You should have gone to a good lawyer. I should have sent you to one."

"No. No. You tried, Jay," she said, sniffling less, reaching for his hand. "What more could you do? What could *anyone* have done? Anyway, to finish the story. . . ."

"Ernest went back to his empty townhouse for the summer." Crossing her legs, she released his hand to smooth her skirt, then sat primly at the table, hands folded on her lap. "The old man hired a divorce lawyer whose only promise was an amicable settlement. And that's what happened. The assets were divided up: Laura got the Whale Rock house and her twenty-five-point-five percent of the company—it's called the Agagroup, now—and the divorce became final."

"Ponti's stock must be worth a few million?" suggested Jay.

"I wouldn't doubt it," said Sally with a shrug, wondering if the old man would ever see a cent of it. "I'll throw on the steaks, but thanks to the mosquitos, we'll be eating inside."

Chapter 53

After dinner, they lingered at the small dining room table over mugs of sweetened Irish coffee. "I'll load the dishwasher tomorrow," said Sally. "Right now I want to hear about you. Where do you stand in that crazy Archibald Shaw business?"

"I'm still out on my own recognizance," replied Jay. "My arraignment was postponed. The assistant D.A., an overt lesbian named Georgene Reilly, insists I'm under indictment for murder, but I've never actually been charged, never had to enter a plea. Of course, they know I didn't do it, but they don't like me because of my *Hotline* and things I said and wrote from the Midwest that defamed Massachusetts. Now they think they've got me where they want me. Now they're trying to make my life miserable—succeeding, too."

"Being with you is like living in a Wagnerian Opera," said Sally, sitting back in her chair and peering over her half-finished glass mug. "First we hear the *leitmotif*, the musical signature, the theme associated with each character, then they appear and we learn their fate. Their unfortunate fate."

She thought for a moment. "Not their death, usually—just

their transmogrification. I've always wanted to use that word in a conversation [she grinned]; this is the first time I've actually done it! Anyway, they're transmogrified into animals; or, some other supernatural thing happens to them."

"Why not their death?" asked Jay.

"Because they're needed for arias in upcoming scenes. Their voices are too valuable to kill off prematurely. They'll die at the end, though."

Jay nodded, smiling. "In my world, the good characters disappear without a trace; the bastards live on forever, or at least it seems like they're always around. In my world, the news is not announced with *leitmotifs*, it comes by way of Certified Mail. I'm required to sign a return receipt proving I received it. When the mailman approaches with a pen, my heart sinks." Jay continued to smile as he spoke. Food. Liquor. Clever conversation. A beautiful woman sitting across from him. And yes, her husband gone for the evening.

"So . . . go on with your story," she urged, also pleased. Easy conversation. Pleasant company. No troubling urgency surrounding—should she even think it?—sex . . . yet. "So, how are they making your life miserable?"

"They continually harass me with trivial, time-consuming procedural court hearings, often at the last minute. It's a *capias* if I don't show up. Arrest. Contempt of court. They say they won't stop until I turn Ricker over to them."

"Why doesn't he—assuming he didn't do it—come forward on his own?" asked Sally. "Clear the air for you?"

"He's afraid they'll jail him, which, of course, they will. In fact, I warned him to stay away. I know I'm letting myself in for conspiracy charges by doing so, but what the hell . . . I see a higher morality here . . . I won't turn him in."

Sally and Jay sat in silence over their empty glasses. Finally, Jay spoke: "Do I detect something not quite right between you and your husband? . . . or am I *way* out of line for mentioning it?"

"You're not *way* out of line," she said, standing, taking her dishes into the kitchen. "Not *way* out of line at all."

"Are you two, um . . . trying to stay together?" He followed her with his own dirty dishes. "Splitting up? What?"

"My Wagnerian Opera poses those very questions," she replied. "Trumpets blare, awaiting my answers.

"But I have few answers to give." Sally's tone had changed to one of summation, as if to wind down their conversation, their evening. "I'm at a crossroads in my marriage—more importantly, in my life—that much I know. I'm facing a personal challenge that I must meet head on. My rite of passage, you could say, before I'd be ready for . . . um, the next step."

"The next step?" asked Jay, hopefully.

She took his hand.

Saying goodby at the door, kissing her tenderly on the lips, Jay smiled. "You're right, of course, not to rush into anything. I know teasing-to-put-a-guy-off-and-lead-him-on-at-the-same-time when I hear it, and I didn't hear it tonight. You know what I heard?

"I heard birds singing. Music. Young grackles calling for food and adults finding and feeding them. I heard a happy ending."

Chapter 54

Ricker's first reaction to Jay's letter was shock. Eve Angel dead. No details—not that any would have helped. Another chapter over. Really over.

And his prospects? Was he never to have his name cleared? Was a fugitive's life all he'd ever have to look forward to? Alas, he'd need time to think over his new situation. He decided to get out of town. Out of Cambridge. Away from people.

Returning to Whale Rock, he first checked the Help Wanted ads in the local paper and noticed some openings for caretakers; no pay, but offers from landlords bartering winter lodging in exchange for custodial services: snow shoveling, preventing freeze-ups and leaks, and performing general maintenance; in effect, tiding their summer residences over for them until spring.

Ricker was hired in that capacity (using Laura as a reference, Ponti's corporate headquarters as her address) to look after a vacant estate not far from the old man's beachfront property. His duties, in payment for the use of the estate's guest house, would be routine: ward off burglars and vandals, keep the main building functioning, and call plumbers and other service people if problems arose. The owners, favorably impressed, also provided a small stipend and the use of their Jeep.

Strolling the neighborhood that winter, Ricker found Ponti's boarded up house accessible to him, virtually at will. Then, at a local bar, he met a security watchman whose employer, he learned, was desperate for help. The understaffed company wasted no time hiring Ricker, even assigned him Ponti's house to patrol. ("It belongs to the 'Ex,' now," they confided, with a wink.) He'd search it at his leisure, he decided (old habits die hard), maybe turn up something to help the old man.

But then, before he had an opportunity to take any action, a major storm appeared on satellite radar: a hurricane with Boston's South Shore as its predicted landfall.

The storm, fueled by an intense low pressure area stalled near Bermuda, organized with alarming speed and ferocity. Its first effects, a tidal surge, took the form of waves crashing onto east-facing beaches. Coming in unobstructed from three-, four-hundred miles out at sea, with hundred-fifty-knot, Category-5, hurricane-force winds behind them, they began battering the shore. Electric power went out in the first few hours, but over transistor radios, the tinny, urgent voices of special-event news-casters could be heard in shops in downtown Whale Rock. Their message to residents: "Evacuate. This storm is headed directly for you."

Sound advice. All along the coast, sea walls began disappearing, swept away like sand castles. Eroding bluffs collapsed into the cauldron, some houses on them merely threatened, others gobbled up by the sea. Even at low tide the assault continued, the surf breaking onto lawns and rolling into the back yards of beachfront cottages. At high tide, flooding proceeded inland for a quarter of a mile—in places, more.

Ricker had long since boarded up all the windows on his estate—that was part of his custodial duties in payment for his lodging—but having sealed himself in his small guest house, with no view of the outside, he soon became claustrophobic. With the eye of the storm still a distance away, he decided to abandon the confines of his post in favor of a somewhat loftier venue.

Laura's enormous house, as he approached it, looked like a castle rising from the sea. He pulled his Jeep into the flooded driveway. At least she has fireplaces, he thought. At least I'll be able to get some heat.

Before long, sitting in front of a roaring fire, a glass of expensive sherry in his hand, he experienced an unaccustomed feeling: satisfaction. The sinister satisfaction of usurping Laura's cozy hearth, to be sure, but also some transcendent satisfaction with the appropriateness of Nature's fury; her violence, her disregard and total lack of respect for anything mere mortals had put in her path.

Indeed, outside, the winds continued to increase, some reports predicting landfall for the eye of the storm within twelve hours, others saying it wouldn't arrive for another day or two. By morning, sets of waves were breaking continuously against the concrete pilings below Laura's back deck. I think I'll take down some plywood, he thought. Get a good look at the show.

No sooner had he unlatched a four-by-eight sheet from the largest picture window in the house than the wind took it, blew it across the street, blew it two or three streets away after that. Inside, reflections in the window moved—the fireplace, the candles—their images distorting. The broad expanse of glass was bowing in and out with each relentless gust of wind.

Ricker was in the bathroom when he heard the explosion. Felt it. Seventy, eighty-five knots of wind and rain pouring in through the wide opening where the window had once been. Funneling through. The pressure inside the house soared. And then the windows on the other side of the house broke out, and he was in a wind tunnel, the roar deafening. The fireplace embers, first burning the rug, the sofa, were finally extinguished by the rain. Everything in the house was drenched, flying around: furniture, pictures, linen, appliances. . . . Ricker decided to get out fast, before the roof blew off. May Laura get what she deserves, he thought, fighting his way, an inch at a time, across

the porch to the flooded driveway. Everything she deserves . . .
and then some.

His Jeep, which he had left with water up to the hubcaps, now
stood with floorboards submerged. He waded out, climbed in,
and turned the key hopefully.

Miraculously, it started, but before he could back out into the
street, a police car pulled up blocking his path. Digging out his
wallet, he approached the cruiser. "What's up?" he ventured.

"Restricted area," the lone officer replied. "Are you the
owner?"

"Security guard," said Ricker, passing a laminated card
through the half-open window. The officer had seen cards iden-
tical to this before; members of his own family had them. The
local company issuing them was so familiar to him that he little
more than glanced at the name typed beside the picture, the
alias under which Ricker had taken the job.

"I'd cut off your patrol early if I were you," said the officer,
handing back the card. "This house may be a lost cause, and
heroic measures by locals are seldom appreciated. There's a
communications center in the high school gym . . . the Red
Cross even has coffee and donuts there. . . ."

Ricker waited him out; then, after the cruiser finally disappeared into a side street of battered cottages and bent-over trees,
he got back into his still-idling Jeep and drove off as well.

Heading inland, he knew somehow that he'd never see the
ocean again. Never, in the heat of the summer, would he ever
again join the hordes of beachgoers gravitating to ocean shore-
lines as if drawn by some inexplicable urge to return back to the
primordial soup from which all life originated. Instead, he saw
himself, on some future summer's day, sweltering in unbearable
heat in some godforsaken jail, feeling, in every cell of his body,
the tug of the ocean, yearning to immerse himself in its life-
sustaining waters, but knowing he would never again be free to
do so.

He saw himself drying up. Desiccating like a cadaver. He saw
himself turning to dust.

It was still raining when Ricker arrived back in Cambridge. His room—the rent two months in arrears—awaited him. His landlady liked him; she planned to wait three months before moving his few possessions to the basement. He peeled off four damp hundreds for her, went up to bed, and slept, more or less for two days straight, then spent another two days considering his options.

He brought the crystal ball down from atop his wardrobe and placed it on his kitchen table. Staring at the inert sphere, he thought he heard his phone ringing.

As he listened, the ringing grew louder. He approached the wall phone and picked up the receiver. Apparently, it had not been disconnected, although he hadn't paid a phone bill for as long as he could remember.

"Ricker," said Jay, on the other end of the line. "I need you. I have an assignment for you."

Chapter 55

A few busy months after her cookout, Sally called Jay suggesting they get together once again. She'd fill him in on how far her rite of passage had taken her. She apologized for not calling sooner, for not keeping in touch, but events left her with little time for herself. She told Jay that she and her husband had separated; later, expeditiously divorced. Perhaps her being unemployed played a part . . . at home with him so much during the day, in his daytime territory . . . or could her loss of income be a factor? . . .

"Any thoughts about the *next step*?" Jay replied, trying to hide his joy at hearing from her. Trying to keep his relief that she hadn't rejected him from revealing itself in his voice. He missed her. Indeed, during their time apart he found himself thinking about her more and more with every passing day. He held off calling her, though. It took all his will power not to reveal himself as needy. Insecure. Weak. It took all his self-control not to pick up the phone and dial her number.

"One thought," she responded, candidly: "You."

"Me?" repeated Jay, smiling into the phone. "You mean my *attraction* to you did not go unnoticed at your backyard cookout?"

She blushed privately, enjoying the feeling as it swept over her. They arranged to meet at her new apartment—a drink first, then the short walk to the North End for an Italian dinner.

Riding up the elevator in her harborview hi-rise building, Jay felt like a schoolboy—excited, nervous, unsure. . . . Unsure sexually. He'd had little sexual contact for almost three years and had no idea whatsoever as to how he would perform. How, if called upon, his penis would perform, that is.

He hugged her warmly at the door. "I hope I don't let my *attraction* get the better of me," he said, not attempting to separate.

"I think I can handle it," she said, squirming away. Then she proceeded, somewhat apprehensively, to show him around her three airy rooms on the twentieth floor. Should she include the bedroom in her tour, she wondered? Where should she invite him to sit? the sofa? the dinette? Should she offer him a drink? And what about their conversation? The word *attraction* still hung in the air between them refusing to go away; wasn't that a kind of verbal foreplay? She hadn't a clue. I've been away from these courtship rituals for too long, she concluded with a secret smile.

Handing Jay a Heineken, she brought her Chablis to the other end of the sofa and sat down primly, her cotton skirt tucked neatly under folded legs. "My divorce was short and sweet," she said. "The house was all he wanted, so I gave it to him. He loved working in the garden. I had the feeling that marriage to him was tending a garden, not a wife. Anyway, I got to keep *all* my money . . . but I'll really miss the birds, the feeder. Up here in the clouds . . . well, there *is* an occasional seagull. . . ."

Jay put down his beer and stared at her. The step from friend to lover would be a long one, he thought. "Should we go out to dinner, get drunk, talk dirty?"

Placing her empty wineglass on the marble coffee table before her, Sally came over to him, and, without ever losing eye contact, melted into his lap. Neither spoke.

The wet stain on the front of Jay's trousers widened. "I'm a failure," he said, knowing all along he would be.

"We'll see about that," she responded with a shy smile. "Want to take a nap with a naked lady?"

Chapter 56

T he next day, Sally found a message on her voice mail
from Jay suggesting another attempt to have dinner
in the North End. He recommended the Trattoria
Sporta, his favorite bar, which was also an excellent Italian
restaurant.

She called him at his office to accept the invitation. "Perhaps
we should meet there," she advised. "If you come up to my
apartment, we might never make it to dinner."

She arrived first and when he walked in, he found her surrounded by regulars and bartenders alike. "I simply told them
that I was waiting for Jay Arsenault, and suddenly I'm a
celebrity!" She accepted his kiss on the lips—quick but tender,
eyes lingering after.

"Poor Jay hasn't had a date in years," said the owner's wife,
with a kindly smile. "I guess he was saving himself for you, *cara
mia* . . . and now I understand why."

Jay introduced Sally all around. "We'll see you folks later," he
said, ushering her toward the maître d' station.

The owner's wife, accompanying them, picked up a couple of
menus along the way. "I have just the table for you," she said,

beckoning to a waitress. She led them to a private corner of a room decorated with urns, ceramic grapes on wall trellises, and ornate chianti bottles lined up on tile shelves.

Resting his briefcase against the leg of his chair, Jay smiled.

"Why the grin?" asked Sally.

He slid the briefcase her way with the toe of his shoe. Peeking in tentatively, she saw a toothbrush, pajamas, and a change of underwear.

Back at her apartment they didn't speak, allowing the harmony of their bodies to determine their movements: The sofa. The kisses. The mysterious urgency taking over, the shedding of clothes. And the smells—he relished them—first her perfume, behind her ears and the back of her neck. Then the moist personal aroma of her from the crevasses under her arms and breasts, and downward toward the most exquisite feast of all, open and beckoning to him.

Red-lipsticked kisses—now he had them—the overwhelming, all-night joy of them. May I never forget this feeling, he thought. Twenty years from now, may I be able to look back and remember this moment. If only a twinge—I'd be grateful for that—just enough to remind me of how lucky I was.

By the weekend, Sally broke the spell with some news: my "Wagnerian Opera," she announced at her dining room table, "Valhalla is in flames." They were sharing the salad he'd made in her tiny kitchen: goat's cheese, paper-thin ham, three kinds of lettuce, balsamic vinegar, triple-virgin olive oil. The bread, fresh-baked, was still warm. Later, she'd make an omelet—secret soft cheese, secret herbs. Romance, he thought: the newness, the mystery—for an all-too-brief moment, the irresistible secrets.

She continued: "The bastards tricked Ponti. They began by liquidating corporation assets. Evidently, you can end-run around the Securities and Exchange people by selling the assets of a company rather than the company itself. By the time the accountants get the figures, you're rich and the company's down the drain. Ponti's twenty-five-point-five percent of the stock isn't worth a plug nickel. He's left with nothing for his old age. . . . He's broke."

"Happens every day," added Jay, sipping the trendy, expensive white wine he had picked up on his way to her apartment. "Ponti's stock deal was probably written to survive as a document separate from his divorce, an independent financial transaction to stand on its own. That way, whatever disaster befalls him, he can't go back to divorce court claiming foul play."

"Well, Mr. Justice Denied," she said with a shrug, "now you can put *his* sad story into your next book, along with the stories of your other *Hotline* victims."

"My writing days may be numbered," confided Jay, swirling his wine, holding it up to the large picture window. "A law firm I worked for years ago has been hounding me to come back. A partner retired recently, and it's trying to improve its image, which had been tainted by accepting clients with ties to Organized Crime. I'm thinking about returning."

"What about its image of having lawyers on its staff who are under indictment for unsolved murders?" interrupted Sally, with a broad grin.

"My darling," responded Jay, relishing his words as he spoke them, "Georgene Reilly will be married and see half a dozen kids through First Communion before she ever brings those charges against me."

Chapter 57

Entwhistle's invitation took Jay by surprise. "I'm not really one of your circle," he said, replying to the RSVP phone number on the bottom of the embossed card. It was a business number. Entwhistle's law firm. "Your golf partners might feel a tad uncomfortable with me around."

"Not so," replied Entwhistle, taking the call without making Jay wait. (A protocol reserved for only a handful: corporation presidents, CEOs, top-echelon superiors, mistresses.) "Rumor has it that Hallsmith & Ingoldsby want you back. They're small potatoes compared to us, Jay. And at least we don't flaunt our underworld clients.

"Anyway, we're not giving up on recruiting you, and this dinner party is the perfect opportunity for you to meet our top brass."

Jay said nothing.

"So they—the top brass, that is—insisted I invite you to this little get-together. It's for insiders only. Partners and their wives, for the most part . . . and you and me."

"What did I do to deserve this?" asked Jay.

"They see you as a celebrity. Don't ask me why, but they do."

"What makes you think I can hold their interest?" asked Jay. "My *Hotline* is defunct. I'm depressing to be around, lately."

"That's not what I heard," claimed Entwhistle. "Anyway, I thought we could treat the old codgers to something different for this party. I was thinking of something *really* different . . . like a seance."

Jay, frowning, said nothing.

"Perhaps you could help in that department," continued Entwhistle. "Do you know any fortune tellers? Gypsies? A client, perhaps? Someone who could serve as the medium, the mistress of ceremonies? Nothing legitimate is expected in the prognostication department, by the way; she doesn't have to bring anyone back from the dead. We'd just like to have some-body colorful to provide a little entertainment."

Still nothing from Jay.

"Think about it, Jay. Some important people will be there. People who could solve all your problems will be there."

"You're invited," Jay told Sally that evening over dinner. They were at their regular table at Trattoria Sporta. "I told Entwhistle about you. He knew Ponti personally. Knew Arthur Tonzillo very well, he claimed. Thought the man was a bastard. Anyway, he insists that you come. He says he can't wait to meet you."

"I thought you hardly knew the man," she replied. "I thought you turned down his job offer in favor of one from your old law firm."

"Not quite," admitted Jay. "Entwhistle's a friend of the judge hearing my case, so I haven't turned him down . . . yet. In any event, this party can only help me. My legal problems. My career. My future. Our future!"

"Oh well," said Sally, as their entrées arrived at the table. "I do have a new cocktail dress that I've been dying to wear. . . ."

He, in a rented tux, and she, ravishing in her peach, off-the-shoulder evening gown, arrived beneath Entwhistle's porte cochere with Stanley at the wheel of their rented Town Car. It was the smallest limousine in the mansion's circular drive.

"We're keeping it intimate," said Entwhistle, after the door-
man announced Jay and Sally to the small group gathered
around the fireplace in an enormous sitting room. "Anyway,
you're the last to arrive. Dinner will be served presently."

After dinner, the guests, ten in number, returned to the sitting
room, now darkened and inhospitable, with table lamps unlit and
the fireplace cold. Finding that the temperature had dropped to
an uncomfortable level, Entwhistle had his staff rekindle the fire.

Once the initial conflagration had moderated, the hearth
became a cozy backdrop for the unsettling business at hand.
Well, not quite cozy. The shadows cast from the flames danced
unpredictably, flickering over the faces of the guests after they
took seats around the medium, an old Gypsy woman, already
seated. Hunched over a cloudy crystal sphere, she was a cheer-
less presence in layers of drab skirts and sweaters, a woolen
kerchief covering her grey wig, dangling earrings and somber
makeup accentuating her disfigured face. The only light in the
room came from the fire and, later, from the sphere as it began
to glow when the participants joined hands around the table.

The unmistakable sound of skaters filled the room. The occasional hollow wooden crack of a hockey stick making contact
with the rock-hard ice surface, a few echoing shouts, but most of
all, skates. Blades. The edges of blades—scraping, scratching,
scoring the ice.

The sphere glowed brightly as the scene within it came into
sharp focus. A skating rink—a large pond, actually—at night. A
municipal skating pond, floodlit. It was closing time, and most
of the skaters had moved to shoreline benches to change from
skates to street shoes. Except for a man and a little girl, the pond
was deserted. Finally, as the last of the skaters disappeared into
the night leaving the benches empty, a custodian arrived to turn
out the floodlights that encircled the pond. "Leave one on,
Harry, if you don't mind," asked Jay. "Ermalyn and I would like
to stay out on the ice a little longer. I'll shut it off when we're
through."

"No problem, Jay," said the custodian. "You know where the switch is. Stay as long as you please." He left a single light on. It was near the bench area. The rest of the pond was in total darkness.

Jay was skating backward circles around his young daughter while watching her from over his shoulder. As a defenseman in his hockey days, he was most comfortable skating backward; now, he took to it automatically, pushing off in lazy arcs, his blades crossing over effortlessly, his body swaying with the fluid motion that propelled him.

Coming from French-Canadian roots, Jay was expected to play hockey in the North Shore town where he grew up; indeed, he continued his winter sport into college on a hockey scholar-ship. His position: defense, the task of shutting down the oppos-ing team's high-flying forwards. Skating backward, he'd meet them face-to-face and, if he couldn't take their puck, he'd at least try to slow down their momentum, throw them off stride, break up their assault.

His backward circles took him farther and farther from the child. "I'm afraid, Daddy," she said, when he'd come close enough to be heard. "When you disappear into the darkness, I get scared."

"Just listen for my skates," Jay told his little girl. "You're the center of my circle, and circles always come back to where they start."

The sound of Jay's skates became fainter and fainter as he spent more and more time outside of his daughter's tiny patch of light. Slowly, the crystal sphere on Entwhistle's table darkened.

Sally, distraught, refused to release Jay's hand, as the barely-detectable sound of his skates lingered, then faded abruptly from the room.

Seated beside Ricker in the back seat of the cruiser, Eve Angel, an ethereal presence in a white, long-skirted cowgirl outfit, tried to comfort him. Taking his dark, Gypsy hand in both of her pale, white ones, she shook it for emphasis as she spoke: "I'll free you when all other measures fail," she said.

"How did you get here?" he asked out loud, disregarding the troopers in the front seat, who seemed indifferent to him and, in any event, oblivious to his visitor or the possibility that he had one.

Without answering, she leaned toward him and kissed his lips. Later she spoke: "When all else fails, I'll be there, Rick. I won't disappoint you."

Chapter 58

Facing charges of murder to justify the anticipated high bail, Ricker waited for Jay in the courthouse holding cell. While in police custody, he felt no depression; in fact, the ride from Entwhistle's after the séance, with Eve Angel by his side, left him elated. Could he conjure her at will . . . his ally, his lover? The thought comforted him. He needed comfort. He was in handcuffs. He was in court.

Court was where the knot in his stomach never failed to tighten while his fate hung in the balance. Not his guilt or innocence—they never really seemed to care about that—just his destiny: how they would dispose of him. First the lawyers' games—the dances they do—the jargon and posturing so he'd *think* justice was being served. Later, during a recess or some other time when no outsiders would be present, they'd slip into the back room and make their deal. Later still, he'd learn his fate: how long he was to be put away.

Before Ricker had ever been to court, back in his early days, he had faith in the System, supported it—more than that—championed it! He was a landowner, was he not? Didn't he run a boarding stable at a profit? Lead a law-abiding life? . . . for the most part.

Sure, he had a tattoo, a motorcycle. Yes, he'd leave his young wife alone while he went on weekend rides with rowdy friends. Was that illegal? Was it grounds for divorce? Sufficient reason to dispossess him of property that had been in his family for more than a hundred years? Apparently. His wife had planned cunning strategy behind his back. She sat down with lawyers. They were in no hurry. They bided their time. They left nothing to chance.

When they pronounced themselves ready, they struck. They hauled him into court and took their assigned places on stage. That was almost six years ago; he remembered it as if it happened yesterday. . . .

His wife, Cantrice: thin, delicate, abused. In a cervical collar. Vulnerable. On the verge of tears. A small white handkerchief clutched in her trembling hands.

The documents: exhibits placed in evidence against him—a foot high, thousands of pages: Xeroxed receipts from porno video rentals, phone company records listing calls to sex lines, sales slips and canceled checks for leather, handcuffs, guns. . . . Pictures: nudity, debauchery. . . . Affidavits from private investigators. No gentleman here, no worthy landowner. Looks of disgust rained down on him.

The judge: admonishing him to be humble, contrite, to keep his courtroom outbursts in check.

Why? he thought. Why not sound the alarm when they lie? His lawyer—mute, restrained—was letting everything get by unchallenged. All their bullshit. Lies. Perjury! Planted evidence. What kind of a game was this?

Then through innuendo and sly sophistry they made their charges stick. Convinced a jury: *Violation of a Restraining Order, Assault With a Deadly Weapon (a beer can), Threatening, Intimidation, Domestic Abuse, Contempt of Court.* . . .

Five years.

And that only opened the door. When they want you in, you

stay in regardless of your sentence. They'll find a way to keep you behind bars, to protect society from you, in perpetuity if need be. Without relatives clamoring on your behalf, you'll go under without a ripple. You'll disappear without a trace.

Would this time be any different, he wondered? Maybe. Jay seemed to have connections. Jay knew him personally. Jay, if he were any kind of a human being, would feel responsible for him. For his well-being. If Fate or God intended him to be saved, Jay would be the instrument by which his salvation would be accomplished.

"We're sorry, Ricker," shouted a guard in the general direction of the large holding cell they call the tank. "Mr. Arsenault cannot be reached. But don't worry, the court will provide counsel to represent you at your arraignment."

After his appearance before a judge (from the prisoner's dock in the courtroom, from where he could say nothing and hear little), Ricker was returned to the holding cell downstairs. A few hours later (hours?—precious time for those on the outside, but a meaningless waiting period to inmates enduring years of confinement), he was taken out, shackled hand and foot, and loaded into a transporting van. Presently, overhead garage doors opened, and the van emerged into the late-afternoon, rush-hour traffic. It headed west into a setting sun. The end of a perfect winter's day for some. A beautiful sunset over snow-covered ski trails for some, but for Ricker, merely a glimpse of blood-red sky between the shoulders of the two guards up front.

The officer at Receiving, looking at his screen, didn't say "Are you back again?" nor did the man in handcuffs on the other side of the desk offer any small talk of his own. This time around, Ricker was grim. He had nobody to please, no favors to ask. They would move him or hold him—the choice was theirs; he had no say in the matter—no more than livestock walking in at one end of some large building to be *processed*, and then, later, emerging at the other end—transformed.

Answering questions: an essential part of *being processed*. Not answering them would mean special treatment for tough meat—

a little meat tenderizer, perhaps. Tougher men than he had balked . . . but not for long, and he was a pussycat, a coward. He'd answer.

Name? Social security number? (They had it all on the screen before them, of course, but they had to ask, anyway.) Parents' names? Addresses? Citizenship? Next of kin? Aliases? Religion? Tattoos? . . . Presently, all his possessions would be taken from him, never to be seen again. They'd hand him a receipt along with a plastic bag containing everything he'd need in prison: orange coverall uniforms, towels, underwear, shaving gear, plastic mirror, soap, toothbrush, toothpaste, toilet paper, bed linen, one blanket. . . . Then he'd be photographed, fingerprinted, and finally led, in handcuffs, to his cell.

The maximum security section of this new prison consisted of a series of pods: three tiers of cells facing in, surrounding an atrium-like central common area that housed guard stations, an assembly section at one end with folding chairs for lectures and watching TV and, on the opposite end, picnic tables for dining and visits. No barbaric conditions here—this was all state-of-the-art, hi-tech. Closed-circuit TV cameras monitored everything. Unarmed guards festooned with radio transmitters, mingled casually with the inmates. Loudspeakers blared.

In his small two-man cell Ricker lay on his bed, the top bunk. A cellmate with whom he had no intention of conversing occupied the bottom—staked it out and defended it with his eyes. The cell door, made of heavy iron bars painted grey, was on hinges. It closed with the solid sound of a door on a large Mercedes-Benz. Indeed, in this modern jail the sound of rolling steel slamming and latching would not be heard. (Though many did, alas—for years, in their dreams.)

The windows, without bars, were narrow unopenable plastic slits above eye level that allowed light in without letting inmates out; or, for that matter, without letting out the stale air surrounding them. The only ventilation came through air conditioning and heating ducts in the ceiling. Each of the nine-by-twelve-foot cells also contained a stainless steel toilet with a cold-water wash basin attached, as a unit, above it.

During his first bid, the domestic abuse frame-up—five years for being out-lawyered—Ricker, innocent of all wrongdoing, was bitter. Sure, he thought revenge, envisioned it—maybe even planned it a little. Year after endless year with only the image of his wife's mutilated body to bring a smile to his face. But what about this time?

This time he had no enemies. None. He hated no one. He wished no one harm. This time he had only himself to blame.

Chapter 59

"**M**y first inclination is to blame myself," said Jay, who had been notified by the court that all charges against him had been dismissed, that Georgene Reilly would remain as prosecuting attorney, and that he would be representing Ricker and would be expected to do everything in his power to safeguard the rights of his client.

"My first inclination is to say, 'You wouldn't be here if it weren't for me;' but, in truth—and I'm not trying to weasel out of anything—in truth, I'm not so sure."

Jay had rehearsed that line before coming to prison. He was informed that Ricker was not only refusing food and water, but rejecting everyone's efforts to communicate with him. Indeed, his own calls to Ricker were not returned, and his messages via the warden produced nothing.

He knew his first visit to his client would be crucial. He'd have an opportunity to open the doors to communication. One chance, perhaps. Possibly only one. Bungle it and he may never get another. He'd have to choose his words carefully. His opening words. His demeanor. His attire (a wrinkled suit), his appearance (a day-old beard). He could take no detail in his approach for granted.

"Give me an alibi, Rick," he pleaded. "Anything to go on. Anything."

They sat facing each other at one of the dozen vacant picnic tables at the far end of the atrium-like common space within the maximum security pod. Although attorney/client conferences, unlike visits from family and friends, could be scheduled anytime, not just during visiting hours, and a private room with a guard posted at the door would be made available, Jay, carefully considering the effect of their surroundings on Ricker, decided to forego privacy for the informality of a picnic table. No matter. As it turned out, none of the other tables were occupied. Their conversation would not be overheard by others. They had their end of the pod all to themselves.

Ricker had lost weight since the séance, since Jay had seen him last. No. More than merely lost weight. His chicken-like neck and the deep hollows below it were revealed grotesquely at the open collar of his loose-fitting, orange coverall uniform. His bony body was stooped over, his back hunched. Jay had noticed his walk—a limp—along with a grimace suggesting pain.

"Is there anything I can do for you to make your life less miserable?" asked the lawyer.

Still nothing from Ricker, whose sunken eyes averted Jay's.

Jay leaned toward him, hoping, if he spoke, to hear his words above the prison din: the slamming of doors, the shouts of inmates, the horns and buzzers, the incessant loudspeaker. Rude, intrusive sounds echoing back and fourth between concrete walls.

"What about the statement I came in with?" persisted Jay. "'Give me an alibi. Anything to go on. Anything.'"

Jay detected no anger from the man sitting silently across from him. Indeed, no emotion of any kind. Could Ricker be drugged? No, he concluded, for a man on a hunger strike, that would be difficult if not impossible to accomplish.

Jay's rehearsed approach continued: "I should have taken responsibility for you when you first came into my office, Rick. Looking back, I would have done things differently:

"I would have investigated your so-called *fugitive* status more closely, gotten that off the books. And I should have gone over what Hurley did, to see if I could find grounds for malpractice. But no, I thought only of myself. I sent you to snoop on Ponti. I'm the one who should be sued for malpractice."

The blaring loudspeaker held him silent: sick-call names this time, mostly foreign, non-alphabetical, endless. . . .

Jay's concentration had been broken. He wished he were elsewhere. When the announcements finally stopped, he tried to pick up the thread of his conversation:

"I was no help to you when you were out—why not?—I ask myself now, too late. I never tried to find out what makes you tick. The loss of your parents, your dropping out of college, your biker friends, your bad marriage, your jail time . . . no, I was no help to you, whatsoever. Now you're broken in spirit, on a hunger strike, anxious to die, refusing to do anything on your own behalf to save yourself."

Still no response from his client. Jay decided on a different approach, one he hadn't rehearsed: "I was in jail too, don't forget. That was how I met your friend Larkin, a man who wouldn't hurt a fly. I know the outrage of unfair punishment. To have a judge sitting beside The Flag of the United States of America jailing you, jailing Larkin, jailing me, punishing innocent men. . . ."

"I killed the bugger," interrupted Ricker, speaking finally, breaking his silence with the most devastating words imaginable. "Fair punishment means finishing me off."

Jay was stopped in his tracks. His plan to draw Ricker out had produced a bombshell. His first reaction was disbelief. Ricker falsely admitting to anything that might warrant capital punishment? "I don't believe you, Rick," Jay told his client. "You're confessing to something you didn't do, hoping that the state will put you out of your misery and execute you."

"Massachusetts has no death penalty," Ricker replied, the hint of a smile at the corner of his dry, receded lips.

What now? Jay wondered. Where do we go from here? His

head was reeling. Finally, he spoke: "I don't want to hear that kind of crap from you ever again, understand? I'm here to get you out of this mess, and I intend to do just that. I don't want any more self-destructive nonsense from you." Jay left quickly— perspiring, light-headed, promising to return after sorting things out for himself.

"I've changed my mind," Jay announced at his next visit, "I'm accepting your confession as valid." Once again they were at a picnic table at one end of the common space within the pod, the central area around which the cells rose in tiers. "I'm glad you confided in me. But I have hope for you, Rick. Hope for your future. You're too valuable a person to be lost to the world forever. And so I plan to proceed, as before, clearing you of all the charges you face. I intend to free you, Rick, and I have no doubt that I can do just that!

"In fact, getting you out won't be the problem," he declared, bending over the table toward his motionless client. "For one thing, there is no indication of foul play in Shaw's death, no signs that a murder was committed. Furthermore, there's no tie-in to you. No evidence against you. Nothing. And finally, it's up to the state to convince a jury . . . to prove beyond a reasonable doubt . . . the unprovable."

Jay gave Ricker some time to consider the implications of his remarks before pressing on to what he really wanted to say: "No. This scrape you're in isn't the problem. I've spent the last few days pondering it—days and nights, in fact—and my question, questions, won't go away. What made you do it, Rick? Why? How did it happen?"

The emaciated, slouching prisoner turned his skull-like head toward Jay and replied in a gravelly whisper: "I saw Archibald Shaw a while back, at a time when I was working as a waiter in a restaurant on Newbury Street. He was having lunch with an elderly woman. He seemed to be trying to force her into some sort of deal. The woman was pleading with him, in a quiet voice; but, the more abject she became, the more intimidating he'd become toward her. The scene was disgusting. Finally he stormed out, leaving her in tears.

"The old woman dried her eyes and just sat there, trembling. She wore one of those kerchiefs that chemotherapy patients wear. When she got up to leave, she apologized to me for tying up the table for such a long time.

"I didn't charge her for the meal, by the way. But I learned later that she returned the next day with the bill and paid it anyway. I knew then that I had to get the bastard. I thought of my Aunt Grace, and that was the clincher."

"Let me get this straight," exclaimed Jay, leaning over the table toward Ricker. "You kill a man because he argues with a stranger who reminds you of your aunt? I give up. I quit. I can't waste my time coming here to listen to that kind of crap! Are you some sort of vigilante for old ladies, or something?"

"I told you I want to take my punishment. I want to plead guilty. You're the one who won't let me."

Jay backed down. "Okay, Rick. I'm sorry I lost my temper. But answer one question for me. Just one. If I got you off, would you do it again? Tell me, Rick. If you got off, could you do something like that again?"

"Sure I could do it again," he whispered, hoarsely. "Do you think I could live out the rest of my life without my property?" His voice gained strength as he spoke. "Do you think I could live with the Ehrlichs, the Dillaways—living in *my* house? Sleeping in *my* bed? Looking out of *my* window . . . at *my* barn?" He was up now, his voice, at full volume, cracking.

"The sons of bitches will pay the price for taking my property. My family property." His fist slammed down on the table. "They'll pay me, not my whore of a wife . . . and they'll pay in blood."

Jay looked around nervously, worried that his client's words might have been overheard by others. Seeing nothing that might indicate that they were, he attempted to calm the man standing, trembling before him: "But the people you mentioned don't even know you, Rick, they have no idea of your suffering.

They're innocent bystanders. Why should they be victims of your revenge?"

Ricker seemed exhausted by his outburst. Spent, he sat down slowly. Then, unsmiling, he shrugged his scrawny shoulders. But mostly he just sat motionless. Sat, and with sunken eyes stared off into the distance.

Driving home in a torrential downpour, Jay felt satisfied. He had done his part for a hopeless client. He had offered *due process* to a murderer. He had acted appropriately, professionally. Indeed, he had struck just the right note in a difficult situation.

Chapter 60

J ay and Georgene Reilly were called into Judge Harlow's
chambers—Georgene as the assistant district attorney in
charge of prosecuting Ricker, Jay as his defense counsel.
"How are we going to resolve this case?" asked the judge, a man
uncomfortable with small talk. "Ladies first."

Georgene fixed her dark green feline eyes on Harlow with
annoyance. Like a cat, she resented adapting to the arbitrariness
of others, accommodating their proclivities, conforming to their
agendas. She sensed paternalism (or worse) from Harlow, whom
she considered one of the *good old boys*, an anti-feminist thorn in
her side, a judge who should have long since retired. "He's a
prime suspect," she responded. "His motive: revenge against his
wife's lawyer, a man who had him convicted on felony charges
and sentenced to five years in the county jail. Ricker's court
record is bulging, Your Honor. We have documents establishing
conspiracy with other inmates to kill his wife as well as Attorney
Shaw. And then his escape. And now, incredibly, his relationship
with my 'brother' here. . . ."

"Hearsay," said Jay, although he had, indeed, attempted to
disqualify himself at the outset. He had *in camera* admitted to

Harlow his conflicts of interest; but the judge, aware of Ricker's previous experiences with dubious counsel and sensitive to the man's insistence on his friend this time, bent the rules to allow Jay to remain. Indeed, to require him to remain.

"Let's dispense with the niceties of court," declared the judge. Harlow preferred to run his courtroom from his chambers, preferred the freedom that only privacy can provide. "Did your client commit murder, Mr. Arsenault? That is what I expect you to tell both of us presently, but before you answer. . . ." Harlow gave the two lawyers sitting in front of his overflowing desk in the large, cluttered office time to absorb the portent of his words before he continued. "But before you answer . . . I'm not sure, if I were you, I could trust your *sister* here with that information."

Georgene bristled but maintained an uneasy silence.

"How about it, Georgene?" said Harlow, pressing on. "Can you be trusted? Do you want Jay to tip his hand?"

"We'll learn the truth in a court of law," she responded, her dark eyes flashing. "Granted, our case is weak, but we have enough to go before a grand jury. . . ."

The judge, taking off his glasses, rubbing his eyes, leaned back in his creaky oak armchair. He was a short man, bald, a little overweight; his doctor had urged him to retire, to leave his stressful, sedentary job before it was too late. He lurched up from his desk without warning, and, with the two surprised lawyers captives in their seats, began to pace the room.

The old man appeared to be staging some sort of drama— timing it with words and the spaces between them. With gestures. Indeed, choreographing it. "You'll learn more in one afternoon from me in here," he said, looking at Georgene, "than you'll learn in twenty years parading around in a court of law. Do you understand what I'm saying?"

Georgene, looking up obediently, held his gaze in silence.

"How many of your family have been police officers, Georgene?" he asked.

"How far back do you want me to go?" she replied. When the

judge only glared, she continued: "Most of the men in my family choose law enforcement for a career. A few are lawyers. Very few are neither."

"Public service characterizes your family, Georgene," said Harlow, stopping in front of her. "Duty, yes, but along the way, heroism too. I can't tell you how much respect I have for the contribution your people have made to our community. I want the same for you, you know. Do you know that?" Walking behind his desk, he gave her time to respond—and if not respond, then at least think about his words. She nodded minimally.

"I want you to have the key to this courthouse, Georgene," he said, rummaging around amid the chaos of bulging file folders and other debris on his desk; then, finding his gavel, picking it up, pointing it around threateningly, he continued his tirade: "Not Jay . . . you!" He banged the gavel down on his desk with a deafening crack, then pointed it at Jay. "He's an outsider, a renegade with his own agenda, not to be trusted, but you . . . well, with your family background, the dues they've paid over the years, you could go all the way to the top!" Once again the gavel slammed down. Again the resounding crack. Some papers flew to the floor. A court officer peeked his head in through the office door, then, assessing the situation, quickly withdrew. "I want any politician to be able to endorse you for anything, Georgene . . . to put your name . . . your respected family name forward for any office in this state with pride."

The judge stopped short. Suddenly he lurched across his desk, his eyes riveted on her. "I WANT YOU TO KNOCK OFF THIS LESBIAN CRAP, YOU HEAR?" he cried, out of control, his face becoming red, a vein in his forehead bulging. "If a priest is horny, the archbishop should kick his ass. I feel the same way about this court, Georgene—you're my priest, and I'm taking you to task." He noisily pushed aside his chair and stormed out of the room, black robes flying, his words left hanging in the air between the two lawyers.

"Fuck him," said Georgene, when he was gone. "What's he in my personal life for?"

"He wants what's best for you," said Jay, with a hangdog scowl. "He's pissed because he cares."

"So, what about your case?" she responded, shrugging. "What does he want me to do?—to say?"

"I'd guess he simply wants to be able to trust you, as a team member, to consider society's interests over your own—but why am I telling you this? When you're mature enough to act responsibly, you'll do what has to be done, and you'll do it automatically, without any prompting from the sidelines."

Georgene digested Jay's words in tense silence; later, though, her tension eased. She relaxed in her chair, folded her hands neatly before her. Later still, she spoke:

"I know Ricker did it."

Startled out of his reverie, Jay looked up at her. "What . . . ? How do you know? Clue me in, Georgene."

"I can't say, exactly. I've interviewed him, of course. There's something about him that gives me the willies. I'm never mistaken when I get that feeling, though, and I got it from Ricker. He did it."

The private door at the back of Harlow's chambers opened noisily. "So what's the verdict?" asked the judge, looking at Jay as he entered the room and headed for his desk. "Did your client poison a respected member of the Massachusetts Bar?"

Jay knew the question would be asked again and fully expected Georgene to be present when it was. He stood, put some space between himself and his two listeners, and finally spoke:

"Absolutely not, Your Honor," he said, dividing his eye contact equally. "Who says a murder was committed? The press? Is that how we conduct ourselves in court nowadays? by public opinion?

"A man dies and all of a sudden it's *murder?* No weapon. No signs of a struggle. No nothing, Your Honor. No case. For all I know, Shaw ate some tainted sushi. In no way did Ricker contribute to that man's premature death."

After Jay and Georgene left the courthouse, Jay returned to the judge's chambers. "He did it, of course," said Jay.

"I know," lied Harlow. "Perhaps you were wise not to trust Georgene. She's young. I hope she settles down before her career is in ruins." Then something about the Judge's demeanor changed. When he leaned forward in his chair, Jay could, once again, see fire in the old man's eyes.

"But what about your client, Arsenault? What are we to do with him? HOW MUCH TIME ARE YOU WILLING TO HAVE HIM SERVE?"

Jay, still standing, suddenly became light-headed. He reached for the back of the nearest chair—for support. Then it passed.

"Georgene said it all," he replied, in control again, sitting down—without asking for permission to be seated—in a chair across from the judge's desk. "There's no evidence against him. She might strong-arm a grand jury to indict, reluctantly, but a real jury will have to let him go."

"I respect your loyalty to a client," said the judge, without conviction—indeed, with a measure of disdain, "but I knew Archibald Shaw personally. He helped my family on numerous occasions. I won't have his cold-blooded murder go unpunished."

"If that's all Archibald Shaw had going for him—his personal, insider connections—then may he burn in the fires of hell—which, incidentally, is where most honest men would consign him, anyway." Jay spoke assertively, but with a pained expression.

"You're an impertinent son of a bitch," responded the judge, not meeting Jay's eyes.

"A throwback from my *Hotline* days, perhaps," said Jay, sheepishly. "But now I have a pregnant wife. I'm at your mercy for my future—practicing law, earning a living. By the way, I'm no longer much of a renegade. In a sense, I don't know who I am, or, as a lawyer, what I'm supposed to do. A powerful, albeit unpopular, man was poisoned—with good reason, if you ask me—an eye for an eye, you might even say—in a way, setting things right. . . ."

"I've never heard such bullshit in my life," interrupted Harlow, rising to his feet. "He killed a friend of . . . this court, not some n-n . . . no account street pimp—but a man who knew senators." The vein again, the reddening face. "Archie was a man to be reckoned with. A legend in his time. TEN YEARS, PAROLE AFTER FIVE."

"My client served almost five years already, on a virtual frame-up," asserted Jay, also rising. "If you can arrange for them to count that time, he'll do another year on some minor offense . . . and . . . well, I'd say justice would be served."

"Get him to accept *manslaughter* and I'll personally guarantee he'll get no more than five," declared Harlow. "Not a day more—you have my word on it."

"If he's forced to do another five—and he's a man who has great difficulty doing time—you know the ones [Harlow nodded]—when he gets out, do you know the first thing he'll do?"

The judge waited in silence for Jay to continue.

"He'll finish off the person or persons who put him there, and then—I feel strongly—he'll take his own life. I invited him to the gathering where he was picked up, you know; in a way, I caused him to be arrested. In years to come, in some jail cell or other, in the middle of the night when he can't sleep, he might lie there thinking that I *intentionally* lured him into a police trap. That I had him ambushed. In any event, I would say his prime target—possibly his *only* target . . . will be me!"

"Then we'll just have to find a way to keep him in permanently," said the judge.

Chapter 61

Ricker's case worker called Jay at home late one afternoon requesting a meeting. "No, it's not an emergency," the man said, but he suggested that at some point they should talk. "The sooner the better, actually."

Does he think my time is up for grabs? thought Jay, driving in on a Saturday, a day he had planned to take Ermalyn to feed the ducks, one of her favorite activities—his, too. Their town had paved an area at a bend in the Concord River, a place that attracted carloads of kids and hungry ducks, geese, and pigeons by day. At night, teenagers with different appetites gazed over the restless water.

The case worker, a young man with thinning hair in a crew-cut, heavy, translucent-framed glasses, and a pocketful of pens, met Jay in the administration building. "Our client is losing weight," he said, escorting Jay into his tiny office. "They tell me he doesn't sleep. Doesn't eat. I fear depression, clinical depression. And then . . . er, you know. . . ."

He waited nervously for Jay to speak. To add something. Anything. But Jay, sitting in the plastic chair next to his desk only stared at him in measured silence.

"If you will allow me to be candid, Mr. Arsenault," said the case worker, "I fear suicide."

"If you will allow *me* to be candid," responded Jay, continuing to stare, "if a man is so despondent he wants to kill himself, why don't you let him? Give him a bottle of pills, for Christ's sake. People pass out when they're tortured, don't they? That's Nature's way of saying they've had enough. So what do you do? Throw a bucket of water on them? Revive them so you can torture them again?" Jay got up to walk out. At the door he stopped. "And, incidentally, what do you want me to do? If you want happy prisoners, put Prozac in their Kool-Aid." He waited for the social worker to respond.

"Your client is dying, Mr. Arsenault. I need your consent for intravenous. Restore his electrolytes. Prevent coma. Force-feeding requires your signature." At those words, Jay turned on his heel and disappeared down the corridor.

Since he was at the prison anyway, Jay decided to visit Ricker, whom he hadn't seen for three weeks. With no news to cheer his client, why make the trip?

"The Shaw investigation is at a standstill," he explained, once they were seated at their usual picnic table in the common area within the pod. "The police are baffled. They're attributing the cause of death to an exotic toxin, about which they know nothing. Their progress in solving this murder is slow. No. Not slow, it's non-existent. They have nothing. No evidence. Nothing for a trial. Zero."

"Did you tell them I did it?" asked a morose Ricker, whose dramatic weight loss had rendered him, in less than a month, almost unrecognizable to Jay. And the beard was back—albeit grey and uneven, but this time on an ashen face. The case worker was right: everything about this man's appearance bespoke death. Indeed, the process transforming him into a grey, desiccated cadaver seemed to be well underway.

Jay met his gaze with a pained look of his own. "Of course not. But I thought I'd warn you about how the case against you is proceeding. Or not proceeding. As things stand now, they could spend years gathering evidence. I don't see your case going to trial for years."

"I won't last years. You know that."

They always return with a deal, thought Harlow, catching a glimpse of Jay waiting in the hall near his chambers. Yes, thought the old man, sooner or later they'll always return with a deal.

"My client wants to die," said Jay settling into one of the many oak side chairs in front of the judge's desk. He wants to *drift away*. Euthanized, like an animal. He wants to go to sleep and never wake up."

Don't we all, thought the judge, fleetingly. "Massachusetts has no death penalty," the old man responded, grimly, but with a sudden urge to smile.

"You know what I mean," said Jay.

Harlow lapsed into silence. Of course he knew. Somehow, basic human needs get satisfied—one way or another, legally or otherwise, some sort of justice prevails. "It will cost you twenty thousand . . . cash. Cheap enough for the peace of mind it will bring to all concerned."

"Lethal Injection?"

"That's how it's done, nowadays. The authorities attribute the cause of death to a drug overdose—which, in a way, it is. But sometimes there's a stink. A furor from the press. Sometimes the inmate's family gets up in arms over the laxity of prison security. Embarrassing problems often arise."

"Not in this case," Jay assured him. "Ricker has no family. No friends, except for me."

"Then get some cash together over the next couple of weeks," said the judge. "Someone will contact you."

Chapter 62

Two horses stood at the far end of the gravel passageway, the no-man's-land between the inner and outer walls of the prison. From a distance they seemed restless, uneasy in their confinement, eager to get going. Horses are so easy to read, thought Ricker. They speak a fully-scored symphony with all the shadings, if you'd care to listen—and what a pleasure!—listening.

A rider sat on one, comfortable in the saddle, holding the other horse's reins. She handed them to Ricker as he approached. Once up, he could see an opening in the wall. They passed through at a walk, the crunching of gravel beneath their hooves giving way to the firm thumping of horseshoes on solid ground as they left the prison behind them forever.

Eve Angel wore a faded denim jacket. Her shiny, straw-colored hair flaring slightly in the wind, bounced at her shoulders as she rode. His eyes rested on her. His heart pounded with excitement. The excitement of freedom, to be sure, but the excitement of something else, as well.

She set the pace, leading him by a half-length. Then she eased into an exceedingly slow canter that his horse matched stride for stride. How can she manage so slow a gait? he wondered. It's almost as if contact with the ground is being lost.

She fell back alongside him. "Don't think about it, Rick," she said, with a radiant smile. "It's perfection. Only animals can do it . . . and only on their own."

I could ride on forever, he thought. If only. . . .

Sensing his euphoria, Eve Angel again turned to him. "Do you love me?" she asked, her smile irresistible. He caught the mysterious fragrance of her perfume as he rode. His breath seized in his throat. Tears welled in his eyes. Love, of course. That's the answer.

Give in to it—it's so easy, he thought. Let them know in court, in the jails—tell those in charge. Spread the word: you're through fighting, you give up, they win, you lose (or do you also win with love?—you're not sure). All you know is that whatever they ask, you're ready to do it. If they want it, you'll give it to them—for love. Superhuman strength—you'll marshal it—the strength of love. Nothing's stronger. The soft kisses—now you yearn for them. You're capable of strength, yes, but also tenderness (ah, the enigmas of love—you appreciate them, the subtleties—nothing is lost on you, now).

Tell them. You'll make any sacrifice for love, you promise; more than that, you're prepared to start over . . . from scratch. Start over as stable boy, as blacksmith's assistant. Tell them. Before it's too late. Tell them.

In court, they wait. "What is it you have to tell us?" says the judge. "Why did you bring *the court* here on a Sunday?" (Did he call *himself* the court? wonders Ricker. Was he serious? Or was that term some sort of inside joke?) "Everyone else is at the seashore," continues the judge. "The city is deserted, the streets empty. The temperature is in the nineties—the high nineties, and the humidity is oppressive. The air conditioning in this building is off for the weekend and, on such short notice, there's no way to turn it on. Guards had to be called in from the county facilities—the county *correctional* facilities, that is—so that we might proceed. The lawyers—notice how they don't even wear suits and ties, excusable under the circumstances. . . . You're excused, gentlemen, feel free to loosen your collars as we agreed before, *in chambers*. We have everyone in place, Mr. Ricker. We're waiting. What is it you have to say?"

Eve Angel, sitting alone in the last row of the courtroom, bestows the smile that everyone seems to expect, indeed, for which everyone has somehow waited. It lights up the dusty room ordinarily kept grim to emphasize the dignity of the judiciary—lofty marble halls, black-robed judges, spectators rising, gavels falling—their aim: respect for the *law* (needless efforts, of course—the guards and the jail provide that respect: the respect engendered by fear—fear of punishment—plain and simple).

Her smile is permitted now, at the end of the ordeal—in a way, encouraged. In fact, it provides the perfect touch in a really difficult case such as his. A release of tension, like applause after an emotionally draining performance; it means the experience has been acknowledged, appreciated, even acclaimed, and is now over. Her smile: a reward; the heartache has ended, the suffering was not in vain.

It's within reach. It's within Ricker's reach. He has only to swear to whatever it is they require, to sign their documents—it's so easy. Everybody wants it. It beckons.

"Is that the answer?" he asks the lawyer sitting next to him (his lawyer?). "Is it *that* simple?"

"It's *that* simple," says the man in the pale green sport shirt.

They wait, staring at him. Again he glances at Eve Angel, her expression of love still in place—love for him, he's sure, with a hint of tender sympathy for his difficult situation. A slight tilt to her head now, barely noticeable except to him.

One man to make things right. What could be easier? To bolt for the door? To take the guard's bullet? To take the sweet ticket out?

Two horses wait beside the courthouse stairs. Both have blue steel on their hooves. Both—without doubt—can fly. Alone or with his beloved Eve Angel, he could put the pain of hard, unforgiving earth behind him forever.

He'd choose her, of course. Every fiber in his body yearned for her. The heartbreaking good fortune of having her love was more than he deserved in one lifetime. Of course he'd endure any ordeal to have her. She knew the power of love. The man with the gavel knew it too. Now Ricker also knew it. If it wasn't too late.

Chapter 63

Bedtime for Ermalyn meant a story—for Jay: one of the tiny rewards that made his life a joy. *Once upon a time there was a little girl. . . .*

"And her name was Baby Marie, right Dad?" said the five-year-old. They were both lying on her small, built-in trundle bed. The previous owner, the man who built many houses in Maine, designed the child's room with his own daughter in mind; indeed, the whole house from basement to attic was like an oversized dollhouse. A delighted Sally, who saw it first, bought it on the spot—from front window awnings to backyard birdfeeder, she had no intention of letting her future residence slip through her fingers. Since they left Massachusetts for Maine she had not felt comfortable—an upscale condo in Portland, notwithstanding—so when this dream house appeared, she gobbled it up.

Jay stretched out on Ermalyn's tiny bed, his feet spilling onto an adjoining built-in chest of drawers. In the three years since Entwhistle had fired him, his life had changed totally. His latest move: joining Jim Ingoldsby.

His former employer was building a law practice in a thriving new market, southern Maine, and wanted Jay in on the ground floor. Ingoldsby had constituted his new firm with squeaky-clean partners—Bangor blue-bloods—then added a staff of young, highly-motivated lawyers. Operating out of fashionable water-front offices, the firm was on the rise, piling success upon success, giving the stodgy old faces in dimly-lit, oak-paneled offices near the courthouse a run for their money. As Ingoldsby's specialist in divorce law, Jay practiced his craft with expertise and without a men's rights agenda behind every case; he even accepted women clients. In fact, the majority of his clients were women.

Relocating to Maine, to another state, the Arsenaults first moved into a comfortable condo—more than comfortable: elegant. Certainly no reason for strife, for discord, thought Jay, returning home to find Sally in tears. Hardly grounds for divorce or reason to threaten it.

"Our neighbors are after you," she declared. "I've seen that flirtatious look in their eyes. They're in heat. They're all divorced. They're your firm's clients, for God's sake! They're *your* clients. They come home late; you come home late. I'm not blind."

Certainly no reason to threaten it.

But when Sally found her dream house, Jay could put those troubling thoughts behind him, consign the condo episode to the scrap-heap of forgettables; he hoped she would do the same.

Ermalyn's bedtime ritual always meant a story, one he'd read —her bookshelves were filled to overflowing—or one he'd invent. The choice was hers, and that night she chose to hear one from her dad's imagination:

"That's right," said Jay . . . *and her name was Baby Marie.*

"But it's really about me, isn't it, Dad?" said Ermalyn. "You call her Baby Marie in case something terrible happens to her, but it's really me in the story."

"When has anything terrible ever happened to her?"

"It hasn't yet . . . but it might. Couldn't it?" The child looked up, half-fearfully.

"No, Ermalyn, it couldn't. Nothing terrible will ever happen to Baby Marie."

"But, Dad," she persisted. "Just *admit* that Baby Marie is me. . . . Please." Ermalyn lay against her dad, on the side of the bed next to the wall. When he read a story, she'd prop her head next to his on the pillow and follow along, or nestle in the crook of his arm; but when he told one, she felt free to move around, try new positions. A favorite: perpendicular to him, her feet on his chest.

"Okay," admitted Jay, "Baby Marie *is* you. Now may I continue with the story?" The child, lost in thought, nodded her assent.

One day she was riding her horse, Sweetster. . . .

"Dad," interrupted Ermalyn, "How did you know I wanted a horse? . . . I never asked for one. I meant to at Christmas, but. . . ."

"All little girls want horses. Now let me continue, or I'll get a book to read." An idle threat. He loved her interruptions—hoped they'd go on forever.

Now, Baby Marie would ride Sweetster to school every day; and after school, when she'd come out, he'd be waiting.

"He?" ventured the child. "Was Sweetster a stallion?"

"What's a stallion?" Jay asked, taken off guard by his daughter's question.

"A daddy horse."

"No," responded Jay. "He's a gelding. He's a male, but not a daddy."

"Oh," said the child.

Everywhere Baby Marie went, she'd go on Sweetster: errands to the store, the post office . . . church.

One day the carnival came to town, and everyone was excited—adults as well as children. There would be amusement rides, tempting treats, games of chance, games of skill.

The highlight of the carnival was to be a horse race in which anybody could enter. So Baby Marie signed up to ride Sweetster in the race.

All the horses with their riders mounted on them waited for the starting gun at one end of the main street in town while at the other end, a quarter mile away, a crowd gathered at the finish line. Since a single burst of speed and not endurance would determine the winner, only quarter horses were entered—working horses, for working cowboys. A murmur arose from the spectators—a problem. Something was holding up the start of the race.

It was Baby Marie. Unlike the cowboys with their heavy western saddles, Baby Marie rode bareback, like an Indian. The racing authorities—the mayor, the sheriff, the carnival owner—all got together and issued new ground rules: for safety's sake, no contestant could ride without a saddle.

"Did she get a saddle?" asked Ermalyn, aware of her father's too-long pause.

"Would you?"

"No, Dad. But I wouldn't race, either. I'd rather ride slowly, on an Indian blanket. Just me and my *gelding* horse, Sweetster."

Sadly, Baby Marie rode home, a tear of disappointment in her eye. "Don't worry, Sweetster," she said. "I won't burden you down with thirty-five pounds of leather and then with all my might pull a girth across your belly to keep it in place." They would travel together through life, she told him. Each trying to make the other's journey as pleasant and comfortable as possible.

Ermalyn lay at a haphazard angle to her dad, her head on a small pillow next to the wall, her feet on his stomach. Occasionally her eyes would close. Jay, with a glance at his watch, continued:

When Baby Marie got home she found that her father, injured by some farm machinery during her absence, needed medical attention. And so, she got back up on Sweetster and galloped to the doctor's house three miles away. The doctor arrived just in time to save her father's life.

"Is that the end of the story?" asked Ermalyn, forcing her eyes to an extraordinary degree of wide-openness.

"For tonight," said Jay, getting up, then bending over and tucking his daughter in and then kissing her, usually in the crevice between her tiny nose and her cheek, but sometimes on her dimple, and sometimes between the corner of her eye and the dark ringlet curls on the side of her head.

"Is she down for the night?" asked Sally, looking up as Jay entered their family room. Sally had papers spread out over a coffee table, an oak bridge table, the floor. . . . She had started her own public relations company, and it consumed most of her time: long days, nights, often late into the night. Weekends.

"You never can tell," responded Jay with a shrug. He watched his wife for a few minutes. Watched her intense concentration as she dealt with the chaos of paperwork around her. Was she secretly watching him watch her? he wondered.

"Should I take a shower?" he finally asked, breaking the long silence. The question was a coded reference to sex. Jay always took a shower before bed, regardless.

Sally was slow in responding. "Sure," she said, changing the rhythm of her activity somewhat, her pattern of organizing giving way to one of preparing her task for later. Perhaps later that night.

Chapter 64

A complimentary copy of Ermalyn's yearbook arrived in the mail three weeks before graduation: another gesture of gratitude from the small New England college for Jay's donations to its Annual Fund. Parents' contributions were small compared to those of alumni, but Jay's generosity had caught their attention. He became the recipient of endless handouts from the college, which seldom passed up an opportunity to foster loyalty and school spirit from its benefactors.

In previous years, Jay, perusing yearbook pictures of his daughter's class, barely looked beyond the "A"s; he'd see what Ermalyn was up to, check out the list of accomplishments under her photograph, then consign the volume to the bottom shelf in his bookcase, the only shelf large enough to accommodate it. Her graduation picture took his breath away:

Although facing sideways, she was not photographed in profile. Instead, something in the direction of the camera had caught her attention. Something caused her to turn forward with an expression of exuberant joy. Her image was captured— delighted—beaming into the lens.

Her likeness betrayed little resemblance to Sally, save that enthusiastic spark, that earnest intensity. Ermalyn had soft features: dark-brown hair, light-brown eyes, durable skin. Similarly, he saw nothing of himself in his daughter's face: neither sharp nose, nor cynical, piercing eyes.

> Ermalyn Arsenault. Honor Society 1,2,3,4, Boots N' Bridle Club 1,2,3, Pres. 4, *Clinical Papers* 1,2, Ed. 3, Sr. Ed. 4, Sunday Choristers 4, Empl.: Berkshire Veterinary Clinic 1,2,3,4, Work-study: Berkshire Veterinary Clinic 1,2, Veterinaires sans Frontieres 3, Bluegrass Breeding Stables (Ridgemont, Ky.) 4.

Sunday Choristers? mused Jay. What's that all about? Then turning randomly, perhaps for clues to his daughter's sudden interest in music, another student's name caught his eye:

> Bernadette Chickie Larkin. Debating Club 1,2,3,4, Sunday Choristers 3,4, Empl.: Mt. Snow Ski Patrol 1,2, Brattleboro District Court 3,4, Work-study: Berkshire County Judicial Intern's Program 3, Women's Legal Defense Collaborative (N.Y.C.) 4.

Could it be? The family of Ben Larkin—a granddaughter, perhaps? The same Larkin who was his friend from Massachusetts?—from prison?—later, a client? Larkin had a son, a doctor practicing down South. . . .

A trip to the bottom shelf solved the mystery. The *Student Register* showed Bernadette's parents to be Mark and Lorraine Larkin of Atlanta, Georgia.

Jay had never met Mark, though he had heard Larkin mention him often, always in glowing terms, always with affection. Now, seeing the name for the first time in almost twenty years, Jay was thrown back into a whirlpool of memories. All bittersweet.

No. All bad.

Sunday Choristers, eh? I'll bet they know each other!

Almost two decades. Everything about Jay had changed since he, Sally, and five-year-old Ermalyn left Boston for Portland, Maine. Now they considered themselves natives; for Jay, his former life in Massachusetts but a vague memory. Success also came with time: promotion to law partner in his firm; later, a senior partnership.

Sally also prospered in the less hectic environment of southern Maine. She had started her own public relations company from scratch; now it employed 27. She was making as much money as Jay; indeed, their combined income was staggering—six figures before taxes. Middle six.

Sally's work required travel: New York, L.A.; later, Europe and Japan. When the Arsenaults' home became an empty nest, Sally found no idle time on her hands.

Plans for a gala graduation dinner were being formulated. Yes, the girls knew each other; in fact, they were close friends. The dinner would bring both families together. Details were worked out in conversations between Portland and Atlanta, and Atlanta and Portland, but the Berkshire Country Inn, the perfect venue, indeed, the only decent restaurant for miles around their small college, proved unable to seat both families together for their graduation dinner. Alas, reservations for so large a party, Jay was told, would be impossible to obtain.

Desperate, Jay called the president of the school's board of trustees, Clayton Badermeister, a lawyer from a firm in New Hampshire doing considerable business in Maine. Jay knew him well. "I need a table for ten," he announced.

"Do I look like the maître d'?" responded the venerable school trustee.

"As a matter of fact you do," joked Jay, "but that's beside the point. Nothing is more important to me than providing the most festive celebration possible for my daughter. The Berkshire Country Inn alone can do it, Clay, but it will take your influence to bring it about. That private room on the first floor, by the way, would be perfect."

The room had been booked solid on graduation day: guest speakers, recipients of honorary degrees. "There's no way they can seat these dignitaries in the main dining room with the general public," said the trustee, a few days later. "How about the day before graduation? Six, seven P.M.; you name it."

"Perfect," replied Jay. "The girls are scheduled to perform in a choral concert that evening. I couldn't ask for more."

The girls looked ravishing—full of the joy of graduation. The mothers, ecstatic, alternated from tears to smiles and back again. Chickie's sisters, Esther with her pediatrician husband, and Ruthie who brought along her boyfriend, hugged their baby sister at every opportunity. Rounding out the party were the fathers.

Waiters standing against the walls of their dining room allowed no bottle of Dom Perignon to go unreplaced, no wineglass to go unfilled. The dads, overflowing with love for their daughters, sat at either end of the table, proposing toasts to them, telling anecdotes from their childhood.

Mark, seated, put down his wine glass and began: "On the maternity ward, before Chickie was born . . . it was about 2 A.M., and nurses were preparing the delivery room. The Chief Obstetrician, a partner in our pediatric group, and a close personal friend of mine, told me to wait in a part of the hospital I never knew existed. It was called the Fathers' Room.

"Stepping inside this dimly-lit room was like entering the parlor of an ornate, Victorian residence. The lighting, near-sepia in its softness, came from heavily shaded table lamps, a sharp contrast to the corridors outside, where harsh fluorescent hospital lighting glared twenty-four hours a day. Furnished with oriental rugs, doilied sofas, and Chippendale chairs, this room had the feeling of a serene haven, a sanctuary amid the atmosphere of crisis and urgency pervading the rest of the hospital.

"Oil paintings hung on the walls between bookcases filled to overflowing, but what really drew my attention was an old-fashioned writing desk; and, on its polished mahogany surface, a blank guest album, a bound journal with blank pages. Its purpose: to collect the thoughts of expectant fathers; or, perhaps, to provide a means for the fathers to collect their own thoughts by writing them down.

"Flipping the pages I noted comments like '. . . two of us came here, but three of us will be leaving. . . .' That sort of thing."

"What did you write, Dad?" asked Chickie.

"I don't recall, Honey. Except that I was impressed by the magnitude of certain events and our human need to immortalize them in words. A keepsake for posterity. A guest book at a birth, a christening. Another at a wedding, of course. . . ."

"Not to mention graduation?" interrupted Chickie's sister Ruthie.

"Perhaps, along with funerals, the most chronicled of all," noted Mark.

"I hope they don't ask me to give a speech at the concert," said Jay. "Clay Badermeister said something about my 'singing for my supper.'"

"You've never been at a loss for words before," noted Sally, grinning.

"What would you say . . . um, if you were called upon to speak?" asked Ermalyn.

"Maybe I'd tell them a . . . a . . . story. An Ermalyn story. A story about my *Baby Marie*," replied her dad, tears appearing in his eyes.

After dinner, both families walked to the auditorium, arm in arm with their graduates. Once there, the girls parted from the group to go backstage, to change into their gowns for the performance, while the others sought seats up front, close to the stage. When the curtain rose, the choir, all women in white, occupied one side of the stage, the orchestra, the other.

During their program, Jay had indeed imagined himself called to the stage, although Badermeister had no such plans for him. During his rare appearances in church (the rites and celebrations of others, mostly) or on Friday evenings at *Symphony* (he and Sally were subscribers to the Portland Symphony Orchestra concert series), Jay's experience would always be the

same: he would lapse into a meditative state similar to a hypnotic trance, and then, as if granted permission to give free rein
to his imagination, he would allow vast fantasies to sweep him
away. While his body, dressed in a suit and tie would be sitting
sedately, often for hours, his mind, in church for example, would
be arranging trysts with women in neighboring pews, interludes
in the cloak room during the sermon. Or, at symphony, during
Mahler or Beethoven, he'd imagine armed terrorists storming
the stage and holding the audience at bay. He saw himself,
alone, intervening with heroic and often ingenious schemes to
end the siege.

This time, while the girls were singing, the imaginary scene
began to unfold—Badermeister's announcement delivered by
the conductor: on behalf of the college, Jay would be offering a
few parting words to the graduates and their families.

He pictured himself rising, and, with all eyes on him, making
his way slowly to the stage. Replacing the conductor at the
podium, he would turn from the Choristers on one side and the
orchestra on the other to face and address his audience:

—When I was young, people . . . at cocktail parties, mostly
. . . would ask me what I did. I'd reply that I was a lawyer. That
response seemed to satisfy them.

—Years later, at intimate gatherings, others asked similar
questions: 'What have you done, creatively? Have your accomplishments improved the world? What do you stand for? . . .
No, I mean it,' they'd say. They'd give me a soul-searching stare
and insist on candor. 'What have you actually *accomplished* in life,
Jay Arsenault?' they'd say, as in some group therapy session
[which is probably where they got the idea for the questions in
the first place]. And, of course, I'd have to look them straight in
the eye, and attempt a measure of honesty.

—In those instances, I'd say I was a man trying to help my
fellow man achieve fair play in court. I'd launch into my well-
worn colloquy about men victimized by unfair judges, a biased
press, their own lawyers' betrayals. My listeners' eyes would
glaze over, their attention drift away. Had they heard it all from

me before? Eventually, they gave up. They stopped asking me about my accomplishments.

—But now, with most of my looking at life amounting to looking *back* at it, I think I finally have an answer to their question; not for them, but for myself:

—I am a husband and a father.

—As long as my wife will have me, I'll be a husband, albeit with failings—many of them, but also with love—my version of it. If the woman I married decides to get rid of me, and I see it happen to others every day, then I'll no longer be a husband.

—But I'll always be a father. And so my answer to the question of accomplishments is this: I'm the father of that girl over there with tears streaming down her cheeks, Ermalyn Arsenault, on this stage, in that white gown.

His words spoken, the podium spotlight would fade leaving the stage in total darkness. But then, after a few moments of uneasy silence for Jay to return to his seat, brilliant lighting would once again come up. The audience would gasp at the sight of the Choristers illuminated on stage in their white gowns as before. Only this time the young women—radiant, dazzling—would form a line at the front of the stage, along the footlights, where each face could be seen clearly and each voice loudly heard:

> O beautiful for heroes proved
> In liberating strife,
> Who more than self their country loved,
> And mercy more than life!
>
> America! America!
> May God thy gold refine,
> 'Til all success be nobleness,
> And every gain divine.

The audience would be on its feet now, ready to sing themselves. Ready to join hands and raise their voices in unison to the first few stanzas of this hymn—the familiar ones, words they knew by heart. Ready to end the concert with their own contribution to this celebration of college and country.

But Jay had no such plans for them. No, he mused, deep within his own reverie, the Choristers alone would be given the last word. For him the concert was over.